First Printing, October 2020.

ISBN 978-1-913716-04-2 (Hardback)

ISBN 978-1-913716-05-9 (Paperback)

ISBN 978-1-913716-06-6 (Ebook)

Book and Cover Design by: ArtByKHuggs

Ink & Fable Publishing, Ltd.

www.inkandfablepublishing.com

For Jac, Mason,
Sophie, and Des

NEVER LANDER

WRITTEN BY

ELORA BURRELL

INK & FABLE PUBLISHING

Skull Rock

Hangman's
Tree

Indian
Camp

Boulderswift
Passage

Neverwood

Neverpeak
Mountains

Stoneshaw

Tiki Forest

Hinview
Thicket

Cannibal
Cove

Evergreen
Shores

The Redbreast

N

W E

S

Black Castle

Mermaid
Lagoon

Crocodile
Creek

Curly's Cave

Fairies
Hollow

The Jolly Roger

CONTENTS

NEVERLANDER

PROLOGUE

They say that my family is cursed.

Whilst some would argue against this profusely, I would have to say that I agree. We're a broken family, haunted by my family's past. Every Darling knows the tales, passed down like a twisted family heirloom. As a child I'd heard the stories—I enjoyed them as my mother spun them to me with words of silk. Her eyes would be alight with wonder and a glint of magic. To this day, I can remember the adventures of the young boy, Peter, and his mismatched crew of Lost Boys. They lived in a world beyond anyone's wildest dreams.

Wild Red Indians and majestic pirate ships, mermaids and mischievous faeries. A world of such wonder that even I fell victim to the delicious call for adventure. Peter was and always had been a part of my family's past; he could be traced all the way back to my great grandmother —not that I had known this back then. No, I would only come to know about Peter and the darkness of those tales when I lived them myself. If only I'd known about the permanent damage it would come to cause my family.

It all started with my great grandmother; she was the first storyteller. And the stories of Peter Pan have followed our family through the generations, ever since. They picked out sisters, cousins, mothers and daughters, and drove each of them to disastrous ends. Of course, since they were all female, some blamed women's wild imaginations, whilst others put it down to unfortunate coincidence. But the rare few knew better.

From whispers on the street and stolen glances, to articles mentioning the Darling name in the weekly papers—our name was everywhere. Children went missing, never to be seen again; mothers and daughters were left with fractured minds, obsessed with a fairy tale place that does not exist.

A place my great grandmother had insisted was real for many years after. Even as her younger brothers, my Great Uncles; John and Michael, lost their same belief of Peter. No matter what, she stood proud and her faith never wavered.

Even to the ripe old age of ninety-four she'd always tell me about her dear old Peter.

Like clockwork, she would lean forward and wink at me as she whispered the words.

"You believe me, don't you Winnie dear?" she would ask, her voice raspy with age. And for a while after, she played idly with the golden acorn charm hanging from her neck.

I remember how vigorously my naïve little head would nod; my eyes wide with childlike wonder.

"Always Grandmamma Wendy," I would chirp, squeezing her wrinkled hand in mine.

I

As I hurry across the cobbled street, picking up my skirts, I steal a glance at the early evening sky. I try hard to collect my muddled thoughts with each step. My breaths are shallow and uneven as I go.

My rising emotions are barely at bay and I quickly remind myself to keep calm and collected. I can't let them get the best of me again, it would only unnerve everyone if my walls were let down.

The colours of dusk sweep across the summer sky in beautiful shades of pale purple and pink. The air is warm, but not uncomfortably so, with a slight soft breeze floating through the streets. The city of London, like always, is bustling with life, even at this late hour. Motor-cars chug by and all walks of life scurry up and down the walkways. The familiar scent of soot, the warm aroma of a nearby food stall, and the overlapping sound of voices, all remind me that I'm right where I belong. I'm home.

I pull my shawl tight over my bare shoulders, clenching it until it crinkles in my fists. I keep my head down as I avoid people's curious glances, as I continue on my way.

I question myself for probably the tenth time. '*Why am I even going?*' And then the familiar snag of years of guilt reminds me exactly why.

The guard barely glances at me as I walk through the tall steel gates. The only sound are my footsteps crunching against the loose gravel as I head towards the looming steps.

My stomach is tying itself into knots and soon there is nothing left but a matted bundle of nerves. Out of habit, I run my fingertips over my palms, now slick with sweat. Anyone who knows me will know that it's a nervous trait of mine.

I don't allow myself to hesitate as I enter the building. Before I can change my mind, I stride up to the reception desk where a Sister sits quietly filing paperwork. Her face is tightly sealed in her black and white attire as her eyes lift to meet mine. A dry mouth threatens to block my speech, but the guilt ushers the words from my lips nonetheless.

"I'm here to see Mrs. Ainsley."

The Sister says nothing, her eyes staring straight through me.

"Charlotte Ainsley?" I continue, hoping for some sort of reaction.

"We have no-one here under that name, young lady, so if you wouldn't mind..." she gestures to the door momentarily before continuing with her task.

I feel myself panic, surely there must be some sort of mistake. Then my mind clicks, and it dawns on me... surely Father would not have been so cruel. I lean over the desk so that my face is inches from the Sister's.

"What I mean to say was, I am here to see Miss Charlotte Darling," I whisper, suppressing the urge to shiver as the Sister meets my eyes and drops her work.

"I see. Come with me." She stands, solemn-faced, walking past me and continuing down the hall.

I follow her quietly as she leads me down lengthy corridors, with darkened hallways and cold marble floors. It all looks so *clinical*. Though the only smell is the odd whiff of damp—not the antiseptic smell I expected. And the walls are bare. How the Sisters don't fall into despair seeing the same dreary thing day in, day out astounds me.

The Sister comes to a stop and I pull myself out of my thoughts just in time to avoid crashing into her. She turns to me with a sombre expression, the look in her eyes almost sad.

"Go gently now with Miss Darling," is all she says before she unlocks the bolted door.

It opens with a painful creak that echoes down the wide hall. The Sister shuffles to one side, gesturing for me to go in.

I take a deep breath and step forward into the room. It's much smaller than imagined—though the same could be said of the woman crouched over in the corner, between the single bed and the white-washed wall. The whole room is simple and minimalistic with the bed one side and a rocking chair on the other. The only decoration on the walls is a small barred window, too high to reach.

My eyes fall back to the woman on the bed just as the Sister calls out from behind me "Miss Charlotte, you have a visitor, my dear."

Through the folds of blonde hair, she lifts her head and her face emerges almost as beautiful and dainty as I remembered it. Only now, the spark in her bright eyes has faded, her skin that was once soft and smooth is now tired and wrinkled in places. She has aged in such a way that I cannot relate to her. A woman of such grace and grandeur left to wither away like a rose with no water. No longer does she look full of life; she is tired and lost.

Her bland eyes look for me through the space between us and I watch as they widen in surprise. The curve of her lips widens into an *O* as she sits up a little straighter. I notice a flicker of movement in her wrists, and watch with slight amusement, as her fingertips run nervously across her palms.

"Bronwyn? Winnie dear, can it really be?" she utters in disbelief.

Her voice sends a rush of warmth and reassurance through me. The sound of it, the strength of it. Her voice is the only part of her that hasn't changed.

A small smile reaches my lips and I feel the knot in my stomach loosen as I take her in. My thoughts reorganize themselves and for a moment we're not in this dark and dreary room, but somewhere else entirely. Far away from this institute and the guilt that lingers in the air.

The words that leave my mouth are quiet, but sure. "Hello, Mother."

Her eyes light up and she rushes towards me, taking me into her arms and spinning us both. "I knew he would send for me; I knew you would come!"

The glee in her voice unnerves me and I step away from her, holding her at arm's length. "What are you talking about?"

"Peter of course, silly girl, don't toy with me, he's sent you here to get me," she explains, her voice giddy with joy.

With those words, my hopes come crashing down around me and the unravelling knot in my stomach tightens once more. She begins to play with the gold acorn pendant around my neck—a parting gift from Grandmamma Wendy—before I pull her hands away and lower them with mine.

"No mother, Peter Pan is not real. He is a character in a story, and no-one has sent me to you other than my own free will," My voice is quiet, disappointment clear in my tone as I run my thumb over the top of her palms, still in my grasp.

"Just like your father. All you do is lie and call me mad," she shouts, frustration leaking into her voice as she rips her hands out of mine and storms back over to the bed. She perches on the edge calmly, though I can see the anger simmering in the way she clenches her tiny hands.

I know I shouldn't let her words pierce me like they do, but their venom cuts right through me and stings in a way I never knew they could.

I walk quietly over to the door with my skirts swishing around me and knock once to be let out. My eyes turn to her one last time and I take in every detail.

"I never thought you mad Mother, only sick," I say earnestly as the door opens and I walk away from her.

II

I wander through the sea of satin skirts and silk suit jackets as I search for the familiar face of my father. Flocks of the upper class have crowded here for the biggest event of the season, and why wouldn't they?

Why Father and his colleagues thought it best to hold such an event in the one of the largest art galleries London has to offer, I don't know. Though I must admit, I'm glad to have something else to talk about besides the higher class drivel and gossip. It was always the latest scandal or some embarrassing rumour.

Emerging from the crowd, I find my father amongst a group of guests, all eager to be acknowledged by one of the upstanding hosts. I step into the group vaguely aware of the conversation, until my father notices me.

"Ah my dear daughter. Bronwyn you know Mr. and Mrs. Clarke, and the Smithson's eldest son, Frederick." He gestures around the group for me.

I smile and tilt my head toward each of them in acknowledgment.

"Frederick here has just been employed by the bank," He continues as he looks from me to his newest staff member.

"Congratulations, Mr. Smithson. Your family must be very proud," I say, directing my gaze to the young man with warm eyes.

"Thank you, Miss Ainsley, and please don't be so formal. Call me Frederick," he says before taking my hand in his and lifting it to his lips.

I feel the heat rise up my neck and colour my cheeks. I let my hand fall to my side once more. I turn my head in time to see the proud look my father passes me as he continues his conversation with the group. I know by that look he intends for Frederick and I to become better acquainted. So, before he can leave the two of us alone, I excuse myself and surge forward through the crowd toward one of the quieter corners of the gallery.

I smile at the odd guest as they greet me, but soon I find myself getting lost in the art. The multitude of colours and styles brightens the otherwise dull space.

I wander along the edges of the room, taking in each piece and appreciating its unique splendour when I feel a presence behind me. Startled, I turn to find Frederick watching me meekly, his palms raised in surrender.

"I'm sorry if I frightened you, I only meant to join you, if you'll let me."

"A ploy from my father no doubt," I reply, my brow raised.

"On my honour, it is of my own free will, I do seek your company," He says exaggeratedly, holding his hand to his heart. I can't help the wry smile that tugs at my lips.

"Well then, by all means," I reply as I continue my slow walk around the gallery.

"That is quite an unusual piece," Frederick comments as I stop to stare at a vibrant canvas.

"Isn't it just?" I reply, lost in the brush strokes of auburn and yellow.

Frederick chuckles to himself and I turn to look at him, confusion written all over my face.

"I was actually referring to your necklace," he explains as his eyes fall back to the golden acorn that I've been fiddling with.

"Oh, it was my great grandmother's," I reply as I look down fondly at it.

As Frederick opens his mouth to reply, the chime of silverware against glass interrupts the moment, pulling our attention from one another, to Mr Edwards, one of my father's associates.

"On behalf of my colleagues and I, I would like to thank each of you for attending our annual gathering. You, our esteemed clientele, are what make our bank great and I thank you all, individually, for your loyal custom."

A brief wave of applause erupts in the room, before the familiar buzz of chatter and subtle background music fill the air once more. My companion and I take this opportunity to continue our stroll, commenting on each piece as we pass it until my eyes fall on a piece that sends a chill right through me.

The picture is a bird's eye view of London. Big Ben towering high to the left side of the painting, the Thames flowing below and the glowing stars in the night sky. Two stars shine much brighter than the others. When I look closely, I see four silhouettes and the tiny shape of a fifth, surrounded by a glowing halo, to the right of the first shadow.

"What an interesting piece. Ah I see it was commissioned by Mr. Ainsley. Your father certainly has unique tastes."

My eyes fall to the title: '*Take Me To Neverland*' and sure enough, underneath, printed in clear letters, is my father's name. The ice in my veins melts as a white-hot fury bubbles up in my throat. I excuse myself tersely from Frederick's company and storm over to where my father is standing, thoroughly engaged with two more guests.

"And when exactly were you going to tell me about the painting?" I cut into the conversation, not caring in the slightest about my brass manner.

My father frowns at me and my lack of manners. "What is so important about a painting that you must interrupt me?"

"You dare to portray our family's history as though it were something to be proud of, as though it were not a curse on our very name," I argue with indignance.

"Your *mother's* history. It seems you forget that you are first and foremost an Ainsley," he replies through gritted teeth.

I sense the mood shift between us and quickly gather that more than a few curious faces are turning our way. I find that I don't care, my anger is too great to care about several nosey people.

"And what you fail to remember, *Father*, is that I am as much an Ainsley as I am a Darling!"

Before he can utter another word, I storm away, fighting my way through the sea of suffocating looks. Taking my skirts into my hands, I run the entire way home, too stubborn to care who sees me.

As soon as I make it back to the house, I slip out of my pinching shoes and sneak past the maids.

The head maid, Nana, in her typical timely fashion, pushes through the kitchen doors as I reach the fourth step. Her eyes find mine for a single moment, before I look away.

"Well dare I say our Winnie looks more like a sourpuss than a respectable young lady," she comments. "Aren't you meant to be at your father's work gala?" she continues when I don't answer.

"I cannot be around that man and his unbearable pretenses," I snip.

I don't give her the chance at a reply as I hurriedly climb the staircase to the first floor. I'm in no mood for light conversation or Nana's pointed questioning, regardless of how well-intentioned they all are.

I pull the countless pins and hair ties from my tresses as I climb the stairs, letting the waves flow freely down to the small of my back. As I reach the landing, I make my leisurely way down the corridor toward my room. As I pass the second room to the left, something causes me to stop.

I push open the door and lean against the doorway, smearing my peach-coloured lipstick with the back of my palm. On stepping in the room, I quickly recognise the space as mother's old nursery. I inhale the musty staleness of the room, looking from the fading wallpaper to the neatly made beds. A generation of Darlings had grown up in this room, and I wonder, idly, if I'll be the last.

As I trace my fingers along the long-forgotten furniture, I see a partially covered mirror standing in the far corner. Without a second thought, I go to it, pulling the white sheet away and letting it sidle to the floor with a soft *whoosh*. I take in the girl staring back at me: her petite frame, the dress fitted to her natural, womanly curves. I stand mesmerised by her wild, blonde locks and her sad green eyes, curtained with thick curled lashes. By the moonlight shining through the nursery window, I see her smeared lipstick, spread across her bottom lip and chin, and the splash of freckles over her nose. The girl who stares back at me resembles, all too much, her mother. The only difference between her and Charlotte Darling is the common trait of an Ainsley; bright green eyes.

I wipe the sudden hot, angry tears from her smooth cheeks and turn away, seating myself by the window. '*So many good memories were had here,*' I think, as I gaze out into the night.

As I cling to the golden pendant resting on my chest, I don't think of the angry words shared with my father tonight, I think of the stories Grandmamma Wendy used to tell me, the ones retold by my grandmother and my mother after her. And with a comforting silence surrounding me, I slip into the realm of dreams.

The odd sensation of something brushing my face causes me to open my eyes. I watch sleepily as the floating lights circle around me and above my head. I smile to myself. This is already a lovely dream.

They are beautiful things. I watch as their white wispy, smoke-like bodies continue to float around me. I hear them call to me and I smile as the satin of my dress brushes my legs when I walk.

The window is wide open, but I don't feel the cold as they beckon me closer. I climb onto the window seat and step outside. It feels as though I'm walking on air.

"Where are we going?" I hear myself ask, a dreamy smile on my lips.

The whisps chime and ebb with a soft light as they surround me, touching my hair, my arms, my hands, guiding me forward. One whisp floats forward and touches the golden acorn hanging from my neck.

"*K...i...s...s*," it murmurs in an odd hushed voice.

A childish giggle bubbles up in my throat as my necklace begins to glow, soft golden sparks falling from it as it rises, tugging at my neck gently. I feel an eagerness deep inside my soul. I feel my arms spread wide as I shout with unsuppressed excitement.

"Take me away!"

And in that moment, I jump from the ledge.

But I don't fall. In a dream so wonderful, how could I do anything but fly? The sensation is as beautiful as it is breath-taking. London below is littered with twinkling lights and streets still bustling with life. I want to shout down to the people to show them what they're missing, but the wind carries my voice away.

As the whisps light the way, my heart races with joy; the rush of adrenaline is deliciously addictive. They surround me with their light as they lead the way through the starry skies and across the path of the crescent moon.

The wind rushes through my hair, sending it sprawling behind my head, and the skirts of my dress ripple around me like wild waves. The coldness of the evening is all around and yet even in my summer gown with sleeves, I don't feel it for a moment. The only sensation that overcomes me is the utter elation of flying further into the stars and leaving the city of London far, far below.

III

My eyes flutter open as the sun's warm rays coat my face and arms. The remnants of last night's dream are foggy in my mind as I sit up, my hands running over what I can only describe as the softest bed I have ever slept on. My eyesight focuses and I take in the staggering blue skies around me. My heart does a somersault in my chest.

I'm not in the nursery, I'm not even in the house.

Shock overwhelms me as I try to think this through logically. Soon though, I feel the panic begin to rise from the pit of my stomach. I squeeze my eyes shut and open them again, only to stare blankly at the white billows of cloud that envelop me.

'This can't be right' my mind argues.

"This is impossible," I mutter to myself.

I pull myself up and slowly crawl to the edge. My heart hammers in my chest and then stops altogether when I take in the view. There, leagues below, sits one large island surrounded by the murky depths of the sea. My mind is incapable of words; the only thing to come out of my mouth is a gasp.

"Ok Wyn, it's time to wake up now," I tell myself.

Suddenly, I feel myself sinking rapidly through the folds of cloud. I try to pull myself back up to safety, but before I can stop it, I'm falling through with nothing but the dark sea to catch my fall.

The scream that escapes my throat is one of sheer terror as I tumble through the sky. My body plummets so fast that I barely register crashing into the water—that is, until the freezing temperature kicks my body into survival mode. It takes what feels like an eternity to break the surface as I gulp in lungfuls of air.

Just as I'm getting my breath back, I'm roughly plucked from the water and thrown onto the deck of a ship. My hair is plastered to my cheeks and neck as I splutter and cough up water. A rough pair of hands hoists me to my feet.

I look up to find a whole crew of rugged, filthy looking men watching me with rotten toothy grins. Their faces are rugged and worn, some with scraggly beards and others with days old stubble. The sight and smell turn my stomach and I fight not to empty the contents on the wooden floors. If I didn't know any better, I would have said that these filthy men were *Pirates*.

"Well lookie' here!" says one of them as he pushes forward.

"What have we nabbed ourselves, boys?" he cackles as he stands in front of me.

He doesn't give me a chance to explain before taking my chin in his hand and lifting my face to his. He scrutinizes me as he tilts my head from side to side, his beady eyes drinking in every detail. He's older than the rest, with greying, scraggly hair and whiskers protruding from his upper lip and chin.

The man's attention shifts as he lowers his gaze to my exposed chest, making my skin crawl. He spots my acorn pendant between his fingers, twisting it in the light as his other hand falls slack from my chin.

"As I live and breathe," he breathes, the stench of rum heavy on his lips.

He takes the golden acorn in his hand and yanks it hard. The clasp breaks and the necklace falls from my neck into his hand.

"That is mine, it's a family heirloom!" I cry, trying to fight the firm grasp of the man gripping my shoulders.

"No need to lie, sweetheart, we all knows that it were Pan who gave you this! Can't fool us eh' boys?" he rallies as he lifts the necklace for the whole crew to see.

"I'm not who you think I am. I've never met this Peter. My name is Wyn, Bronwyn Ainsley!" I plea, fear taking root in my stomach.

"You can't fool us, Darling girl." He leers at me, before turning back to the crew.

"Scully, have The Jolly Roger head for The Redbreast! I'm sure Pirate Captain Kage'll be thrilled to have his Wendy back. Kram, tie her up and take her down to see'im." He waves a hand at my captor and walks away, my pendant tight in his grasp.

"No, please! You're making a mistake!" I scream, as I fight mercilessly to escape Kram's tight grip as he drags me over to the mast.

Kram ignores my desperate pleas as he ties my wrists to the mast. He sneers at me as frightened tears cascade down my cheeks. I start to shiver, though I can't tell if it's due to fear or the harsh winds.

"The Cap'n will be seeing you real soon."

I look up to the sky, praying to whatever god to help me wake up from this nightmare, when a shadow in the left corner of the sail catches my eye. I can tell from the way he's moving he isn't one of these thuggish men.

The figure dives out of his hiding spot and swings down on a thick rope, landing effortlessly on the deck. The stunned pirates take in the intruder as he gets to his feet and wipes his palms on his knees.

"Now that's no way to treat a lady."

In moments they're on him with swords unsheathed. The clash of metal reverberates through me. I watch in horror as they keep coming toward him from all sides. He's outmanned a dozen to one, and my mind tells me that he is sure to lose. Yet, one by one, the pirates are being defeated.

I watch helplessly as some are flung overboard, while others are knocked unconscious. All the while, my mysterious hero remains standing. Once most of them are down, he rushes to my side.

"Who are you?" I ask, warily.

"There'll be time for introductions later," he says, lifting his sword above his head.

I bite back a gasp as the sword comes down, searing the rope in half and setting me free. Before I can get my bearings, he takes my hand and rushes to the other end of the ship. I risk a glance behind to discover several of the pirates on our tail.

"What is the meaning of this!" a voice bellows.

Time seems to stop as I glance over my shoulder at the presumed Captain. His face is shrouded in shadow from his overly dramatic hat. That, matched with the deep red coat fashioned with brass buttons, he is a sight to behold. His presence fills me with a sense of dread, and I look away quickly.

"There's no time, can you swim?" the stranger asks as we reach the bow.

I barely have time to nod before he has me in his arms and is throwing me overboard. I hit the water too fast for any sound to escape my mouth. The water is deafening in its silence. Luckily there are no pirates to pull me out, this time I'm pulled to the surface by a dolphin. I've already swallowed an impressive amount of seawater by the time I breathe in air again.

Just as I'm getting my bearings, using the dolphin for support, I hear a large roar from above and then a splash, the stranger resurfaces at my side. He gives me a reassuring wink before I can speak.

"Hold tight, we need to be quick. Don't want to be caught by any sirens," he warns as he wraps himself around me, his hand curled in a firm grasp on the dolphin's fin.

"Sirens?!"

No reply. The stranger laughs at my incredulous tone and the dolphin takes off, flying through the waves effortlessly, leaving the pirates and their ship far behind.

The dolphin drops us a bit of a way offshore and my mysterious saviour tells me to swim for land. By the time I reach the sandy shores,

I'm exhausted. I try to catch my breath as the aftershock sets in. As I get to my feet, my wet hair and dress plastered to my small frame, I see the stranger surging along the beach and disappearing into the line of trees.

"Hey, wait!" I call after him, squeezing the water from my hair as I make my way across the sand after him.

As I stumble through the greenery, I stop and gape at the sheer immensity of my surroundings. I turn back to see his outline is getting smaller and try my best to run after him, my bare feet catching on thorns and sharp twigs.

"Please!" I call out after him.

I watch as he stops and turns his head in my direction. To my surprise, he waits for me to catch up. When he deems me close enough, he disappears into the undergrowth again, and without another hesitation I soon follow.

"Take me home," I plead, my hair and my now ripped gown getting tangled in the foliage.

"No can-do, sweetheart, I'm not really the hero type," he argues, keeping his pace.

"Well what on earth would you call that back there?!" I exclaim, throwing my arm out to emphasise my point.

He doesn't turn around, he merely chuckles under his breath. "Let's just say I like to get under their skin, and by the looks of it, so do you. Kage though, well I wasn't expecting him there," he says calmly.

"Hardly, they took me prisoner!" I scoff, tugging my tattered skirts from a large thorn bush.

"Oh, had they now, I hadn't noticed," he replies, sarcasm dripping from his words. I don't need to see his face to know that he's rolling his eyes.

"And whose Kage? Is he their Captain?" I question.

"Look, you don't want to get on the wrong side of him. So best just to stay out of his way"

I stop and throw my hands up in the air in frustration as I blow several loose strands of hair from out of my face. "Well if you aren't going to help, you could at least point me in the right direction!"

I watch him as he slows mid stride, his shoulders sinking as he lets out a deep, frustrated sigh.

"Alright, fine. Where you headed?"

"London," I reply indignantly.

I watch as he stops dead in his tracks, his body stiff. He looks back at her over his shoulder. His voice is soft but clear. "What did you say?"

"I said London. I need to get home," I repeat, an uneasy feeling settling in my stomach.

Before I can react, he doubles back and pins my shoulders against a tree. His closeness has my heart racing, fearful of his next move. I turn my head away slightly, trying to put some distance between the stranger's face and mine.

I watch breathlessly as he looks me over, taking in every detail with a furrowed brow. He doesn't speak for what feels like a lifetime before he finally focuses his eyes on mine. And with a single whispered breath he utters a question that stops the heart in my chest.

"Wendy?"

My throat closes up and I feel myself trembling under his gaze. He notices the heaviness of his hold on me, and backs away, his eyes still watching me warily.

"Y—you knew Wendy?" I stammer when I finally regain my voice.

I watch as he runs a hand through his hair. My memories come alive as I recall the stories from my childhood.

"Yes, but it was a long time ago." He breathes out a disappointed sigh.

"Clearly I got the wrong girl," he adds, lifting his eyes to meet mine.

"A few generations too late I'd say," I counter, unable to look away.

"What the hell does that mean?"

"You really knew her?" I ask, ignoring him and stepping closer.

I study him closely as my head swirls with the stories she'd told me, the stories my grandmother had retold, and my mother after that.

"That's why they captured me; they must have thought I was her..."

"But wait... that would make you," I trail off, my head focusing on the math.

"Pretty damn old, but who really counts these days?" he replies, his eyes still trained on me.

I shake my head in disbelief. In the back of my mind, I can hear my mother's voice and the way she would build the tale; excited beyond reason. My stomach twists with guilt as I realise the consequence of refuting her fanciful tales. Tales which were in fact true.

"Who are you?" I demand, unable to stand the suspense any longer.

"The name's Curly, but Wendy used to know me as—"

"—Cubby," I finish, my eyes wide with wonder.

His brow furrows as he surveys me, tilting his head to one side. I see his hand slowly lift to where his sword hangs at his waist. "And how the hell would you know that?"

"She told me," I say, my voice quiet as I fall back against the trunk of the tree.

"How is this possible?" I whisper to no-one, staring through him.

"Who are you? How do you know my name?" Curly repeats, his voice louder than before.

"Wendy. She was my great grandmother."

He blinks in shock, dropping his hand from his belt. Stepping forward, he regards me closely. I feel the question bubbling up inside me as he watches me. There's chatter in my head that I can't block out and my temples throb in time with my pounding heart.

"Where am I?" I ask.

"Well you're a long way from home, sweetheart," he replies, the corner of his mouth twisting into a slight smirk.

"Curly, where am I?" I reply, my voice louder as I drawl the words.

Curly steps back and opens his arms wide as he turns from left to right.

"Well, you're in Neverland of course. Or rather, what's left of it," his arms drop back to his sides with a grin.

I start hyperventilating. The revelation causes my head to pound. In my deepest of hearts, I knew it could be nothing but the truth, but yet how could that be?

This information is more that I can take. Before I know what's happening, the world around me blurs into several shades of finger-painted green and my mind plummets into darkness.

IV

When the unconscious haze lifts, I awake to find myself in a large cave. My mind is drowsy and far too disorientated to feel any sort of fear. I sit up, furs falling off me as I stretch. My hand lifts to my aching head as I take in my surroundings.

I watch as Curly makes his way over to a leather bag on the far side of the cave, partially hidden by rocks, and pulls it out from its hiding place. He strides over, taking the contents out of the bag as he draws closer. As he sits beside me, he unwraps a few large leaves to show the contents inside: a few rolls of bread, dried fish and some sort of fruit. He hands me a few pieces of each.

"You should eat something."

"Thank you," I mutter as I take a tentative bite of the fruit.

It's much juicier than I expected and extremely sweet, though not in a sickly way. My stomach rumbles with pleasure. With all that had happened, food certainly hadn't been on the forefront of my mind. I chew quickly, savouring the taste before I take another bite. I didn't realise how ravenous I was until now.

"Woah, slow down or you'll make yourself sick," Curly warns, smirking despite himself.

I give him an apologetic smile as I wipe the juice that trickles down my chin. Now that I'm somewhat rested, I take the chance to really look at him. His face is tan and rugged, lined with days old stubble across his jawline and upper lip. His hair is the shade of wet sand and curls over his forehead to brush his thick, dark eyelashes. I can just make out his eyebrows through his curls and they're as dark as his lashes. His eyes are the colour of slate blue, piercing through me as though delving into my soul. I have to remind myself not to stare.

"Some young lady you are," He remarks with a laugh.

"Says the roguish young man with animal skins for clothes," I laugh.

"The roguish young man who saved you from certain doom," he counters.

I lower my hand from my mouth. "Thank you for coming to my rescue, and for bringing me with you. I am in your debt." I say earnestly.

He shrugs, his face failing to mask his embarrassment.

"I see the likeness, you know. Between you and Wendy," he changes the subject, focusing his attention on the fire crackling before us.

I smile in acknowledgement as I take another bite.

"Where are we?" I ask once I've finished my meal.

"Somewhere safe," is all he replies, his eyes lost in the flames.

I scoff, getting to my feet. "This place isn't real. Her stories weren't real; they were just stories," I argue, more to myself than to him.

Curly turns his gaze to me, the light of the fire flickering in his hard eyes.

"Sorry to burst your bubble, sweetheart, but this place is as real as you and me, what Kage has left of it at least."

"My name isn't, *sweetheart*, it's Wyn," I reply indignantly.

"And who on earth is this Kage?"

"He's bad news."

"Care to elaborate?" I press.

He chooses not to reply so I assume the conversation is over. I take in the state of my dress, the soft fabric now rough from the seawater and wilderness. The rips and tears are irreparable and I sigh. Pulling a few leaves and twigs from my hair, I walk over to the mouth of the cave to take in the landscape.

I can hear the sea despite the surrounding, dense woodlands that block it from view. The sheer size of the forested area is overwhelming, and I wouldn't dare attempt to navigate it by myself, besides where would I go? The chances of getting lost, or kidnapped are too high to risk it.

Looking around at Neverland, I sense an underlying danger. Grandmamma Wendy always portrayed it as such a wondrous and magical place, but from what I can see, it's rather haunting and not at all what it seems. As I search the immense foliage for signs of life, I notice small lights floating through the trees towards me. Frowning, I watch as more appear and my eyes widen as I place them in my memory.

"You're from my dream!" I cry as they come closer.

I step backwards into the cave as they surround me, taking in the sheer number of them as they come close, lighting up my arms and face with their dim glow.

"God damn whisps!" Curly complains behind me.

I turn to see him swat at one as they attempt to float closer to him.

"I think they're what brought me here," I say slowly, trying to recall what I thought a dream.

"They called to me," I murmur. *'Just like my mother.'*

I feel his eyes trained on me for a moment before he speaks.

"Then I'm afraid you're as linked to this place as the rest of us, sweetheart. Though talking to whisps is a little strange, even by our standards."

I remember how they lured me in, how they drew me outside, and what they called my necklace. My hand flies to my throat and tears sting my eyes.

"My pendant!"

"You aren't wearing one," Curly argues, turning his focus back to tending the fire, while swatting at the whisps.

"I was until that scoundrel ripped it from my neck. I have to get it back!"

"I doubt they'll give you a chance and I'm not going back to find out," he argues with a shrug.

I slump to the floor, my tears spilling over my cheeks. "It was Grandmamma Wendy's; she gave it to me on her deathbed when I was a little girl."

"Ah crap, well I'm sorry."

"It was a beautiful golden acorn, I've never seen another like it," I explain, staring sadly at the empty hands in my lap.

The whisps float closer to me, their hushed voices speaking almost in unison and I lift my head to listen. As I do, I see Curly flinch and turn his head to face me, an urgency in his eyes.

"The kiss!" he breathes.

"*K...i...s...s,*" the whisps murmur over and over.

"That was what she used to call it. How do you know that?" I ask warily.

A cloud passes over Curly's face and he turns away, his fists clenched as he does. A thick silence shrouds us, the only sound the crackling of the fire, until my curiosity gets the better of me.

"Curly?" I probe.

"Pan gave it to Wendy. It's what they called it." He tells me, his back still turned.

"Where is he? Maybe he could help me get home," I suggest.

Curly shrugs. "The hell should I know, he disappeared years ago."

"This isn't how she described this place to me when I was a child. You, Peter, and the rest of the Lost Boys were all children, Hook and his pirates were the adults." I say, trying to understand.

Curly lets out a heavy sigh and turns to me, a sadness and anger in his eyes that stops me from uttering another word.

"Pan was never the same once Wendy and her brothers left. We all saw it, we all felt it. Then Kage came along. All of a sudden, we weren't kids no more. It was slow going but we grew up. That crook has a lot to answer for. Came from nowhere and cut Hook down faster than Pan could blink, and he burnt our hideout down to the ground," he explains bitterly.

"That's where they were going to take me. They said Kage would be happy to have his Wendy back or something like that," I tell him.

"Like I said, he's bad news. Do me a favour and steer clear of him," he warns.

"Anyway, Kage drove Pan away the minute he stepped foot on Neverland's shores. No-one really knows what happened to Pan, not even the Lost Boys. Not that we go by that name anymore."

"Where are the rest of you?" My voice is gentle, tentative.

"We all went our separate ways. Sure, we bump into each other once in a while, but I'm not looking to get reacquainted. Pan was the glue that held us together. With Neverland and the magic going to crap, and Peter gone, there was nothing to keep us united.

"Haven't you tried to find Pan?" I ask. "You could fight Kage together." Curly lifts his head and laughs before shaking his head. He turns to look at me, a playful smirk on his lips, and for a moment, the warmth of his gaze unnerves me. So much so that I feel a blush rise up my neck.

"You really are Wendy's granddaughter, aren't ya?"

"Great Granddaughter," I correct, my lips lifting into a small smile.

I gaze out to the mouth of the cave and beyond, listening to the crackle of the fire as I watch the sky. The day fades slowly into night as the pale pink clouds blend into the peaches and oranges of the sky, the mountains in the distance reach high to touch them. I watch silently as the sun lowers through the trees and somewhere through the dense forest, kisses the horizon before sinking into the sea.

"I didn't think it were possible that this place could truly exist," I say quietly.

"And yet here we are," Curly responds with a slight chuckle.

I turn to look at him, grabbing his arm. "I have to find a way home, Curly."

"I know, I figured you'd say that eventually. But there ain't no magic anymore so you can't just fly home," he replies, watching my hand as I retract it.

"And I suppose you have a plan?"

"We'll head over to the Indian camp where the Piccaninny tribe live in the morning, they may have some ideas. Besides, it was on my to-do list anyway."

"Hell, they can even help you with some new clothes too."

I look down at my worn attire and I can't help but agree. A new set of clothes wouldn't go amiss.

"I don't understand what it is with you Darlings and coming here in your nightgowns," Curly remarks. His tan cheeks colour even more with what I can only assume is a blush.

"It is not a nightgown! Wait, Grandmamma Wendy came here in her nightgown?" I scoff, trying my best not to laugh at the idea of the utter indecency.

Curly points to the tattered cerise gown I'm wearing. "*That's* a nightgown. I don't care how much you deny it. I know what a nightgown is Wyn."

"Well you are mistaken. It is in fact a ballgown," I argue.

"A ballgown?" He raises a brow, unconvinced.

"Yes, it's what you wear to parties," I explain.

"You wore that to a party?!"

"Well, I admit it didn't look quite this bad at the party. Besides, I've been swimming in it and chasing after you through the wilderness. Things most young ladies don't do—nevermind in ballgowns!"

"I'm sure where you're from that's a perfectly valid point," Curly replies with a snort.

"It is a perfectly valid point regardless of where I'm from," I retort.

"Stubborn like her too," he mutters.

"Excuse me?"

"Wendy," is all he replies.

V

I awake with a jolt to Curly gathering supplies around the cave, shoving them into a bulging rucksack. Rubbing my face, I sit up to glance out of the mouth of the cave. I try to focus my eyes on the dark trees; dawn hasn't risen yet.

"What time do you call this?" I groan, turning in Curly's direction.

"I let you sleep in," he retorts, amusement laced through his tone.

"You would call this sleeping in? It's hardly the break of dawn, Curly," I argue, pointing to the mouth of the cave.

"Journeying to the Indian's camp is long and hard, it will be even longer if we sit around here," Curly says, giving me a pointed look.

"How far is it?"

"The other side of the island," his voice is strained as he tightens the knots on the rucksack.

Reluctantly, I drag myself out from under the blankets of fur. As I try to ignore the way my skin prickles from the cold, I gather the furs up and fold them into a neat pile.

I brush the long tresses from my eyes and rip off a length of fabric from the bottom of my tattered dress. I use it to tie back my locks into a manageable ponytail, a few flyaways tickling my cheeks and curling at my ears.

"Where are your shoes?" Curly says, behind me.

I turn to face him, his eyes trained on my bare feet. I stare at them for a moment as I try to remember the last time that I was wearing something on my feet.

"I left them by the stairs, at home!" I gasp with dismay.

Curly sighs heavily, accompanied by an eyeroll as he unfastens the rucksack and flings a pair of leather slippers my way. I pick them up gingerly, my eyes returning to him as he re-ties his bag.

"They were meant to be a gift for Lily but they should fit you," he grumbles.

"Lily...?"

"Yes, Tiger Lily, Pr—"

"—Princess Tiger Lily?!" I cry, my eyes widening as I burst into laughter that echoes through the cave.

"What's so funny?"

"I remember Grandmamma Wendy telling me about Princess Tiger Lily, oh how frightfully jealous she was of her," I explain before another chuckle slips from my lips.

"Jealous?"

"They were both seeking Peter's affections, were they not?" I ask.

I notice the subtle blush spread across Curly's cheeks and a knowing smirk forms on my lips. My eyes fall to the slippers in my hands and my smirk turns to a grin. I casually stroke the slippers, my voice teasing.

"Something I see you'd understand. Wouldn't you, Curly?"

"What are you talking about?" he scoffs, his voice breaking slightly.

I look up to find a very flustered Curly, his eyes averted from mine and his cheekbones a defined pink. I chuckle quietly.

"Well one could argue that these slippers were made with the princess in mind." I put to him, lifting the leather slippers.

For the first time since I've met him, Curly is lost for words. I step towards him, closing the space between us as he watches warily. I smile warmly at him, before planting a soft kiss on his cheek.

"Thank you for the slippers, it's very sweet of you to give them to me instead of the girl they were intended for."

I watch in silent amusement as the blush deepens on his cheeks.

"You'll need them more than she will. I can always make another pair along the way," he shrugs.

"Well, either way, I appreciate the gesture," I reply, slipping on the handmade shoes. They fit perfectly.

The forest cradles us as we trudge through the wild undergrowth. Light creeps into the sky and though the hum of the forest is almost inaudible at first, as the hours slip by, the sound becomes more noticeable.

Curly is practically silent as he weaves in and out of the trees. His left arm is fixed in the same position: hovering above the hilt of the blade tucked into his side. I see how easily he blends in and how at home he is in this wilderness, and my heart pangs with envy.

I had never fit in with my father and his aristocrat friends, nor did I belong in an institution alongside my mother. Home, while a comforting place, was not something that felt truly *mine*. It was no more than a family heirloom passed down in my grandfather's will. One day, since I don't have a brother, it will be mine. Though this had never sat well with me either, my home became a shell after mother was taken away. A sorry state from the very day her nimble steps echoed the halls.

But here in the wilderness, it's almost laughable how much I stand out. Curly's quiet yet quick pace is not something we share; my slippered feet crack twigs and rustle leaves with every step. I sound more cumbersome than he does—and that is not how a young lady should be.

As I follow behind, I snag my dress on a loose tree root and tangle my foot in the fabric. With a cry of surprise, I fall to the ground as Curly doubles back to find me trying to untangle myself. He crouches down to my level and unhooks the snagged fabric before looking at me.

"You really should be more careful."

"Easy for you to say, you aren't wearing a tattered dress," I huff as he helps me to my feet.

He drops back down and grips the worn fabric in his hands.

"Hey! What do you think you're doing!?" I cry in dismay as he begins to rip at the fabric.

I watch in silent horror as he rips away the bottom few inches of my dress, so that it falls just above my ankles rather than trailing on the floor.

"There," he sighs as he rolls the loose fabric around his hand.

"That solves that problem."

"You didn't have to be such a brute about it," I argue, crossing my arms.

"A thank you would suffice, sweetheart," he rolls his eyes as he turns away and surges forward.

"My *name* is Wyn."

Trundling through the wilderness, I find myself lost in thought. Curly doesn't speak much as he surges forward down the path that only he sees. Dawn broke hours ago, but the snippets of sky that I see through the canopy are grey and dull.

I listen as the wind rustles the leaves and the birds chirp from high above. My feet pad more quietly now, a sign that I'm adapting to my surroundings. Though I'm unsure how it makes me feel. I wonder if Father has noticed me missing, I wonder briefly what he's doing and how long I'll be stuck here before I'm home.

"*Wyn.*"

I stop in my tracks, snapping my head up as I search ahead for Curly, but he hasn't spoken, his back is still facing me as he moves forward through the trees.

"*Wyn.*"

The voice is soft as it floats by me, deep and yet gentle. I turn my head to my left, staring into the lush foliage. It calls to me again, the curiosity to follow it makes me turn inland. I take a single step forward, onto the sand.

"Wyn, what are you doing?" Curly asks as he grabs my elbow.

I freeze at his touch and shrink back for a moment before the shock subsides.

"Goodness, Curly, you startled me!"

He looks from where I was headed and back to me, with a solemn expression on his face.

"What were you doing?"

"I heard someone. It sounded like it was calling to me. Was it you?" I turn to face him, curiosity written on my face.

Concern clouds his eyes, changing them from slate blue to more of a grey. He watches me warily before looking inland, his eyes carefully scanning the trees and their shadows.

"What is it?" I ask, searching his face for answers.

"Nothing, just stay close. We need to keep moving."

I think back to what Curly said in the cave and notice the path that we're on takes us around the island, instead of cutting through the island's inner stretches.

"You said where we're going is on the other side of the island though, surely it would be faster to cut inland," I reason.

"It's safer this way, trust me." Is all he replies.

I nod silently, not daring to argue, and we continue on our way.

The afternoon has welcomed us with a lazy downpour of drizzle. I'm tired and achy from walking for hours with no break. My skin is slick from the rain and my blonde waves stick to my cheeks, becoming uncomfortably plastered to my neck and back.

Wordlessly, I follow Curly, hoping he'll stop us soon to rest before we carry on. But he doesn't slow and so I find myself having difficulty keeping up.

This carries on for what I can only assume is an hour or so, before he stops and turns to me, dropping his rucksack and delving into the contents.

"How much further?" I ask, my voice whiny.

"After this next stretch, I promise."

"Why is it so imperative the Picaninny people help me?"

"It just is. They're more knowing than me, and like I said I was planning to go anyway. Unlucky for you, you're stuck with me. So, where I go, you go."

He takes something out and gets up, his face serious as he watches me closely.

"This is the dangerous part," he tells me.

"I thought you said this way was safer," I tease, a small smile playing on my lips.

"It is. But we're almost at Mermaid Lagoon," he says as though this were an explanation.

"There are actual mermaids here?" I ask, unable to hide the excitement leaking into my voice.

"There used to be," he replies, his tone sombre.

"Take these," he says softly as he hands me what looks like a handful of moss.

"What is this for?"

"To keep you safe. Put it in your ears and don't take it out until I tell you," he explains.

I look at him dubiously.

"Trust me," is all he says, his face earnest.

With a small shrug I do as he says. He keeps his eyes on me until he's satisfied that I've pressed the even portions of the sponge-like substance into my ears. He does the same. I watch as he remounts his sack before giving me a reassuring nod. Before I can respond, he turns on his heels and strides forward, with me hot on his tail.

The thick trees soon grow sparse as we walk towards an opening. All of a sudden, I can see the sky and feel the wind on my face. The sensation is refreshing. I take in the change of scenery gratefully, drinking the salty air into my lungs.

The open plane is a lagoon. Jagged rocks encircle the shore and its waters, embracing the soft waves as they wash in. The water is a clear turquoise, the colour deepening as it meets the open sea.

I'm happy to see something other than trees and vines. Even with the soft downpour of rain, the lagoon is beautifully serene. When Grandmamma Wendy told me tales of Neverland, this is the sort of place I imagined. It seems so otherworldly compared to the rest of the island. Though it's beautiful, there is an underlying darkness that I can't quite put my finger on.

I watch on as Curly surges ahead, his head down. I can almost envision the focus on his face. Within a moment, I'm reaching down and slipping off my shoes to feel the wet sand soothe my aching feet. As I tuck my hair behind my ear, some strands catch and I feel the sponge's grip loosen. I watch as it falls out onto the sand.

I look up in a panic, but luckily Curly is too focused to notice. The sound of the waves and the wind rushes into my head as I bend down to pick it up. Before I can replace it, something sidles its way into my ear and captures my attention.

'I know of a place which calls to me,
A burden that I must bear,
And when my name sounds from her sweet call,
Temptation I cannot fight.'

The voice is eerily familiar and the tune so soft that I shouldn't be able to hear it at all over the waves, yet I hear it clear as day. The sound of the voice is soothing and beautiful with each note and each word, I feel myself being drawn to it.

'Her influence like a siren to men,
A beckoning plea for me,
Answer her call this darling must do,
Beware should she come for you,
Beware of her call to you.'

My mind travels back as I step forward, following the voice into the waves, the cold water pooling around my ankles, but I hardly notice. I listen to the words, the voice becoming a figure in my mind, one I recognise as she grows clearer in my mind's eye.

"Mother."

The water rises and I sink further into its depths as the pull of my mother's voice beckons me closer. My skin prickles from the cold, but my mind doesn't register it; my brain is foggy. I see my mother in the distance, her silhouette balanced on a rock, inviting me closer. She slips off the rock and swims closer to me. The pull of the current urges me forward until the banking gives way to the open waters and I'm pulled under.

The water is dark and much deeper than I expected, my mind is still cloudy, the remnants of the song still echoing through my mind as I sink further. I see the silhouette come closer, her shape changing as she closes the space between us. As my eyes start to make her out, I notice her hair isn't blonde like mother's, it's dark like a raven's plumage. Her eyes are equally black, soulless and slanted. Her face is grey and her chin sharp and pointed. And where her legs should be... is a long, thick, scaled tail.

She flashes a wide grin, showing me the rows of jagged teeth behind her thin lips. It's enough to break her spell over me and I scream. Sea water pours down my throat, burning my oxygen-starved lungs as I panic. My heart drums in my chest as I realise that I'm drowning.

The creature crashes into me in an attempt to disorientate me. As black spots begin to dot my eyesight, I fight to swim to the surface. Just as I break through, she circles back and bats me again with her tail, and I thrash around in the water once more.

I feel myself weakening and about ready to give up when I hear an unearthly screech. Moments later, an arm hooks itself around my chest and I feel myself being dragged to the surface.

I'm still choking and spurting out water as I'm pulled onto the wet sand, my body soaked through and shivering from shock. I sense Curly stooping over me, his hand roughly pushing the hair away from my face and I gasp in mouthfuls of air.

My ears are ringing, but I can just about make out the words he's yelling at me. I open my eyes and immediately regret it, as when I look at his face, it's clear that he's furious. He clogs my ears with the moss once more as he continues to reprimand me.

"What the hell were you thinking? You could've drowned!"

He pulls me to my feet as he yells, the fury rolling off him in waves while I stand there like a dishevelled child. I try to apologise, but the words are lost as the lump in my throat grows bigger as I fight the tears that threaten to spill.

All of a sudden, his face goes slack, and the words on his tongue are lost to the wind. His eyes shroud over with an odd milky whiteness, his alluring blue irises lost underneath the white film. He turns, taking slow but meaningful steps back towards the water. I notice with instant dread, that his ears are clear of their plugs and without hesitating, I surge toward him to tug him back, but it's no use.

"Curly, no!" I scream, even though he can't hear me.

I pull at his arms and stand in front of him, pushing against his hardened torso with all the force I can muster, but he doesn't move an inch. I scream at him to stop, and pound my fists against his chest, but he doesn't acknowledge me.

"Curly, snap out of it, please!"

I realise all too soon, that we're now waist-deep in the water, and I feel the blood roaring in my ears. Frantically scanning our surroundings, I search the beach for anyone who could help, but come up empty-handed.

"He needs a distraction," I think out loud.

I sense the water's current change, the bank beneath us ready to give out from under us in the next few steps, and somehow in that moment of pure terror, I know what to do.

Planting my palms strongly against each of his ears, I reach up and press my lips hard against his. I feel his slow pace stop completely as I press against him and almost hesitantly, his hands move around me. Tears of relief and fear slip down my frozen cheeks as I realise it's working.

I pull away, my hands still firmly pressed against his ears, and watch his eyes closely. They meet mine and to my relief, are back to their regular shade of blue. He watches me, his eyes conveying the confusion and bewilderment he feels.

As I stare at them, I feel the water ripple around me and see the figure of the siren in their reflection. Before Curly has another moment to react, my hands are on the hilt of his sword. I swing it up and around, and with all of my might, plunge the blade into the murky depths below. The tip pierces her tail, drawing blood which bubbles to the surface.

The screech that erupts from her is blindsiding and even with my makeshift earplugs, the sound sears through my brain like a white-hot blade. My survival instincts suddenly kick in and I fight through the pain and grab Curly's hand. I practically drag him back to shore with me, barely stopping to swoop up his rucksack as we hurry into the safety of the forest, leaving the lagoon far behind us.

VI

The sky is now a deep blue and the clouds have cleared. The stars sparkle and shine their light for those of us below. Hours later, I'm still soaked through as I wait for Curly to return with the firewood.

After dragging him through the forest blindly, he'd silently redirected our route. As night fell, he'd decided it was best to stop and set up camp in a small clearing we'd stumbled across.

Though I know we're far from the lagoon, I can still hear the faint sound of crashing waves and the hiss of the sea. The memory of earlier sends a chill through my already trembling body and I shake my head roughly, as though that would shake the memory from my mind.

The sound of cracking twigs startles me and my eyes spring open, my gaze lifting to meet Curly's as he emerges from the trees. As soon as he notices me staring, he drops his gaze and busies himself with making the fire. I feel heat rise up my neck and look away, shifting uncomfortably in my seat.

The tension between us is thick and uncomfortable and I'm not sure how to break the awkward silence between us. Instead, I shift my gaze up toward the sky. I watch the stars glisten and I wonder if this is the same sky above London. A deep ache settles in my chest as I think of home, of my mother alone in an empty colourless room, of Nana fretting over my disappearance. Then the homesickness develops into guilt.

All those years I doubted my mother, all this time she had been right and I had dismissed her. I allowed my father to lock her away as though she was a shameful secret. Now here I was in the place she'd told me stories about, one all too real, and hardly the child's fairy tale I thought it was.

I wrap my arms around myself with a sigh as I lose myself in the stars. The noise from the crackling fire eventually pulls me back to the present and my thoughts of home are momentarily pushed to one side. Curly watches me through the flames, his eyes reflecting the warm glow.

"Curly, about before," I start, my voice uneasy.

He casts his eyes downward and remains silent for a few moments before he opens his mouth.

"Don't." He growls.

I open my mouth to speak, but I think better of it.

The night is silent, the fire now a pile of dull embers. The sky is breathtakingly beautiful and alive with stars, the air is cool and fresh, and yet I find that I'm comfortably warm. My mind is wide awake and even as I hear Curly's breathing deepen as he slips into a deep slumber, I'm unable to follow suit.

My mind trickles back to the song the siren had sung, her voice twisting and morphing into the sweet sound of my mother's. She'd sung the words to the lullaby my mother used to sing to me. In my mind's eye I see her how she was, full-faced and beautiful. Full of life and song. Then before I can stop myself, my mind takes me back to that small, white room of the institution. My mother curled up on the bed, her sunken face turned up at the tiny window, her hollow eyes staring fixedly at the bars. I see the familiar far away expression etched into the lines on her face, I feel rather than see her deep need for freedom, for fresh air.

Hushed whispers bring me back to reality, and I bolt upright. Hurriedly, I wipe away the tears that cling to my cheeks and bury the guilt pressing against my chest. I look up to find a whisp directly in front of me, and I jump in surprise.

As I calm down, I notice how a group of them have gathered around me. They float silently, a few pulling gently at my hair. Confused, I slowly get to my feet as I look around at them all.

"C...o...m...e," they whisper to me.

I watch silently as they beckon me away from the clearing and into the thick foliage. For a moment, I stop and look back at the tiny camp, my eyes falling on Curly. His breaths are slow and even. For a split second, I wonder whether to wake him. Remembering his tone earlier, I think better of it.

"C...o...m...e," the whisps beckon once more.

With a deep breath, I turn and follow them into the trees, leaving Curly fast asleep.

The whisps lead me through the forest. The starry sky above is shrouded by the wide branches of the trees and so I am guided by the dim light that the whisps provide. Though my curiosity is piqued, I bite back my questions and follow willingly.

Keeping close behind them, the tiny creatures guide me for what feels like quite some time. The ground softens beneath my feet, changing from rock and stone to mud and dirt, and before I know it, the trees are opening up to a small circular clearing. The night sky illuminates the space and I hold my breath in awe as I see the branches above bending around the small opening in a perfect circle.

I step forward into the centre, the tall grass reaching my knees, and lift my face to bask in the light of the moons. I feel the soft flutter of the whisps as they hum around me, brushing against my bare skin.

"Why have you brought me here?" I ask, my voice gentle for fear of frightening them away.

"*W...a...i...t*," they reply in unison.

"*S...e...e*," they continue.

I nod and take in my surroundings once more. The natural curve of the trees, their branches entwined like vines above, the tall grass sways freely with my movements. I inhale the fresh earthiness of the ground under my feet with a smile. The cool night air strokes my bare skin. I take in it all but see nothing save for the whisps that continue to float around me.

"What am I meant to be seeing, what am I waiting for?" I ask, frustration leaking into my softened voice.

"*P...a...t...i...e...n...c...e*," they utter in unison, their combined voices a lilting mix of whispers.

With a deep breath, I fluff my ragged skirts and seat myself amongst the tall grass. I twirl my blonde tresses around my fingers as I wait in silence.

Some time has passed by the time I notice a pink light emerging from the darkness. My heart stops in my chest as it draws closer. It's no bigger than the palm of my hand, nevertheless it shines as bright as a lamp. I hold my breath as it comes closer, until it's close enough for me to see it clearly.

I fight back a gasp as I take in the creature emitting the pink light. Her little body is perfectly tiny, as are her delicate hands and pixie face. Her violet eyes are wide and eerily beautiful, yet her mouth is so small that I can barely register it on her petite face. Tight pink curls cling to her head and bounce as she cocks her head to one side. Her dress, made from what looks like flower petals and bits of leaves, fits her form perfectly.

I'm already amazed by her when I notice her wings. Perfectly formed, delicate as a spider's newly woven web, and shimmering all the colours imaginable as they flutter behind her. She is eerily beautiful and I'm silenced by her presence.

Without realising it, I lift my arm and slowly reach out to her with my palm flat and facing up. I feel the whisps continue to circle us as she hesitantly lowers herself onto my open hand. I'm afraid to breathe as she does so. Our eyes are trained on each other as she sits in my hand. I watch in stunned silence as she smooths her skirts and folds her wings behind her.

"She's beautiful," I breathe.

At this, she chimes like hundreds of tiny bells in unison. While it takes me aback for a moment, I quickly compose myself and consider it a thank you.

"D...o...Y...o...u....B...e...l...i...e...v...e?" The whisps question me, their individual voices overlapping.

"I do, I do believe," I whisper, my eyes unable to veer from the tiny fairy in my hand.

As soon as the words leave my lips, she chimes once more and leaps into the air, her wings spread wide. A laugh bubbles up in my throat, but before it escapes, the surrounding trees come alive with colour. Spheres of light draw closer: red, green, yellow, all the colours I could imagine. More fae materialize in the small clearing, each of them bringing a new chime to the mixture and creating a beautiful musical sound that rings sweetly in my ears.

They rush past me, around and around until all I can see is a tornado of blended colours, lighting me up like a rainbow, and leaving me breathless. My hair swirls up with the current they've created, and the excitement of it renders me speechless.

"T...h...e...r...e...A...r...e...S...o...F...e...w...O...f...U...s...L...e...f...t," the whisps explain through blends of colour.

As they say this, the fae stop their light show and hang in the air like beautiful, multicoloured lanterns, dotted around the clearing, all their violet eyes trained on me. I spin slowly, as I take them all in, a few dozen, but not nearly as many as Grandmamma Wendy would tell me of in her stories. And as I do, I notice one fairy in particular isn't amongst the dozens I see.

I'm about to ask them where Tinkerbell is when a cry cuts through the night's silence. My heart stops as the sound pierces me. I whip my head around to the direction of the sound, my gut telling me it's Curly.

I spin back to the fae to find that the sound has startled them and they've scarpered back into the safety of the deep woods, the whisps along with them. The clearing is unsettlingly quiet, void of all the musical chimes that just a moment ago filled this space. The stars no longer brighten the clearing like before; the lack of colour and light has transformed this tranquil place into something unwelcoming and cold.

A second cry, cuts through the silence and draws me back to the thought of Curly. Without another thought for the fairies, I'm rushing through the trees and back to the camp as fast as my legs will carry me.

I make it back to camp in minutes, the embers are still glowing as I rush to Curly's side. His face is scrunched up, a low groan sounds in his throat as he tosses in his sleep. I notice the beads of sweat forming on his forehead and the way his chest rises and falls rapidly. He's having a nightmare.

I hush him and do my best to soothe him as I try to wake him up gently. I call to him, dabbing the sweat from his forehead as I caress his face, a sadness spreading through me as I watch him suffer. He calls out and the pain in his voice cuts through me, making me feel utterly helpless.

As I continue to hush his moans and wipe the sweat away from his face, his eyes dart open, the steely blue of his iris' changing ice cold as they focus on me. I have no time to distance myself from him and almost instantly, he grabs me by my scalp, and I hear the familiar sound of a metal blade being unsheathed. Before I can scream for him to stop, I feel the cold edge of his sword pressed against my throat.

The blade stings as the sharpened edge cuts into my skin, causing a small trickle of blood to bubble up against the metal and run down my throat. A suppressed whimper from my throat causes his eyes flicker as he jolts back to reality. The icy sheen over his eyes melts away to shock as he takes in the blade at my throat and the way he's scrunching a fistful of hair.

The horror in his eyes drowns out the harshness of his stare. Curly shrinks back and drops his sword with a soft *thud* on the mossy ground as he scuffles back, away from me. Terror has me rooted to the spot; I can't even bring myself to move.

"Wyn, I..." he begins, his voice wracked with guilt.

As soon as my name leaves his lips, life comes back to my frozen limbs and I dart into the trees, running with all my might. I bring my fingertips to my neck and when I pull them away, they're smeared with blood. Frightened tears cloud my vision as I crash mindlessly through the trees. I have no sense of direction, the urgency to run set deep in my bones. I need to get away from the feel of cold steel by any means necessary.

I hear him as he calls after me, his voice drowned out by the hammering in my chest. It doesn't take long for him to catch up with me. As he wraps his arms around me to stop me from running, a hair-raising scream escapes me and rips through the night.

As though touching me has scalded him, he quickly lets me go, a pained expression burned into his features. I stumble forward, clutching the nearest tree trunk to stabilise myself. My breathing is ragged and now that I've stopped running, I feel my body shaking uncontrollably and violently.

"Wyn, I—I'm sorry. I didn't mean it," he rambles, rushing through his words like a terrified child.

I turn to face him, more fearful tears threatening to spill. I can't calm my nerves enough to stand still, let alone string a sentence.

"I was having a bad dream and I lashed out. I didn't mean it," he continues, his voice drips with guilt.

I look into his eyes and notice his gaze fall to the small cut on my throat, before eventually meeting my gaze. I see the remorse in his eyes, but I'm unable to stop myself from trembling, unable to forgive him just yet. He tentatively holds out his hand to me and I shrink back without thinking. The hurt in his eyes is unavoidable, but I can't get the earlier scene out of my head—the icy stare, the deadly stance, how easy it could have been for him to kill me in that moment of lost clarity.

With a defeated sigh, he drops his hand back to his side and turns back, taking long slow strides back to the camp. I watch him purpose-fully slow down and look over his shoulder to where I'm standing. He's visibly waiting, hoping for me to follow. I look out at the dark woods and for a moment I wonder how long I could survive without him, and the thought takes me back to the encounter with the siren.

With a jagged breath, I turn to him and follow in silence. He waits for me to catch up to him before he moves forward, stopping every few metres and waiting patiently for me.

When I'm close enough to hear, his pained, quiet voice reaches me. His tone is gentle, yet firm.

"You have my word that I will never hurt you again."

And somehow, with that promise, the knot in my stomach loosens.

VII

The sun is peering through the trees when I finally wake. I sit bolt upright, my eyes falling on Curly who watches me tentatively from a safe distance. I can tell he doesn't want to startle me, and I'm grateful for the distance. I quickly realise how late in the morning it is, though it doesn't take long for me to realise that this is Curly's way of regaining my trust.

Subconsciously I reach for my throat, my fingertips grazing the flaked dried blood. Luckily, the wound is only superficial, but I still feel on edge after last night's incident.

"Will you let me take a look?" his voice drifts over to me from the other side of the fire pit.

I slowly turn to meet his gaze, and as I do my heart quickens its pace. I know that I will eventually have to trust him, but my body betrays the anxiety that I feel. I bite my lip and get to my feet, slowly stepping around the ashen fire pit and seating myself across from him, an arm's length away. His gaze stays with me as he cautiously inches forward so that he's close enough to touch.

My breath hitches and he senses the change, quickly showing me his hands, his face earnest.

"I won't hurt you, Wyn. I gave my word."

I give Curly a quick, silent nod, once again, not trusting myself to speak. I watch as he assesses the wound. He reaches over to his satchel and draws out a thick piece of cloth, a handful of what looks to be crushed herbs, and finally, his water pouch.

I watch, fascinated as he sprinkles a handful of herbs onto the cloth and douses it with water. He then scrunches the wet cloth into a ball and squeezes out the excess fluid before pressing it against my neck, wiping and dabbing. I flinch as the cloth comes into contact with the cut, but I soon relax into the gentle method of his touch.

"I should've warned you not to wake me, this is my fault," he comments, cutting through the silence.

My eyes fall on him, but he keeps his attention focused on my injury. I feel my unease start to thaw as I watch him and how attentive he's being.

"Accidents happen," I murmur.

His hand falters and his eyes lift to meet mine, a seriousness in them that stops me in my tracks. "I could've killed you."

I'm surprised how calm my voice sounds as I reply. "I know."

The morning has quickly drawn into the afternoon when we finally set off. Though there's still a slight tension between Curly and I, the mood seems to have brightened considerably.

I follow closely, at a steady pace, but as the sun beats down on us, the forest temperature rises, and I begin to feel my skin turn sticky and slick with sweat.

I do my best to put up with it, but as the minutes roll into hours I find myself struggling with the thought of it more and more. We just reached the second hour mark of having left our previous camp when I finally speak up.

I pull a twig from my greasy locks and grimace. "Is there anywhere we can clean ourselves? I've never felt so filthy in all my life!"

"Alright, Princess. Not all of us live in ivory towers," Curly teases, his humour apparently returned with his lightened mood.

"There's a stream somewhere through this way. We'll stop there for a while."

"Thank heavens," I sigh with relief.

True to his word, a few hours later through the calming noises of the natural environment, I hear the familiar sound of running water. As we get closer, the sound grows louder and the smell of wet grass and moss fills my lungs.

"Lucky for us, it seems we're close to a waterfall." Curly calls over his shoulder.

"A waterfall?" I repeat.

"Yeah, there's tons of them scattered around the island."

He stops and turns to me with a playful smirk on his lips.

"Don't tell me you've never heard of a waterfall."

"Of course, I have!" I scoff, turning my nose up at him.

"...Though I've never seen one before."

At this, he lets out a hearty laugh and shakes his head before continuing. I pull a face at him, sticking my tongue out like a petulant child rather than the respectable young lady I am.

I follow him through a cluster of trees and carefully climb the slight gradient toward two large boulders covered in a mossy coat. I slip through the slim opening between them and walk straight into a tight clearing.

The trees from before are replaced with high walls of stone, slick with water and slimy moss. The air is fresh and damp and the sun sneaks through the branches that stretch high over our heads. The rich sound of rushing water fills my ears as my senses are enriched by the feeling of life around me.

I inhale sharply as I take in the waterfall. The fresh water cascades over the stone wall and rushes down into the shallow pool below. I watch as bubbles surface and float along the stream, bursting with each ripple and bend.

"Is this the sort of thing you were after?" Curly teases as he kneels by the stream, collecting the water in his pouch.

"I think... this is better," I breathe, my attention still drawn to the water.

"Well we still have a fair way to go, so we can't stay long," he tells me, as he twists the cap onto the enlarged water pouch.

"The only way in and out of here is the way we came in, so we shouldn't be bothered by anyone either."

I watch in silence as he drops his satchel and unties his scabbard, dropping it to the ground with a soft clang, the sword still sheathed. Folding my arms, I wait for him to notice me.

When he finally stops and looks up, his expression turns to confusion.

"What?"

I give him a stern look and say nothing as his eyes trail slowly down my body, before looking up again. Moments later his eyes widen as he realises what I'm hinting at.

"Oh, right!"

He turns away from the waterfall, and me, abruptly and walks toward the bubbling stream connected to it.

"Don't panic, I won't look," he tells me, his back still facing me.

I hesitate for a moment, unfolding my arms and dropping them back down to my sides. I feel satisfied when he continues to keep his back to me.

With a slight spring in my step, I turn to the pool of water. I spin around, expecting to see Curly looking my way, but he's crouched down, focused on the stream.

I slip off my handmade shoes and peel my dress away from my skin, throwing it to one side. I glance down at my undergarments and decide to rid myself of those too, all the while trying to ignore the fact that I'm sharing the space with Curly.

I dip my foot in and inhale in surprise at the coolness of the water, and before I can think twice, I jump straight in. The middle of the pool is deeper than I had anticipated, reaching just over my breasts as I stand up.

"Oh! It's *freezing*," I gasp as I resurface, my skin prickling all over.

I just about hear Curly's chuckle over the roaring waterfall, but I decide to ignore him, and focus on the task at hand. I wade over to the waterfall and dive under quickly as it pounds down over my head. I emerge from the water and keep close to the overhang where the flow is most powerful. I wash my body thoroughly until I feel the cold begin to seep into my bones.

"So, I suppose you're interested in the princess, then?" I pry, my back still to Curly as I wash my skin.

"What's it to you?"

"Curiosity mostly," I shrug.

"How long have you cared for her?"

"Long enough," he responds after a moment of silence.

"So then, you're courting her?" I press, dipping my head back to remove the grease.

"Courting?"

"Yes. You've made your intentions clear to her," I explain.

"What? No!" He replies defensively.

"Then how is she to know your feelings if you don't tell her?"

I hear a sigh behind me. "It's complicated I guess."

Deciding not to press further, I stay quiet and finish bathing. As I check to see the coast is clear of wandering eyes, I notice Curly's focused on me. I immediately crouch down in the water again so only my face is showing.

"What happened to *not* looking?" I demand, embarrassment leaking into my voice.

Water drips from his chiselled chin as heat rises up his neck. Curly averts his eyes, and I take the opportunity to clamber out of the water and clothe myself. I take no time in dressing, once more as presentable as my tattered clothes will allow.

I stride over to Curly as I squeeze the water from my drenched hair.

"Well it would seem somebody has wandering eyes! And if there is ever a next time, I hope you understand that I won't tolerate being stared at like some common harlot!"

Curly says nothing.

"Well? Do you have anything to say fo—" the words shrivel up in my mouth as he stands up straight, his tunic gripped in his fist.

In my embarrassment and fury, I hadn't noticed the fact that he was shirtless, but as he turns to face me, it's all I can focus on. His smooth skin is taut with the rippled muscle underneath. Between that and his broad shoulders, my attention is captured. That is, until my eyes catch the jagged scar that starts under his right collarbone. The scar stretches diagonally across his chest and torso, all the way down to his navel.

Even though I can see that it's fully healed, the glossy skin is angry and raised. It stands out starkly against his smooth chest and the lines of muscle down his torso. I try to look away but my eyes won't listen.

"Well *now* who's the hypocrite?" Curly chides.

He heaves the tunic over his head, his muscled frame tense from stretching upwards. The sizable scar pales as the skin becomes taut, before it disappears under his clothing.

"You scold me for stealing a mere glimpse at you, which if you'd asked instead of assumed, you'd know it was to check if you were safe! And yet, you stand here gaping at me as though you've never seen a naked man!" he continues, his eyes stony.

With my mind still hazy, I open my mouth before shutting it again, unable to defend myself.

At my expression, he laughs, a bitterness to his tone. "You haven't, have you? My god, what sort of sheltered upbringing did you have?"

"How did you get that scar?" I ask, my voice low but steady.

I realise I've caught him off guard when his eyes widen in surprise. The colour of his eyes dull and I sense rather than see the aura of solemnity that blankets him.

Eventually, he speaks.

"That's a long story."

He swerves around my body and moves past me, heading back towards his belongings. I turn around to face him, his back to me.

"I'm sorry for staring. But... tell me what happened, please?"

I watch as he stops in his tracks, his broad shoulders slumping slightly in defeat. He exhales heavily as he crouches down by his bag. I tentatively walk over, lowering myself onto the carpet of grass. My eyes are focused on his face, noting how every part of him screams serious.

"It was a long time ago."

I rush through the trees in the direction of the hideout. Even with the speed I'm travelling at, I know no-one is following. I dart in and out of the trees, my feet familiar with the woodland track. The sounds of the forest echo all around me, but my mind is elsewhere; the news I'm so eager to share with the others balances on the very tip of my tongue. Tinkerbell follows close behind, her glow lighting up the path home as she flits through the greenery.

The hideout is teeming with activity; the twins are busy playing Pirates and Indians, Tootles is unsurprisingly occupied with his marbles, while Nibs and Slightly are nowhere to be seen, and so naturally, I assume they're inside with Peter.

Both the twins and Tootles look up as they see me approach Hangman's Tree.

"Come on you lot, I've got news and you're all gunna wanna hear it!" I holler at them before jumping through one of the entrances of the hollowed out tree and sliding down to the lower level of the hideout.

I drop and roll as I land inside, and it's not long before I hear the boys follow down after. As I guessed, both Nibs and Slightly are here, one carving something out of a piece of wood, while the other picks at his teeth with a pocket-sized blade.

"And where the hell have you been, Curly?" Nibs questions, pointing his knife at me.

A smirk forms on my lips and I give him a knowing stare.

"Well if you gave me a minute, I'd tell ya!" I counter.

I look around the space, searching for the leader of our little band of misfits.

"Where's Peter?"

Without looking up from his carving, Slightly points to the ladder leading further down into the den. "Wendy's room."

I rush over to the ladder and look over my shoulder at the boys. The surge of excitement rushes through me, causing my hands to jitter somewhat.

"Well lads, Tink, you coming or what?" I ask as I grab hold of the poles on each side of the ladder and slide down into the room below.

I hear them call after me as I drop down, landing in a pile of fur blankets with a hearty laugh. True to Slightly's words, I find Peter lounging around Wendy's room, boredom plastered heavily on his face.

"Peter, boy do I have some news for you!" I blurt, striding into the room.

He turns to me, as the boys all crowd in after me, his slack expression animated as he hears my words.

"Well go on then, Curly, tell us!" He pushes, leaning forward.

"Do you want the bad news first, or the good?" I ask.

"Bad first," Peter replies, his eyes glinting as the eagerness leaks into his voice.

"Well I was out scouting like you asked when I stumbled across some good-fer-nothin pirates out by Cannibal Cove," I explain, looking around the group as I speak.

"Gosh, is that it? Way to drag out a dull story, Curly," Nibs scoffs.

"Pirates are always lurking around Cannibal Cove," Tootles adds.

"I hadn't finished!" I argue.

"Well go on then!" the twins shout in unison.

"As I was saying, I overheard them talking about some new bad guy, been terrorizing the locals and all sorts."

The Lost Boys and Peter lean in, the curiosity clear on their faces. I can tell that I've caught their attention. I can't help feeling pleased with myself as I continue my story.

"I even heard one of them admit this guy is worse than Hook, if you can believe it!"

Peter scoffs. "I don't believe it for a minute!"

"We'll teach him a lesson, just like we did Hook! I bet he's not worth those rumours," Slightly jeers, digging a playful elbow at Nibs.

"Yeah, we can take him!" the twins add.

"Well go on then, Curly, tell us the good news,"

"Brace yourselves boys," I tease, looking around the room, taking in each of their faces as I do.

"Hook is dead!"

Silence shrouds the room for a moment, before the boys erupt into a barrage of questions and cheers, their voices overlapping each other.

"Hook's tricks were getting old anyhow, at least with this new guy we might get a bit of a challenge, eh boys?"

"The old codfish is dead!"

"Took him long enough!"

I turn to Peter expecting a grin or even one of his pixie-like smirks, but instead all I see is a hollow stare and a daunted expression painted onto a pale face. The excitement seems to die as each of the boys in turn notice Peter's sombre manner.

The air is so thick with silence that no-one dares to breathe. The words tumble from Peter's mouth in an accusatory whisper.

"He can't be, you're lying."

"Well that's just it, Peter, I heard the Pirates say it. Hook's dead—this new threat killed him. Tink was there too, she heard the same thing I did, right Tink?" I counter.

"Do you remember what they called him, Tink? The something Master was it?" I ask, clicking my fingers as I try to remember their words.

Tinkerbell chimes in, her voice ringing true to her name.

"The Shadow Master! Yes, that's it!" I answer.

"The Shadow Master? Pfft, what a silly name!" Nibs interjects.

"I'm sure he's no match for us, Peter! We'll have him begging for mercy," Slightly adds, his voice raised and excited.

"That's the spirit boys, looks like we have a new enemy to face!" I cheer.

"What do ya say, Peter?" I ask as I turn back to Peter.

I stop short as I watch the blood drain from his face. Silence envelopes the room once again as all eyes fall to our eerily quiet leader. I'm about to open my mouth to speak when his hazel eyes lift to meet mine.

The fury in his eyes is fierce and unrelenting and his stare pierces through me like a fiery blade. The boys shrink away as Peter slowly gets to his feet, his body floating millimetres above the ground as his eyes remain trained on me.

"Hook is dead and you're cracking jokes about some new threat to Neverland, to us!" he roars, lifting his dagger above his head before bringing it down fast, flying towards me with unmatched speed.

Instinctively, I drop back and unsheathe my sword, quickly lifting it above my head to block his next vicious blow.

"But I don't understand... Hook is dead, why aren't you happy?" I argue, baffled at his behaviour.

"Happy?!" Peter cries incredulously.

The boys back into a corner, unwilling to help as Pan flies at me, throwing punches at my face and chest, whilst swinging his blade at me, the metallic sound cutting through the air as he continues to surge toward me.

I twist and duck away from him, blocking his blows with my arms whilst simultaneously attempting to thwart his vicious knife-wielding. But he's unrelenting and pushes me through the doors and back into the larger underground room.

"What is wrong with you?" I yell as I block another one of his attacks.

"You should be happy, you hated him above all else!"

"You utter fool! How can you not see, it was all a game!" he bellows, throwing another punch my way.

I'm not quick enough to deflect it, and the blow sends me sprawling backwards, the room spinning rather heavily from the impact.

I can hear the other's calling for Peter to stop, but their voices are lost in the background as Peter's words ring in my ears.

"A game?! God man, he tried to kill you, and you him! So many times, in fact I've lost count!" I argue, anger filling me with newfound strength.

"He and I, we were an even balance!" He yells as our blades meet with an unyielding clash.

"And now that has been eradicated by something far worse, the likes of which none of you have ever seen or could ever hope to vanquish!"

We split apart, two heaving bodies fuelled by anger and pride. His words were confusing. I know that he's using his anger as a substitute for pain, and yet I can't get my head around it. Peter Pan and Captain Hook had been sworn enemies for all of time—since the beginning of time! And not one person lived without knowing of their rivalry, of their constant battle of wit and skill. We all knew that eventually one of them would vanquish the other somehow.

And yet as I watch Peter lash out at me, his violent emotions rolling off of him like a tidal wave, I can see that he is hiding something sinister. Without a doubt. A secret that is so close to being spilled.

"What is it you're hiding, Pan?" I ask aloud, my brows furrowed as I watch him.

Before I can predict his next movements, he's suddenly on me, his knuckles *colliding with the bridge of my nose in a loud, sickening crunch. I'm reeling from the strength of his punch when, all of a sudden, I feel the unmistakable cool metal of his blade slice down my torso like a hot knife through butter. I watch Peter as his anger slowly starts to dissipate. He starts to realise what he's just done as he glances over at the horrified faces of the Lost Boys, and finally down at the wound he just inflicted on me. The length of the cut stretches across my body, starting under my collarbone and ending at my navel. Even from where I stand, I can see the wound isn't fatal, but blood has already begun to well up out of the opening, drenching my already damaged clothes in blood.*

I feel the shock begin to numb my body and I fall back against the padded floor, my eyes still trained on Peter. There is a deadly silence as he moves over to the ladder, wiping his bloodied blade on the fabric of his trousers. He stops when he reaches the steps, throwing his gaze over his shoulder at me.

"You have no idea of the level of evil that has been unleashed on Never-land," His voice dark and his face shrouded in shadow.

"You're not my leader. You're a coward!" I spit full of malice, blood coating my lips.

As the words leave my mouth, Peter silently floats upwards and out of the room. There's a loud swoosh and I know that he's gone for good.

Slightly and the others rush over to me, their voices overlap as they each shout orders at each other, but I'm not listening. My ears are ringing and a cold-ness spreads through my chest, though I'm unsure whether it's because of my wound, or if it's because of the hostile words shared with Peter—the person I'd idolised since the day I arrived in Neverland.

I stare at Curly in disbelief, my mouth hanging open as he finishes his story. I fight the urge to peek at his chest, but I fail, eventually drawing my eyes back up to meet his stony blue ones.

"Peter did that to you?" I murmur, disbelief in my tone.

"Unfortunately," he replies, his tone hard to depict.

"But how could he, I mean did he ever apologise?" I ask, scrambling through my words as though I had lost my ability to speak.

"He never came back, I haven't seen him since that day," Curly replies, his tone sombre.

I watch as his eyes cloud over, and I don't need to be told to realise that in his mind's eye, he's back there, reliving that day. The tragedy of it leaves a hollowness in the pit of my stomach.

"How awful! He's nothing like Grandmamma Wendy described, if he is capable of that level of violence," I mutter quietly.

Curly turns and watches me in silence for a moment or two, as though choosing his words carefully.

"The Peter that Wendy met was a very different person to the one he became. After she, John and Michael left for London, he turned into a completely different version of himself. An entirely new entity."

I fall silent as he speaks, taking in every word, his tone wary and guarded. I could almost hear the defensive note in his voice, as though after everything, he was still defending Pan.

"And what of this evil, greater than the dreaded Captain James Hook?" I ask.

"We never hung around long enough to find out. Though it became apparent the Shadow Master was Kage after rumours spread. After Peter left and we realised he wasn't coming back, there was little keeping us Lost Boys banded together." He replies, his eyes distant.

"You could have stayed together!" I argue.

Curly gives me a sincere yet sad smile. "We agreed it was more dangerous for us to stay together, than to stay apart."

"But that makes no sense, I don't understand," I reply, watching him closely.

"If you had as many enemies as we did, Wyn, you'd understand our reasoning. Besides, I don't miss the arguing," he says before collecting his things and walking away.

VIII

It's on the fourth day of travelling through the wilderness, late in the afternoon, when Curly tells me that we've arrived at the border between Neverwood and the Indian camp. The knowledge gives me a strong sense of satisfaction. Whilst we continued through the woods, Curly told me that the land sits on a gradient—which leaves the Indian camp sat on the cliffside.

I imagine a humble camp of teepees huddled in a circle, a raging bonfire in the centre, and a totem pole guarding their humble little space. I'm taken aback when we reach the camp gates; I was so wrong.

The tightly woven walls reach high above, grazing the sky with their pointed heads. They stretch as far as my eyes can see, encircling the entirety of the camp in a protective embrace. As we reach the opening, I notice the two guards on either side of the entrance. Their wide shoulders are heavy with quivers of arrows and each of their bows are fitted with a sharpened arrow. The weapons are pulled taut as we approach.

Curly holds up his hands as he sends a lazy smile in the direction of the guard on the right.

"We come as friends. We're here to see the chief and the princess. Urgent business," he explains, slowing his pace.

I stop at his side as the guards regard us warily for a moment. After a few seconds, they lower their bows and I release the breath I didn't realise I had been holding. They gesture us in and Curly gives them a simple nod of the head before he struts into the camp.

I rush to keep up with him, but as soon I get through the gate, I stop in my tracks. It's nothing like anything I could have imagined. Even this late in the afternoon, the camp is buzzing with life. I watch in wonder as people come and go around me, at a glance, they're all the same. Yet if you look closer, they're all unique. Their skin is beautifully tan and their hair as black as the raven feathers that some wear atop their heads. They look like the Red Indians I was taught about in my history classes as a child, though not quite; they are happier, thriving in their bustling community.

Occasionally one of them will do a double-take when they see me. Their head whips round to stare at me, until I notice more and more stopping and staring as I follow after Curly with my head bowed. They whisper to each other, their eyes never leaving me as they speak to one another. I can sense the buzz of excitement that fills the camp as we walk through.

"They're all staring at us," I whisper to Curly.

He glances over at me with a knowing smirk. "Not at us, at you."

"But why?" I ask.

"We don't get a lot of newcomers around Neverland," he replied, amusement laced through his voice.

By the time we stop, I've caught the attention of almost half of the camp and a crowd has gathered behind us. Curly stops us outside a teepee decorated in rich colours: red, brown, and gold are woven into the fabric in intricate and beautiful patterns.

He turns to me and grasps my shoulders in a gentle hold. I notice his eyes flicker briefly to the commotion behind me before focusing his attention back on me.

"Wait here, I need to speak with the chief."

"Wait, why can't I come in with you?" I argue.

"Just stay here. It's about matters that don't concern you. Don't move from this spot, got it?"

I let out a loud huff as he releases his grip on me and turns back to the teepee, hesitating before ducking through the curtained doors. As he disappears from my view, I turn around to find an army of people standing behind me.

I step back in surprise as a few of them take wary steps forward, their hands reaching out to touch my face and arms. The children tug eagerly at my dress, while the elderly women twist my golden locks around their worn fingers. I say nothing, afraid of startling them as they explore me. Every pair of eyes is tinted with a childlike curiosity.

I'm so distracted by the crowds of people encircling me that, at first, I don't feel the tug at my skirts. When I eventually do, I look down to a little girl's face staring up at me, in one hand a handmade doll, the other gripping my dress, tightly.

"What is your name?" I question.

She tugs at my skirts again, pointing through the crowd with her doll.

"I'm not allowed to leave this spot," I try to explain.

She says nothing and tugs at my dress again, her beautiful, wide eyes boring into mine until I feel myself relent. I glance nervously over my shoulder at the teepee before shifting my focus to the young girl.

"Alright, what is it you want to show me?" I ask with a small, friendly smile.

I let her guide me through the crowd of people, her hand still wrapped tightly around the fabric as she pulls me along with her. In silence, I let her guide me through the teepees, winding down a path that only she sees.

She stops abruptly in front of a humble-looking teepee and looks searchingly at me for a long moment before gently letting go of my hand. The fabric on this one is older and much more worn than the one that Curly disappeared under. Whilst it's still beautiful, the detail has faded with time. I turn to look at the little girl and find her pointing toward the entrance of the tent.

I take a small step toward the tent and nod. The little girl doesn't say a word, She simply drops her arm and skips away, still clutching her doll. I watch her until she disappears behind another teepee. After she's gone, I push aside the folded fabric that marks the entrance.

"Hello?"

I don't let myself stop long enough to question the little girl. Instead, I take a deep breath and make my way into the teepee.

The smell of sweet smoke fills my nostrils as my eyes become accustomed to the dim lighting. The inside is larger than I imagined— various belongings are dotted around, each one beautifully crafted.

"How quaint," I murmur as I look around.

There's a rolled-up bed stashed to one side and a small fireplace in the centre of the carpeted floor, and across from me is an elderly woman, her once raven waves now ashen and grey from a lifetime of living. Her wrinkled face shapes into a welcoming smile as she regards me, her hands outstretched.

"Neverlander, you have finally come," she says, her voice gentle yet raspy.

Unsure of what to do, I shuffle around the embers to stand closer to her. I begin to feel awkward standing up, so I lower myself onto my knees in front of her, mimicking her.

"I'm not sure what a Neverlander is, but my name is Wyn. Bronwyn Ainsley," I explain as I introduce myself.

"You are a traveller of worlds, yes?" she counters.

"Well I suppose—"

"—Then a Neverlander is what you are," she tells me.

"And who might you be?" I ask, as her worn hands find my face.

"I am Shikoba, Shaman of this place, seeker of all knowledge," she offers, her fingertips tracing my cheekbones.

She pulls her hands away from my face, her warm eyes still trained on me as she reaches into one of the many bowls beside her, filling her palm with a yellow powder.

"You must prepare yourself," she says cryptically.

"Prepare for what?" I ask.

But the Shaman doesn't reply, her attention is focused on the crackling embers in the centre of the room. Before I can push her for an answer, she tosses the yellow powder onto them, the room filling with yellowed smoke, as the spices sizzle into ash on the embers. I inhale deeply, breathing in the sweet scent of amber and something that smells a lot like cedar. As I exhale, my head starts to spin and my skin prickles as I fall into darkness.

I'm floating in a vast nothingness.

The world is non-existent in this apparition... or if it does exist, it is a world void of colour, sound, and smell. It holds nothing but myself, until all of a sudden it doesn't.

I'm whisked into the lush greenery of the forest and dumped in the centre of the trees. I breathe in expecting the fresh smell of the surrounding nature, but all I smell is amber and cedar. It's eerily familiar to me and yet I cannot place it in my mind.

I spin in a slow circle as I take in the colours and details, I feel cocooned, safe within the circle of trees that reach around me. The place feels familiar and I feel my heart rate slow, my body relax.

Then out of the corner of my eye, I notice a figure standing alone. As I turn to face it, the bright daylight shifts and twists into blood orange colour, tinging the woodlands in a dark red, the trees are menacing.

I can't distinguish any features on the figure; their entire body is shrouded in an unnatural black shadow. Their eyes, however, burn a bright violet and send a shiver down my spine.

"Who are you?" I call out.

The figure remains silent, an unspoken challenge brewing between us. The unnerving scene causes goosebumps to erupt over the smooth skin across my back.

Before I can repeat myself, I feel something heavy knock against my ankle. I look down to see Curly's mangled, blood-soaked body at my feet, his face covered in deep cuts and mottled bruises, his ocean eyes wide and lifeless.

The scream that rips from my throat is raw and piercing. I stumble backwards, my heels connect with something hard and I'm sent sprawling onto my back. I bolt upright, and to my horror, discover that I've tripped over another dead body in the same condition. I don't recognise this one; he's a stranger to me.

Scrambling to my feet, I scour the forest floor, taking in countless piles of bloodied limbs. The numbers pile up in my mind as the blood roars in my ears. As I take in the arrangement of twisted, mutilated bodies, I noticed the dark figure growing. Its bright eyes burn into me as it doubles, then triples in size.

"Stop this," I scream as fearful tears plummet down my cheeks.

A deep, dark laughter erupts from the figure as I search the trees blindly for a way out. The bodies around me seem to multiply with every passing moment. The faces elude me, strange yet familiar.

The menacing figure continues to grow in size as the fear suffocates me. Then just as I think I can't take discovering any more bodies, just as I think the figure can't grow any bigger, it surges towards me, its violet eyes turning red as they sear into my mind.

And I scream until the world around me fades back into darkness.

I'm still screaming and flailing when I come to, Shikoba talking to me in a foreign tongue, her voice calm and soothing.

As I realise that I'm back in the teepee, I take in the comforting smells of spices and look around the tent, memorising the colours and the detail of the fabric housing us. I focus on the dying embers in the centre of the tent and watch the tiny flames dance until my heart returns to a steady rhythm.

"The path ahead is one of hardship and pain," the Shaman utters, her tone grave.

I turn to face her, my hands shaking in my lap. "What *was* that?"

"Your purpose is clear, now you must decide whether to accept it or not." She states.

Before I can ask her any more questions, she gestures to the entrance. And even though I have thousands of questions swirling around my head, I realise that my time with her has come to an end, for now.

Shakily, I get to my feet and walk toward the doorway, holding the rippling fabric to one side so that the cool early evening air brushes my face. I hesitate and look back.

"What I saw..." I begin.

"When you are ready, return to me," is all she replies.

I nod silently, understanding nothing and leave the tent with the dream, or hallucination, whatever *that* was, still clinging to me.

As soon as I leave the tent and breathe in the fresh air, the pounding in my head lessens and the fumes from within Shikoba's tent dissipate. The sky is a picturesque painting of purples, peaches and pinks as the dusk slips into night. The images from before stick in my mind with intent and I notice the shaking in my hands hasn't lessened.

With an increasing feeling of dread, I wonder how long I've been away from where Curly left me. I chew on my bottom lip nervously as I wonder whether he's noticed that I'm gone yet. Just as I'm about to attempt to find my way back to the chief's teepee, a voice floats over to me.

"Damn, well aren't you a sight for sore eyes!"

I turn to face the owner of the voice and find a young man, who is decidedly not Curly, walking toward me. His dark hair falls over his forehead, matching his large brown eyes. His sharp chin is masked by a sparse-looking beard, and there is an arrogant confidence in the way he walks toward me.

"What's it been, a lifetime?" he asks, stopping in front of me, arms crossed as he looks me over.

"I'm sorry, you must have me confused with someone else," I reply, averting my eyes from his gaze.

"Oh, I don't think so. I never forget a face, Wendy," he scoffs.

I'm about to reply, when out of the corner of my eye I notice Curly striding towards me, anger plastered all over his face.

"Where the hell have you been?" he demands as he reaches me, his temper directed solely at me.

I open my mouth to reply, but think better of it as an image of blood and corpses flashes through my mind.

"I've been looking all over for you. When I tell you to stay put—" he growls.

"—Well I'll be damned! Curly?"

I start as I realise who he is. The young man is still standing beside me, amusement dancing in his eyes. Curly stops short, momentarily thrown off as we both turn to look at him. I send the stranger a grateful smile, but his eyes are now on Curly.

"Slightly," Curly breathes, surprise written all over his expression.

I gape at the young man as the two of them grab each other's hand and pull into a brief one-sided embrace before they pull away. The tension between the two could be cut with a knife. Curly's uneasiness is loud and clear, though Slightly is harder to read just by looking at him.

"You're Slightly?"

They spin around as I turn to Curly.

"As in one of the Lost Boys, Slightly?" I continue, unable to comprehend it.

"Don't tell me you've forgotten me, love?" he retorts, holding a hand to his heart mockingly.

"She's not Wendy," Curly cuts in.

"Well, you could've fooled me," he replies, peering at me with interest.

"I'm her Great Granddaughter."

Slightly stares at me in disbelief, his mouth gaping.

"Look, we'll have plenty of time for introductions later," Curly cuts in, grabbing hold of my wrist.

"Wait a minute," Slightly starts, still in a state of bewilderment.

"We don't have *time*, the chief is waiting for us, Wyn," Curly continues, dragging me forward with him.

I look over my shoulder at Slightly and give him an apologetic smile. As Curly and I disappear around the pathway of teepees, I glance back a final time to see Slightly still rooted to the spot, surprise etched into his handsome features.

"Well that was rude of you," I comment, raising my brow at the back of his head.

"We're trying to get you home, remember, not stand around making pleasantries with old friends." He argues, pulling me roughly.

He realises how rough he's being and releases his hold on me. Gratefully, I pull my arm to my chest and rub my wrist as I fall into step beside him.

"Besides, Slightly can wait. The chief isn't someone you want to keep waiting," he points out as he leads us through the twisting maze of fabric houses.

When I finally begin to recognise my surroundings, we're back in front of the chief's teepee. I feel an uneasiness begin to spread through my chest, tightening it quickly.

I watch as Curly steps forward and grabs hold of the heavy fabric, lifting it to one side so I can pass through. He watches me and tilts his head toward the entrance.

"After you," he says, a hint of impatience in his tone.

I give him a measured look and he sighs, the sharpness in his eyes softening.

"I'll be right behind you, don't worry."

I take a deep breath and let it out, feeling the tightness in my chest ease faintly. I send a nervous glance in Curly's direction before tentatively moving forward. I duck under his arm and make my way into the tent to meet the Indian chief.

IX

The air is warm and stuffy inside. The remnants of burnt incense still wafts about the room, filling the air with a smoky pungency. The air is misty from the layers of smoke accumulating within the space.

The layout of the room is similar to that of the Shaman's tent— though this room is much larger. It has the air of wealthiness, with rich thick rugs carpeting the floor and the bedding area piled high with colourful satin cushions, and blankets with intricate details along the hems.

There is a fire pit in the centre of the teepee, and behind it, a man who I presume is the chief. The sight of him alone is enough to intimidate me. As he slowly gets to his feet, I take in every detail. He is a large, tall man with long raven hair, half-braided with leather and wooden beads. His skin is a dark tanned colour, slightly creased with age. His eyes are dark and direct as he assesses me, his full lips set in a straight line. His face is an emotionless mask. I feel Curly come up beside me, but the tribe's leader has my undivided attention.

"Chief Great Big Little Panther, I present to you, Wendy's relative, Wyn," he voices, gesturing towards me as he speaks.

"Daughter of Wendy, welcome," the chief says, his voice as deep as it is loud.

"I'm not her—what I mean to say is—I'm her Great Granddaughter," I utter, my voice uneven from nerves.

I feel a small jab in my side as Curly subtly leans over.

"Just go with it," he hisses.

I return my gaze to the chief and give him a small smile and curtsy.

"Thank you for allowing me into your camp, Chief Great Big Little Panther."

"Please, know me as Big Chief. Come," he replies, unfolding his arms and gesturing for us to come closer.

We step further into the room and sit on the flat cushions set around the fire pit, opposite Big Chief. For a few long moments, no-one says anything. I sit silently as I wait for him to speak. I feel increasingly awkward as he stares fixedly at me, regarding me carefully. Once satisfied, he speaks up.

"Daughter of Wendy, so far from home."

He takes a long pipe in his hands, and sucks in a long breath, before releasing it in a puff of bitter smoke.

"What is it you come to me for?" He asks, tendrils of smoke leaking from his mouth and flared nostrils.

I glance over at Curly noticing his distracted expression, his focus directed elsewhere, before turning to the chief with my answer.

"I'm here by mistake. When I arrived here, Curly said that you may be able to help me find a way back to London," I explain.

"She speaks the truth?" Big Chief asks Curly.

"It's just as I said earlier Big Chief, Wyn here is just trying to get back home," Curly confirms, his eyes flicking over to me briefly before returning to the chief.

"Can you help me, Big Chief?" I add, searching his face eagerly for an answer.

The chief ponders my question as he puffs on his pipe. Rings of smoke float into the air, rippling as they lose shape and fade into nothing. The silence is punctuated by the crackling of the small flames dancing in the pit between us.

"Yes, and no," he utters finally, his voice husky from smoking.

"I'm sorry, I don't understand," I tell him.

"You have been brought here for a reason. Kage seems to have use for you. Big Chief can only help with part of this journey, you must seek out another in the quest for home."

His words ring in my ears as a sinking feeling grows in the pit of my stomach. "Who is it that can help me get back home?"

"Little Flying Eagle."

"Peter?" Curly says, stunned.

"Peter is Little Flying Eagle," he explains, seeing the confusion on my face.

"Where can I find him?" I ask Big Chief.

"But that's just it, Wyn," Curly cuts in. "No-one knows where he is. He disappeared years ago!"

All my hopes of finding my way home are dashed and I fall silent. Getting home feels impossible now as defeat washes over me. The chief's words keep repeating themselves in my head and I think back to the visions in Shikoba's tent. The black figure, the scattered bodies painting the forest floor red with blood, the impending sense of doom I felt as I watched it happen.

"There must be another way," I hear Curly plead, his voice cutting through the haze of my thoughts.

"The chief is right," my voice is surprisingly strong as the words leave my mouth.

Both men stop their conversation and turn abruptly toward me. I look at each of them in turn, my gaze steady and determined.

"Me being brought here was no accident, and even though I can hardly understand why, there must be a reason for it. I do need to get home, but I need to know why I'm here first."

Neither of them speaks; Big Chief smokes silently while Curly stares at me, his mouth set in a thin line.

"So, let's just worry about our next steps before we concern ourselves with finding Peter, Curly," I say to reassure him.

I turn back to the chief, directing my words at him. "Big Chief, I appreciate any help you can give me."

"I can give you supplies, weapons and shelter. My daughter, Princess Tiger Lily, will find you some suitable clothing. You're welcome to stay as long as you need," he tells me, billows of smoke floating toward me with his words.

The chief then holds his hand out, gesturing towards the entrance of the teepee and I realise our meeting with him is over. We both thank him for his time, disappearing through the folds of thick fabric and out into the open.

The camp is in dark when we emerge from the chief's teepee. The sky is shrouded with clouds, blocking the light from the stars above. The air is crisp and clean; a refreshing sensation after the stuffiness and smoky, polluted air within the chief's quarters.

I turn to Curly who is quiet and sullen. He opens his mouth to say something, but for some reason decides against it.

"The princess's tent is over there, just explain to her that Big Chief sent you," he tells me, pointing to a teepee not dissimilar to the chief's—other than being smaller in size.

I follow his outstretched arm to where he's pointing before turning back to face him, giving him a quick nod.

"I'll come find you after," he says quietly, his eyes glued to the floor.

Before I have a chance to respond, he's turned on his heel and trudged away, his head hanging low. I watch him until he disappears into the sea of tents and tribe members. I take a deep breath and make my way over to the princess' teepee.

"Princess Tiger Lily?" I call, listening closely for a reply.

"Your father, Big Chief, sent me," I add after a few moments of silence.

"You may enter," I hear after a few moments.

I pull back the thick hide covering the entrance and make my way inside. My eyes become accustomed to the dim light as I look about the space, watching quietly as she silently lights the candles one by one. The room consists of the same materials and similar colours to the other teepees. However, instead of a fire pit in the centre, there's a seating area made out of a pile of flat cushions.

Once the candles are lit, the princess turns to me and I find that I can't help but stare. She's beautiful, with caramel-coloured skin and wide, dark eyes framed by thick curling eyelashes. Her nose is petite and pretty, her lips small, yet plump and rosy. Her long dark tresses of hair are split into two and tied into low pigtails with small leather straps. Around her forehead is a blue leather headband with a full speckled feather attached at the back, perfectly centred against her hair parting. Her colourful dress fits to her womanly curves and reaches just past her knees, synched with a belt wrapped around her small waist. I'm once again in awe of the detail threaded into the hem and all around the bottom of her dress.

She couldn't be anything other than the crown jewel of the Piccaninny Tribe.

"Who are you?" she asks bluntly, her voice snapping me out of my daze.

"I'm Wyn, Princess, it's a pleasure to meet you," I reply, dipping into a small curtsy.

I watch her eyes as they drop down to my attire and I feel every inch of heat as it crawls up my neck in embarrassment.

"What are you *wearing?*" she then asks, distaste dancing in her eyes.

"Your father told me that you could maybe help me with that," I explain, a sheepish smile on my lips.

Her haughty expression softens and she gives me a reassuring smile. She reaches out for my hand and I take it.

"I can."

I'm not sure how much time has passed, but I don't concern myself with it too much as Tiger Lily keeps me busy. I actually find myself enjoying my time with her as she helps me with new clothes.

Two young women join us in her teepee to help with my transformation. They giggle amongst themselves as they touch and play with my long blonde waves—when the princess doesn't tut at them disapprovingly.

Eventually, Princess Tiger Lily hands me a pair of brown trousers and a rich red-coloured tunic, leaving the teepee momentarily to allow me to change. She ushers the girls out with her until I call them back in. As soon as they return, both of the young women take what is left of my poor dress and disappear from the tent. The princess then passes me a handmade belt, which I fasten around my waist, and a leather band that I'm instructed to wear on my arm.

The young women return once more with a sturdy looking pair of handmade boots, made from animal hide.

"For you," they tell me shyly as they encourage me to take them.

I thank them as I do so, slipping off the ones Curly gave me and putting my new ones on. As they try to take them, I explain that I'd prefer to keep them and with a smile and quick nod, they leave me alone with Tiger Lily.

Just as I think I'm finished and ready to thank her for her kindness, she gestures to the cushions.

"Please sit," she tells me.

I'm curious but decide not to question it and seat myself. She walks over to a corner of the room and rummages around for a few moments before returning with her hands full of different items. Wordlessly, she seats herself behind me and begins to brush my hair. The sensation feels alien to me for a few moments before I'm mentally transported back to my childhood, when mother would brush my hair and tell me stories before bedtime.

Princess Tiger Lily says nothing as she brushes through the long handfuls of hair and I'm grateful for the quiet after several days of craziness. My mind wanders as she works away, teasing the brush through the knots and matted sections.

After a little while, she seems satisfied and gets to her feet, returning the used items back to the corner where she retrieved them, before returning to me, her hands outstretched. With a warm smile I take her hands and get to my feet.

"Come," she beckons, guiding me over to the far side of the room.

She stops and pulls back a sheer curtain to reveal a large mirror, a satisfied look on her face as she looks at her handiwork.

I'm speechless as I stare at the stranger in the mirror. The last time I had gazed upon myself, I saw a teary-eyed girl in a posh frock. Now I see someone new.

The girl in front of me wears ankle-length trousers and thick boots. Her sleeveless tunic curves over her breasts and splits at her hips, the length of the fabric dangling down between her legs and just above her knees, with a belt wrapped around her petite waist. A leather band adorns her right arm and another woven strap sits on her forehead.

I turn my head from left to right, to catch a glimpse of my neatly styled hair. I draw it over my shoulder gently before setting it back to rest between my shoulder blades.

My silence continues as I feel the braid woven against the right side of my temple, careful not to ruin it. The beautiful strand of hair runs all the way down the length of my head, before falling loosely past my shoulders with the rest of my hair. The other side is decorated with two small loose braids starting behind the top of my ear, with red ribbon woven through each of them.

Thoughts of home disappear momentarily as I stare forwards. The girl I see is a true Neverlander. There is a boldness in her eyes, and a confidence in her stance that wasn't there before. She is one of them, she belongs here. I draw my gaze away from the girl in the mirror and turn to Tiger Lily, taking her hands in mine.

"Thank you," is all I can muster.

She seems pleased nonetheless and gives me a bright smile before stepping away from the mirror.

"There is a feast tonight, you must come as my guest," she tells me.

"I'd be honoured. Though I'll need to find Curly first," I explain.

"You are a friend of Curly?" she asks, her tone curious.

"I am," is all I reply, intrigued by her reaction.

She contemplates something for a moment before she speaks. "Bring him too."

"I will," I reply as I leave.

I meander around the camp, wondering where Curly could be. I've reached the heart of the camp as the tribesmen busy themselves with stacking firewood in the impressively large bonfire for the festivities later on. The large totem pole in the middle of the camp draws my attention away from the busy workers, its many faces staring out over the entirety of the Piccaninny Tribe. I study each animal, amazed at the intricacy of the carving and the soulfulness of each pair of eyes casting out a wide gaze over the tribe's territory.

"Well don't you look the part," Slightly's voice cuts through the bustle.

I scan around me to pinpoint where the voice came from. It doesn't take long to notice him leant against the bottom of the totem pole I had just been admiring.

"Well it's certainly better than that tatty thing I had on before," I counter with a playful smirk.

"Well give us a twirl and I can see for myself," he replies with a glint in his eye as he steps away from his leaning post.

"Don't pay him any mind, he'd flirt with anything that moves, given the chance," a voice interjects.

I turn to see a young woman walking towards us with fiery hair and a face full of freckles, her smile as bright as her auburn hair. Her clothes are not dissimilar to my own, only seemingly tighter against her broad frame and made completely from leather and animal hide. Slightly holds his hands to his heart in mock pain, pulling a face.

"Oh Khara, do you really think so little of me?"

"I just know too much, Slightly, or would you rather me call you Mister Charming?" she teases.

"Wyn, I don't believe you've met my dear friend, and accomplice, Khara," Slightly, shifting the focus back to me.

"I don't believe I've had the pleasure of formally meeting you either," I retort before smiling at Khara.

"You're completely right, love. We have Curly to thank for that," he replies with a wink and a smile.

"Speaking of, do you know where he is," I ask, looking around for any sight of him.

I glance over to Slightly and Khara, whose eyes flit past me. I follow their gaze to find a furious looking Curly heading our way.

"Why do you always wander off, I've been looking all over—" he starts, trailing off as he gets closer.

Curly stops short, his words lost to the wind and his jaw slack as he takes me in. Heat rises up my neck as he prolongs his unwavering stare, his eyes lingering on my body.

"Didn't they ever teach you boys that it's rude to stare," Khara cuts in, shattering the moment.

Curly's eyes refocus, and settle on Khara, casting a stony glance her way. "Khara."

"Curly," she replies in acknowledgment.

"Well now that we're all reacquainted, shall we prepare for tonight's festivities?" Slightly asks as he claps his hands together.

Behind Slightly, a native lights the bonfire and the smell of cooked meats wafts through the air, making my mouth water and my stomach growl. Out of the corner of my eye, I see Curly open his mouth to speak. I know by his expression that the next words to flow from his mouth will be ones of protest, and so I quickly interject before he gets a chance.

"Princess Tiger Lily invited us as her personal guests, it would be rude to turn the offer down."

Surprise registers on Curly's face and for a moment he doesn't say anything, I notice the colour rising in his cheeks but I say nothing.

"I suppose it *would* be rude to turn down her invitation," he says, his tone revealing his defeat.

"Quite," is all I reply with a satisfied grin.

The festivities are in full swing in no time and I'm enjoying the spectacle as we stand around the dancing flames. Curly hasn't said much since we joined the crowd around the bonfire, but I notice his eyes trained on the princess and a knowing smile forms on my lips. I lean over and bring my mouth to his ear.

"I can see the appeal," I say before leaning away again, anticipating his reaction.

He rolls his eyes and mutters something. I can tell by the way he shifts that he's embarrassed. Though I'm secretly glad to see him relaxed and finally enjoy himself for the first time since we've met.

All of a sudden, the music dies down and Chief Great Big Little Panther steps forward, his arms raised for everyone's attention.

"Daughter of Wendy, please step forward," his voice carries over the crowd.

All eyes fall on me as I step forward, and after a reassuring look from Curly, I walk over to where the chief and the princess are standing. The Big Chief takes another step forward with Tiger Lily at his side, gesturing for me to stand in front of him. I do so and he begins to make symbols with his hands for all the people of the tribe to see.

I watch partly mesmerised, partly confused and glance over at Curly, who's now standing with Slightly, before returning my attention to the chief.

"I name thee, Wyn, Daughter of Wendy, Shenandoah of the Piccaninny Tribe."

The tribe erupts into applause and cheers as I accept the facial paint, spread across my cheeks and forehead by Tiger Lily.

"You are now one of us, Shenandoah," she utters to me, her voice soft yet still audible.

With a small curtsy, I make my leave and begin my way around the bonfire and over to the boys as the festivities and music are revived.

"What is a Shenandoah?" I ask when I reach them.

"It means Daughter of the Stars," Curly explains with a grin.

"You're now an honorary tribeswoman, congratulations," Slightly adds, giving me a gentle knock on the shoulder.

Curly quickly excuses himself and I watch as he makes his way over to Princess Tiger Lily.

"You might want to watch out, it looks like the princess has her eye on your fella," Slightly teases.

"Curly isn't mine," I correct.

Slightly holds his hands up. "Whatever you say."

"I guess this means I've still got a chance," he responds with a wink.

I roll my eyes before turning my attention back to Curly and Tiger Lily. I watch on as they talk, the princess laughing every so often while Curly grins bashfully from ear to ear. It's curious to see him act so friendly, when all I'm used to is him acting aloof. As I watch, I wonder what they could be talking about and my mind flashes back to that day at the lagoon, an odd feeling settling in my stomach. Suddenly, I can't bear to watch and quickly avert my eyes, my cheeks warming.

X

The next morning is quiet, and the weather dreary when I finally emerge from my slumber. As I wipe the sleep from my weary eyes, I look around. The room is quiet, the teepee empty of everyone but me.

Slowly, I get to my feet and pull on my boots, making my way outside. The air is cool and refreshing on my face. I find myself surprised at how early I've risen when I see that the camp is quiet and dawn is just rising over the horizon.

I wander through the camp, making my way past the remains of last night's bonfire. All that is left is a pile of ash being swept across the ground by the morning breeze. I lose myself in my thoughts, reliving the hallucination from the day before, over and over. I weave in and out of teepees until I surprise myself by stopping outside of Shikoba's teepee.

Before I talk myself out of it, I make my way inside, not bothering to make myself known to her. Unsurprisingly, she's up and alert as I walk in, her eyes trained on me expectantly.

"Please, I must know. Can you explain what I saw?" I ask, cutting to the chase.

"Are you willing to learn of things greater than yourself?" She questions.

Wordlessly, I step forward and seat myself on the cushioned seat in front of her. I feel Shikoba's eyes trained on me with such intensity that I can't bear to meet them. I shuffle ever so slightly in my seat, feeling uneasy as the quiet crackling of the fire pit fills the silence between us.

"I need to understand why I'm here and how I can get back home," I say, finally breaking the silence.

"There are forces bigger than you that have been set in motion," she explains.

"What forces? I don't understand."

She turns away from me for a moment and picks out two small handleless cups carved from clay. She then lifts a small teapot from the pit and pours hot liquid into the two cups before silently handing me one.

"Neverland is in your blood, Shenandoah, it is a part of who you are," she tells me before taking a long sip from her cup.

"But what I saw, what has that got to do with any of this?" I take a sip, the hot liquid burning as it slides down my throat.

"What you saw was a future," she tells me.

"But surely—" I begin.

She holds up her hand and interjects as I swallow my words.

"Neverland is dying, the threat to this world is great, the magic all but gone. It is up to you to help stop this, to restore the balance."

"But what I saw was the opposite of that," I respond, shaking my head.

"It was a warning."

"But you just said I saw the future."

"Many futures, many outcomes. Only your actions will decide the true line of events." Her eyes watching me as she takes another sip.

I follow suit before I continue with my questioning.

"So, what I saw may not happen, depending on my own choices?"

"The path you have been placed on is not for the faint-hearted. You will have to fight for this world. It is a part of you as much as you are of it," she says as she scatters a handful of spices onto the fire pit.

Before I can voice my next question, the familiar scent of amber and cedar wafts up into the air and I inhale deeply. The world around me spins rapidly as I cave in and fall under its influence, entering the strange realm of dreams once again.

When I come to, I'm soaring through the clouds with an amazing view of the land below. I dive through the white, billowy clouds with joy. The luscious green of the forest gives way to the snow-capped mountains that surge high into the sky, and the rippling seas embrace the surrounding coast. I feel myself drop lower through the air, landing softly on the high slopes of Neverpeak Mountains.

The air is icy cold and the wind rushes past me with immense strength and yet I don't feel it; my body is numb to the elements.

I look around and I'm taken aback by the sheer size of my surroundings. From the edge of the mountain, Neverland looks as though it could go on forever. I can just about make out the wide blue seas touching the horizon. The wind howls through the passage in the mountains—a natural route carved out of the rock, splitting one peak into three.

I step forward toward the narrow passage, glancing up at the walls nervously. The strength of the wind causes huge rocks to come tumbling down the walls, crashing in the middle of the narrow path. I step back, scared to go any further.

A menacing laugh rips through the mountains and I swivel around. As soon as my eyes meet a familiar pair that glow violet, my blood turns to ice and my heart thrums in my chest.

I stand completely still as I watch the black figure standing a few metres away, hovering right on the edge of the second peak. Right behind him, the mountainside gives way to a sheer drop to the forest below. In the second that it takes for me to blink, bodies have appeared, scattered all around me. I take in all their faces, recognising Curly, Slightly, and Khara amongst many others. Faces of deceased innocents cloud my vision, their lifeless eyes boring into me as blood trickles from every orifice.

The sight turns my stomach and I drop to my knees, dry heaving into the mounds of snow. Just like the previous time the figure gets bigger, its menacing laugh piercing through me as I stand on wobbly legs.

"Who are you?" I yell, my voice echoing through the passage behind me.

"What do you want?"

The figure says nothing, its eyes once again turning violet and boring into me. Before I can prepare myself, it lurches forward, surging through the ice and snow toward me. I shield my face with my arms and inhale sharply, unable to muster a scream before the world around me tumbles into darkness.

I awake suddenly with a sharp inhale. My hands still hold the cup in my now shaking grip, the lukewarm liquid rippling from the movement. My eyes fall on the Shaman, her eyes serious and unwavering as they meet my gaze.

Without breaking the connection, Shikoba hands me a cloth and for a moment I wonder why, until I look down to see blood dripping onto my hand. I bring my hand to my face and brush my fingertips against my upper lip. I draw them back to find blood staining the swirls in my skin.

I take the cloth with a grateful smile and clean away the blood. A heavy silence envelopes us both, but I can't bring myself to break it. Once I've finished with the cloth and have handed it back, she leans forward and gently lifts my shaking hands, bringing the cup closer to my lips until I drink the last of my beverage, the liquid warming my stomach. Once I finish, she gently takes the cup and sets it down beside hers.

"This time was different to the last," I utter, finally breaking the thick silence.

She sits back and waits for me to continue, her patience reassuring me.

"The first time I was in the forest, but this time I was high up in the mountains at the opening of a long, narrow passage through rock and stone."

"You speak of Boulderswift Passage," she tells me, her voice even.

"Both times my surroundings have been different, but ultimately it ends the same," I explain, looking down at my hands balled into loose fists in my lap.

"What does it mean?" I ask, lifting my eyes to meet hers, searching them for an answer.

She says silent, her face void of emotion as she regards me carefully. The fire spits and crackles next to us as the flames dance their final dance.

"There is much to do," she says.

"How am I meant to defeat a threat that I don't recognise? I can't fight, I've never so much as raised a fist," I cry, frustrated.

"All in good time, you will find a way," she reassures me. "Find those who can balance you. Those who are able to strengthen your weaknesses, can also draw from your strengths," she adds, her words twisted into some form of riddle.

I sense the finality of her words and I know that our time has come to an end. Though I still have more questions than answers, I decide to stay quiet on the matter. And so, despite the confusion and frustration coursing through me, I thank her and leave the tent. I don't look back as the fabric swishes closed behind me and I walk away.

The remnants of each vision ring clear in my mind, their hidden meanings and frightening imagery as daunting as ever.

The dawn has broken into a beautiful morning, but I'm unable to appreciate the bright sun and open blue skies as my mind races through everything that has happened. For the hundredth time I question how I got here... how I will ever find a way home, if I even get the chance to?

The natives are up and alert, busying themselves with the list of today's many tasks. I stare through them as they move through the camp this way and that, focused in the present. The sizzling smell of cooking fish wafts through the air and my lungs are filled with its savoury aroma. After this morning's events, I've lost my appetite.

I think back to Big Chief's words and I wonder how they are connected to the visions. I pace slowly through the winding paths of the camp, staring at the ground as I try to fit the mismatched pieces together to understand it all.

As I come out of my cloud of thought, I realise I have made my way to the camp entrance. The dense forest is so open and inviting from where I stand. I acknowledge the guards as I leave the camp, nodding at each of them before I make my way across the stretch of land to my right. The alluring trees are to my left, while the wooden fence separating the Piccaninny Tribe's camp from the rest of the surrounding area, stands tall to my right. I eventually come to a stop at the cliff edge and gently lower myself down so my legs dangle over the edge.

I stare out at the open sea, admiring the place where the ocean kisses the sky to meet the horizon. The water shimmers like a huge pool of stars, shining throughout the day.

My mind flits through the past few days and I wonder if anyone from home has even realised that I'm missing. I wonder if they've carried on with their everyday lives as though I had never even existed. I think of my mother, alone in her room dreaming of the world that

I've found myself in. I dare to consider what might happen if I fail this unknown mission, what might happen to this world if I find myself trapped here, what will happen if I succeed.

As I sit with this stunning view of the open water, I think of all of the people that I have met since arriving here, and how their fate is inexplicably tied to my own. The images of each of their lifeless bodies play on repeat in my mind.

I contemplate my supposed position in all this and the words that the Shaman had to offer me, and as I do so, I wonder what it is that Grandmamma Wendy would have done if she had faced such peril on her adventures here.

I'm so wrapped up in my own thoughts and the feeling of impending doom that the echoing clunk of something hitting a tree trunk startles me. I almost slip off the edge of the cliff and fall onto the jagged rocks below.

I scramble to my feet and decide to investigate, secretly glad for the distraction. My feet move towards the cover of the trees and I remain quiet, listening intently for the sound to reappear.

After a moment or two, I hear the sound again and follow its trail through the trees until I spot a figure through the foliage. She stands rigidly, her legs spread apart, one behind the other. She holds the beautifully crafted bow close to her chest, pulling back the string slowly, an arrow settled in the nock point. I watch in awe as she takes a steadying breath in through her nose and releases it slowly from her pursed lips.

In a single moment, her fingers release and the arrow speeds through the air, burying itself in the centre of a tree trunk several metres away. I'm astounded by the fluidity of her movements, considering her stiff posture before.

As she drops the bow at her side, something in my brain clicks and I recognise the auburn hair instantly. She has it tied into a loose braid that stretches down her back.

"Khara," I greet her as I emerge from my hiding spot.

She turns to face me, her expression serious until she realises it's me.

"Hey there."

She frowns as I come closer, concern leaking into her eyes.

"You look like you've seen a ghost, everything ok?"

I nod and tilt my head toward the arrow now embedded in the tree target.

"Quite the shot you have," I compliment, a small, friendly smile spreading across my lips.

"That was nothing," she replies with a laugh.

"I bet you're quite the skilled warrior," I continue, an idea forming in my head.

"You could say that," she laughs, light dancing in her amber eyes as she grins at me.

"Could you teach me?" I ask, my gaze steady.

Her grin widens for a moment before her expression turns to one of surprise. She lifts the bow onto her shoulder and walks toward me, stopping a few paces short as she looks me in the eye.

"You're serious?"

"Of course, I'm serious," I bridle.

"But why? I mean I'm flattered you'd even ask, but why the need?" she asks, cocking her head to the side.

"This isn't London. So far, I've been attacked by pirates and followed a complete stranger through miles of forest. I'd just like to know that I can rely on myself to stay alive," I respond, gesturing to our surroundings.

"Fair point," Khara replies with a shrug.

"Besides, Curly is far too sullen and protective to teach me anything of use and as for Slightly, well, I'm sure you of all people can understand why that would be a recipe for disaster," I laugh.

"Yeah, I do see what you mean," she says with a chuckle.

"So, will you help me?" I plead.

I watch as she considers it for a moment, her eyes searching the surrounding woodland as though it holds the answer she needs. After a few long moments, she looks back at me and gives me a wide smile. She tilts her head in a bid for me to follow.

"Come with me."

I let out the breath I didn't realise I'd been holding and give her a grateful smile before following her closely as she moves deeper into the forest.

XI

The midday sun blasts down through the tree branches, burning the nape of my neck as I launch myself at Khara with twin daggers gripped tightly in my hands. As I come close enough for contact, I swing my arms around toward her, the sun glinting off the metal blade as it slices through the air.

Birds fly through the trees above, chirping their sweet little melodies that echo through the branches. It's a nice distraction from the gruelling effort and thwarted attempts to get the better of Khara.

In mere moments she has effortlessly disarmed me and returned my attack with a spinning kick to my chest. I fly back against the trunk of a tall pine, landing on my backside, sore, winded, and irritated. I get up and throw myself at her again and again, each time landing in an uncomfortable heap.

Sweat beads on my brow as I fight my own frustration and swallow the bitterness of each missed blow. Each time Khara beats me effortlessly and I find it harder to maintain my calm.

"Give yourself a moment, then try again," Khara calls as she investigates her nail beds.

"I'm not learning anything; all I'm doing is getting battered and bruised!" I snap as I fight to catch my breath.

"Oh, come on, Wyn, I barely touched you!" Khara retorts. "You're just gonna have to toughen up if you want to learn all this combat stuff." She shrugs. "Next time don't ask if you can't hack it."

I glare at her from where I'm sat and she returns the gesture with a wicked grin, her eyes glinting with humour. We both know she's got my full attention, and a new surge of energy rushes through me as her words ring loud in my ears. Scrambling to my feet, I throw the daggers down and run at her, determined to win this time.

She's prepared for me as my fist flies, ducking under my arm, and I'm sent sprawling. I quickly re-establish myself and swing around, bringing up my arm to block her oncoming blow. As she takes another swing I duck down and kick out my leg causing her to lose her balance momentarily. I quickly use her setback to my advantage and punch her, my fist connecting with her jaw, *hard*.

She flies to the ground as I scowl, shaking the pain from my knuckles as she sits and stares at me dumbfounded, while nursing her injured jaw. After a moment or two, she chuckles and gets to her feet.

"Not bad, not bad at all," she says, clearly impressed with me.

"I got in one good punch, hardly anything to be raving about," I argue as I rub the throbbing sensation from my hand.

"You have a point, but as this is your very first lesson in combat, I think it's fair of me to be a little impressed," she points out with a smirk.

I return the smile and casually walk over to where I'd thrown down Khara's blades, wiping them off before I return them to her.

"You know there is definitely something quite alluring about two women running off into the depths of the forest together," Slightly's voice rings out through the trees.

We turn our heads around to see Slightly emerge from behind the trees, with Curly close behind.

"You know, those are the kinds of thoughts one would keep to themselves, not share, Slightly," I retort.

He shrugs indifferently as he and Curly close the gap between us.

"What can I say, I'm just curious to know what you two are doing frolicking about the woods."

Khara and I look at each other, our brows raised simultaneously as we both break into laughter. The boys watch on in confused silence as they wait for our laughter to die down.

"You know, Slightly, you have a very warped idea of women," I tell him, patting his shoulder amicably as he walks past and seats himself on the grassy floor.

"I'll say," Khara adds, with a shake of her head.

The laughter dies in my throat as my gaze falls on Curly. His face is serious, his eyes dark with masked anger. The smile slips from my face as he steps closer.

"You can't keep disappearing into thin air Wyn, it isn't safe," he growls.

"Oh, would you relax already, Curly, she was with me," Khara cuts in, shaking her head at him.

"I'll deal with you in a minute," he hisses at her, before returning his stern gaze back to me.

"What were you even doing out here?" he asks as he gestures to our surroundings.

"Well—" I begin.

"If you must know... we were in the middle of a training session, which, might I add, you two so rudely interrupted," Khara interjects, directing a dirty look at Curly.

"You're kidding," Slightly says, highly amused by the thought.

"Shut up, meat brain," Khara yells at him.

I turn back to Curly and notice the brief look of surprise in his eyes, before the same stern look resurfaces.

"You should have come to find me first."

"I do not have to run every little thing I do past you, I'm not a child," I reproach.

"You're out of your depth, how can I protect you long enough for you to make it back home if you keep—" he argues.

"—If you hadn't noticed, Curly, I was busy learning how to do that myself before you interrupted with your high and mighty routine," I retort, my voice getting louder with my growing temper.

"Ha! Right!" he mocks, throwing his head back in harsh laughter.

I feel the fury burn through my veins and I'm suddenly filled with a fierce resentment. Before I can stop myself, I roughly shove him in his chest. He drops back a few paces and as he regains his balance, I come flying toward him with the roundhouse kick I had just been practising.

It doesn't send him sprawling backwards like I'd hoped, and I wobble a little as I bring my leg back down, but it does catch him off guard and he stumbles back a few steps before composing himself. Surprise registers on his face as he looks up at me, his hand holding his ribs where my foot hit.

Somewhere in the background, I hear Slightly burst into laughter. I ignore him and keep my venomous stare on Curly, anger rolling off me in waves.

"Save your heroics for the princess, Curly. Let's hope she doesn't come to think of you as an overbearing, blundering buffoon!" I yell at him before storming off through the trees and back toward the camp.

I'm making my way uphill towards the camp entrance, my anger slowly subsiding with every step I take away from the others, when I hear a loud gong sound. I stop in my tracks, immediately on alert. Looking around, I hear the noise again and realise it's coming from the camp.

Out of nowhere, Curly, Slightly and Khara all rush past me, running relentlessly towards the camp. A sinking sensation takes over my stomach and I'm filled with an unexplainable dread as I pick up the pace and rush after them into the Piccaninny Tribe's camp.

When I finally reach the gates, I notice the guards have disappeared from their posts and the winding pathways are heaving with people. I push my way forward in the direction of Big Chief's teepee in an attempt to find out what all this commotion is about. When I reach the teepee, the gong is still sounding throughout the camp, the vibrations ripple through the air even after the gong has sounded out.

Big Chief stands high on a tree stump for all to see. He speaks loud and clear, though the dialect he uses is foreign to me. I manage to spot Khara through the masses of concerned looking tribespeople and make my way through the crowd until I'm by her side.

"What's going on?" I whisper to her, my eyes trained on the chief.

"The Jolly Roger is just outside the native's territory, scouts have said it's circling the waters around the far side of the camp," she informs me, her tone hushed.

"Hook's ship?" I question, wondering what it could be doing there.

"It's Kage's ship now, but something's not right, they're in attack positions," she continues, eyes trained ahead on the chief.

"What do you mean?"

"Big Chief seems to think that their attack on the tribe is to do with you," Khara explains as she nods toward the chief, who's still talking.

"But what would they want with me?"

"Kage clearly wants you for something. If they threaten an attack, they'd expect the Chief to hand you over."

I pause wide-eyed for a moment before I ask my next question.

"So, what is the chief saying now?"

"Telling everyone to be on guard and to be vigilant. You are one of them now, and they will not surrender you to Kage and his filthy pirates without a fight."

Khara and I return our full attention back to the chief, just as a loud bang interrupts his speech. Uneasy murmurs spread like a wave through the crowd as we all look around to find the source of the noise. I notice a small whistling sound coming from behind the tall walls that enclose the camp. I'm about to move towards it when a large object crashes through the seemingly impenetrable walls and into the Piccaninny camp, crushing tribe members and injuring those left in its wake.

Chaos breaks out in the camp, people screaming and rushing around in all directions. Amidst the confusion, I'm dragged away from Khara by a current of people, and I'm soon lost in the terrified crowd.

Another loud bang erupts as another cannonball soars through the air directly at us and this time I do my best to run for cover and avoid the blast, others however, aren't as lucky.

All around me I hear wails of pain and screams of terror as the constant rush of terrified natives scatter like ants around me. I'm disorientated and afraid, but I'm determined to find the others and regroup.

I dash through the crowds of frightened people searching for shelter, my eyes darting left and right for a familiar face. The smell of gunpowder fills my nostrils and I choke on the acrid taste. Fire spreads along the teepees rapidly with each new shot. I hear mothers screaming for their children and others wailing for those that they have lost all too suddenly, and my heart breaks for them. I replay the last words that I said to Curly in my mind and my heart shrinks. I pray to myself that those won't be the last words he ever hears from me. A new surge of determination courses through me as I keep searching, desperately trying to seek any of them out amongst the utter chaos.

I weave through the crowds, calling each of them by name with the feeble hope that somehow, they might hear me through all the noise. I feel the ground shudder beneath my feet as another cannonball makes contact with the camp, chunks of earth fly in all directions as another lot of innocent lives are violently snuffed out.

When I take in the destruction from the latest shot, my blood runs cold as my eyes fall on her broken body and bloodied face lying in the dirt. Shikoba beckons me with a shaky hand and I rush to her side, taking her trembling hand in mine. Her palm is still warm as she looks at me, her dark, caring eyes full of hope.

"This is only the beginning, you must restore the balance to our world," she utters, her lips trembling from the effort.

"No please, you can't die. Not like this," I beg, my voice uneven.

"Discover who you are," she continues.

"But I have so many more questions," I ramble, tears flooding my eyes.

She releases her hand from my grasp and with strenuous effort, covers her shaking hands over mine. Her eyes bore into mine with kindness and certainty.

"Make your mark."

With these words, the light in her eyes fade and her warm hands fall limp, dropping to the ground with a soundless thud. My heart drops in my chest and for what feels like forever, I'm locked in the moment. The pandemonium continues all around me, but I feel stuck in my own little time bubble until someone runs straight into me, bringing me back to my senses—and the realization that I'm knelt in the middle of a war zone.

Rushing to my feet, I allow myself one last glance at Shikoba, uttering my goodbye before I get swept up in the mayhem.

The crowds have died down, but there are still enough frantic bodies to disorientate me. I call out for the others again but can't find them anywhere. I search every face of every person I pass in their rush to safety, but not one of them resembles Curly, Khara, or Slightly.

I'm beginning to lose hope of ever finding them alive, when I see a head of mousey-blonde curls. I breathe out a sigh of relief, the threat of tears resurfacing as I take in Curly. I can see from where I'm standing that he's crouched over tending to a wounded child. Even though he's several metres or so away, I can see the focus on his face and the furrow in his brow as he wraps the child's leg tightly to stop the bleeding.

I can't move. I'm unable to break out of my frozen state as I watch him, his hands busy at work as he rushes through first aid. He knows all too well that the threat of another shot is practically imminent. My mind contemplates the day and somehow, I want to laugh at the ludicrosity of it all. To think I had started the day in such a peaceful manner, only for it to end in bloodshed and destruction, mere hours later. In the short space of time it has taken, the anger I felt earlier suddenly feels childish and irrelevant after such a traumatic turn of events.

I begin to rethink everything I've done as I realise how shockingly thin the line is between life and death. All I want is to walk over to Curly and wrap him in an embrace and yet, I can't bring myself to move.

As I stand motionless, a part of me wonders where the others could be, whether they're hurt or helping others like Curly is. I can only hope that they're together and they're safe until I find them and our little group is back together once more.

Then as the familiar sound of a cannon firing erupts through the screams, I'm jolted back to life. I turn to my left to look, just as the cannonball blasts through another section of the surrounding wall.

My heart slows in my chest as the scene unfolds in slow motion, splinters of wood fly in every direction as tribesmen throw themselves to the ground, out of the way of the oversized bullet. I see the cannonball erupt through the air with diabolical speed and strength. I turn my focus back to where Curly is knelt, and to my horror, I realise that he's directly in the path of destruction. I try to warn him but he's too focused on the injured child and too far from me to hear my warning, let alone notice the impending danger.

Out of nowhere, my body has its own ideas as a new surge of energy courses through me. I can barely hear the words that rip from my screaming lungs as I warn him. I break into a desperate sprint toward Curly. His attention shifts to me and as he lifts his eyes to meet mine, he's drawn to what he sees out of the corner of his eye. His expression shifts from one of determination into one of shock and before he has a second to react, I barrel into him knocking him and his young patient clear of the blast and safely out of the way.

Unfortunately for me, however, the metal ball catches me just enough and at such an angle, that it sends me sprawling through the air. I feel myself spin for a few seconds before my body connects with something hard and sturdy with a sickening crunch, and I crumple to the ground.

I open my eyes to find the world is spinning from the impact. My stomach churns and I feel like I'm going to be sick, until I cough up warm liquid that runs down my lips and drips off my chin.

I feel myself weaving in and out of consciousness as I hear muffled shouts and blurred figures rush towards me. Though I try my best to make each of them out, my sight is far too blurry to make out anything of any kind of detail.

I sense rather than see one of the figures circling me bend down to examine me, their fingertips grazing my cheek. But their voice floats right through me as the only thing that is tangible right now, is the pain ebbing through my body.

My ears ring from the blow, and the chaos around me fades into a loud hum. The noise surrounds me from all sides, getting louder as I succumb to the dark folds of unconsciousness, which all too suddenly mutes the world around me.

XII

The world around me is black, yet I hear the quiet murmur of voices nearby, their hushed tones seem urgent, but the words are just out of my reach. I strain my hearing, and I can just about make out the conversation. One of the voices belongs to a female, and I recognise it, however try as I might, I cannot put a face to it.

"Any change?"

Someone sighs.

"No, not yet. Any confirmation on why the Pirates attacked?"

"There's a party out trailing The Jolly Roger as we speak. They were after Wyn."

"What does Kage want with Wyn?"

"Whatever the reason, it isn't good. She's in more danger than we realised."

I hear a pause in their conversation and wonder if they've left me alone. The thought unnerves me slightly until I hear their voices pick up once more.

"Do you think she'll wake up soon?"

"I'm really not sure, she's healing but it's slow going. How's Curly?"

"Not good."

"I don't blame him really, after what happened."

"I just hope she comes around soon."

"Me too."

With excruciating effort, I try to move my lips to speak, but I remain motionless, frustration coursing through me as I try to signal to them that I'm awake. But as I try to move, my body ebbs with pain and nausea consumes me. As the torment on my body reaches new heights, it pulls me back under the safe sheets of unconsciousness.

I see the figure with violet eyes looming over me, its menacing laugh echoing through my dreamscape as a darkness is cast over me. As I try to get away, I realise that the place I'm in is none other than the Picaninny Tribe's camp. Teepees burn and bodies litter the floor as I run through the surrounding destruction. The sea of dead faces stare through me as I run, the path getting longer and windier as the figure grows in size behind me, its laugh becoming a warped cackle.

I keep running, but I feel as though I'm getting nowhere, the face-less figure right behind me. I cry out for help, but the only people around me are the lifeless.

My mind screams for me to run, but I know that it's no use. I come to a stop, heavy breaths rushing from my open lips as my heart pounds incessantly. I look around, taking in each face, until my eyes fall on Curly. When my eyes flicker to the young woman lying beside him, my blood runs cold.

Her green eyes are wide with muted horror. Her pale skin is flecked with drying blood, and her braided hair singed from the surrounding flames. Her body is crumpled by the touch of death, her mouth opens slightly as though her final words had not yet parted her lips.

A chill runs down my spine. That woman is me. I wonder absently

You can either help me or you can watch," I tell her, as I grunt the pain.

rdlessly, she helps me to my feet. My knees threaten to buckle y to stand up straight. I fight the urge not to groan as I breathe y ribs screaming as my lungs expand. I pull away from Khara and my tunic, choking on the gasp caught in my throat. My ribs are a p mixture of purple and black that spreads across the entirety of chest. The mottled skin stretches down toward my stomach, fading st below my navel into my normal skin tone.

"I told you. Your face seems just about the only thing untouched," Khara comments. "Kahuna told us you had bruised your ribs and gotten a concussion from the blow," she adds, motioning to my bruised torso.

"Wonderful," I hiss as I lower the tunic back over the bruise.

Khara watches me warily as I amble out of the teepee and out into the open. The air is cool and wet thanks to a light drizzle, but I relish the water as it hits my face.

I open my eyes and let out a shaky breath as I take in my surroundings. What was once a sea of teepees is now a deserted warzone. Burnt fabric and the remnants of people's belongings litter the floor, scattered amongst the ash and splinters of wood. I watch helplessly as members of the Piccaninny Tribe wander through the wreckage, some recovering bodies of fallen brothers and sisters, while others try to salvage anything and everything they can. I scan the whole scene, picking out movements far off in the distance, where a group of the stronger members have begun fixing the surrounding wall.

As I set my sights on them, a wave of determination causes me to surge forward. People of the tribe stop and lift their gaze to me as I slowly stumble through the wreckage. I feel Khara join me, keeping close to my left as I tread through the puddles and avoid the large chunks of wood dotted about.

I can feel Khara's eyes burning a hole into my face and with a sigh, I stop, turning to face her.

"Khara, *I'm fine*."

"You wouldn't be saying that if you could see the state of you, besides you should eat first. You haven't eaten in days," she argues.

if this is yet another in a string of threatening hallucinations, warning me of what is to come. I take a deep breath and turn to front the faceless threat.

"What do you want," I yell at the top of my lungs.

The same creepy laugh echoes through the vestiges of the abandoned camp. Bright flames lick the rich fabric of the teepees, the fire igniting pathways littered with the bodies of the fallen, twisted and scattered as far as my eyes can travel.

"You!" It bellows.

The darkness rushes toward me and envelopes me in a black, suffocating emptiness. My surroundings quickly disappear behind the black curtain, until there is nothing left but me.

I gasp in air as I jolt upright. I immediately regret it as I groan from the pain of my bruised body, my stomach flipping with nausea. I lift a shaky hand to my head and feel the bandages wrapped around it. As my eyes focus, a voice rattles through my disorientated mind.

"Woah there, Wyn, take it easy," the voice warns, care laced into the words.

I turn my head as she bridges the gap between us, blinking at the blinding light from behind her. I squint, trying to take in the familiar features of her pixie-like face.

"Where am I?" I croak.

"The Picaninny Tribe's camp, or rather, what's left of it," Khara replies softly.

Flashbacks detonate in my mind with a confusing rush of colour and sound. The bitter memory of gun powder stings my nose. I can hear the screams of despair echoing across the camp as I recall the pirates' attack. I remember the words told to me by Shikoba before the light left her eyes and death took her as her own.

'Restore balance to our world...'

'...Discover who you are...'

'...Make your mark.'

I contemplate her words and their meaning as I try to sit up properly, my arms shaking as I attempt to hold myself up. Khara takes over, propping me up with a stack of pillows, and pulling the blankets further up my body. She leans back watching me, concern etched into her face.

For the first time since waking, I notice the cuts and bruises on her face. The blue and green tinges spread across her chin toward the moderate swelling of her right cheekbone. Her hair is mostly tied back, but the sections that fall around her face are unnaturally short in comparison to the rest of her thick, fiery waves. I realise with a shock that half of her hair has been singed off by fire.

"Kahuna said you may be disoriented when you woke. Do you remember what happened?" she asks gently, her split lip catching my attention as she speaks.

My mind flits back to the moment my eyes fell on Curly, seeing his selflessness even in the face of imminent danger. I'm brought back into the teepee by the urgency of Khara's tone, and my mind spins from the number of questions that want to burst from my lips.

"Curly?" I utter, unsure if I'm prepared for the answer.

"Yes, he's fine, thanks to you."

Air I didn't know I was holding in, escapes my lungs in one heavy sigh of relief. I fight to keep the smile threatening to spread across my lips from Khara, her eyes watching me closely.

"How long have I been out of it?" I continue, as I glance down at the bed, I find myself in.

"Three days," she answers, her voice soft as she speaks.

"Three days?!"

She gives me a small smile, kindness in her amber eyes.

"You gave us quite the scare."

"The last thing I remember is the cannonball, then it all goes fuzzy," I recall, shaking my head slowly.

"Yeah you got Curly clear of the blast, but you weren't so lucky

yourself," she tells me, averting happened.

"When we got separated, I gathe̶ safety while Slightly went searching for yo̶

"Slightly found you two just as you ̶ harm's way. Said the blast sent you flying Neither he, nor Curly, could get to you in time. pretty hefty damage and you fell like a ragdoll. ̶ tell if you were breathing and Curly wasn't much he̶ him. Shock does funny things to people."

She pauses for a moment. A dark look clouds her e̶ back up at me, her face serious.

"Slightly brought you to where we'd regrouped, and̶ there we thought you weren't going to make it. It's lucky y̶ alive! Kahuna really worked her magic on you."

"Who is Kahuna?"

"The healing woman here," she explains.

"Well I'm grateful of course, but I hardly feel lucky at the mome̶ More like I've been pummelled to the brink of death," I reply jokingly.

"Well it was close," she frowns.

I quickly realise the two of us are alone in the room and my next question bubbles up without thinking.

"Where are the boys?"

'The boys.' I smile at my own words and at how quickly accustomed I've become to life here.

"Out there with the tribe's strongest, trying to salvage anything from the wreckage to fix the fallen parts of the wall," she responds, jerking her chin toward the outside.

At this, I throw the blankets covering me to one side and feebly try to get to my feet. Khara watches with widened eyes, protesting as I try to get up.

"Wyn, you've bruised your body... and badly. You need to rest."

"Khara, I've rested for days. I've wasted enough time. What I need is to get up and get moving," I argue.

"I really don't think—"

"I'll eat later, I'm fine really," I give her a reassuring smile before continuing on.

By the time we reach the small crowd helping to restore the looming walls, my whole body is throbbing. A dull ache spreads through my chest and I do my best to ignore it as I scour each face, searching for the two I'm looking for. I'm about to give in and relent to Khara's demands that I rest, when I finally spot one of them.

A sense of relief floods through me and I manage a small smile as I head towards him. At first, he doesn't see me, too focused on chucking fractured wood to one side. But as we near him, he stands up straight and his eyes fall on Khara and me.

"Well I'll be," Slightly mutters under his breath.

He waves his arms in the air in some odd show of triumph and laughs as he walks to meet us, a huge grin plastered on his wet face. His dark hair sticks flat to his forehead, dripping from the rain, though his eyes shine with delight.

"It's good to finally see you conscious, beautiful," he tells me with a wink.

I almost laugh but think better of it, instead I roll my eyes and send him a warm smile.

"It's nice to see you still possess that charming personality of yours," I reply sarcastically, shaking my head.

"That's it, focus on the positives," he responds cheerily.

I can't help but chuckle. The pain that bubbles in my chest makes me regret it instantly and I visibly wince at the sharp pain.

"Hey now, all jokes aside, shouldn't you be resting?" he presses gently, the playfulness disappearing from his eyes as he moves closer, putting a hand on my shoulder.

"I've been telling her this, she won't listen," Khara says sullenly.

"Where's Curly?" I ask, deciding to ignore Khara's comment.

Slightly doesn't say anything, he simply points in the direction of a couple of men lifting logs over their shoulders. Amongst them is Curly, his face strained with effort. Just like Slightly, his curls are saturated with water and falling over his eyes. Even from where I stand, I can see the strain on his muscles, his shirt is soaked through, though I'm unsure if it's from the rain or sweat.

I'm momentarily distracted by the sight, until I realise that both Khara and Slightly are watching me. I look away in embarrassment and quickly thank Slightly before making my way over to Curly.

The drizzle begins to fall harder and the water soaking through my clothes and hair, making the ground slippery underfoot. I slow my pace even more, not wanting to fall and cause more damage to my already long list of injuries.

Curly walks away with two other men carrying a huge log. I watch as they step in unison, straining under the weight of the newly carved tree trunk as they lift it over to the gap in the wall. They lower it from where it's perched on their shoulders and slowly stand it upright, filling in the gap perfectly.

As he turns, his eyes fall on me and he stops dead. I stop walking and search his face, suddenly unsure whether I should get any closer. For some reason, my mind flits back to the moment in the woods before the attack. The words I had hurled at him resurface as a bitter reminder of our last encounter before the pirate's attack on the Indian camp.

'Save your heroics for the princess, let's hope she doesn't come to think you're an overbearing, blundering buffoon!'

Shame settles in my stomach as I push myself forward a few paces so that there are only a couple of yards between us.

"So, about before..." I begin, breaking the thick silence between us.

Curly just stares at me, motionless, his face guarded. When I look down at his hands, I notice that he is clenching into fists and unclenching them again as he stares at me.

"Well I just wanted to apologise for those awful words back in the forest. It was wrong of me to speak to you in the manner I did, regardless of how frustrated I was with you," I say, rushing through my apology.

I stop my rambling and sigh, taking a slow, deep breath before starting again.

"I just—I hope you can forgive me," I finish, my voice low.

Through the entirety of my apology, Curly says nothing. He remains mute, barely moving. I wait for a few moments to see if he says anything, but he doesn't; it's as though he were frozen in the spot that I found him in.

As I turn to leave, he surprises me by stepping towards me, bridging the gap between us. His mouth is set in a thin line as he comes closer, the blue of his eyes bright and intense. Before I can open my mouth to speak, he wraps his arms around me and buries his face in my neck. The unexpected gesture stuns me into silence and I stand motionless, enveloped in his arms. I can feel the heat from his chest seep into my now icy skin, and the rise and fall of his chest with each breath that he takes.

As his arms tighten around me, an excruciating pain sears through my body, and I wince trying to bite back the cry that desperately wants to be released. Curly releases me in an instant and takes a step back. As he lets go, my knees buckle and I collapse into the mud. I hear Khara cry out my name and two sets of rushed steps as both she and Slightly rush over to me.

I try my best to muster up some reassuring words but I can't find my voice as the coppery taste of blood moistens my dry mouth. I hear Curly apologising profusely and when I look up at him, I see the panic-stricken expression on his face. I give him a weak smile and hold my trembling hand out to him. He takes it gently, and with his other arm wrapped around my waist, slowly guides me back to my feet.

"It would seem that I'm not quite as well as I'd like to think I am," I say playfully, attempting to lighten the mood.

"Wyn, you're freezing," he notes, his arm still around me.

"I have the rain to thank for that," I utter as I notice my shivering hands.

"I'm taking you back," Curly informs me, his ocean eyes filled with concern as he gently lifts me into his arms.

"You know, I can walk," I argue, just as the others reach me.

"Would you stop being so damn stubborn and rest already?" Khara asks in exasperation.

I give her a weak smile too, while Slightly chuckles to himself, shaking his head.

"You really are something, Wyn." Slightly says with a snort.

He pats Curly on the shoulder. "We're gonna have to watch out for this one, huh Curly?"

"Yeah. I'll catch up with you two later," Curly replies, distracted.

Slightly gives him a quick nod and turns to leave. Khara watches us both carefully for a moment before she follows Slightly. Curly turns back toward what's left of the camp, and without a word, makes his way back with me still balanced in his arms.

XIII

The days blur into each other while I'm convinced by the others to remain on bed rest until most of the swelling and bruising has gone. By the time I convince them to let me help restore the camp grounds, it's only my ribs that are causing some grief. After the hugging incident, Curly keeps a closer eye on me from what he deems a safe distance. I notice the change in him and the space he's keeping between us, and I can't help but wonder why. Until I notice that the less time he spends around me, the more time he spends with the princess. After the realisation hits me that I almost died for him, I'm unsure how to feel about that, and so I bury it.

After the days blur into weeks, I'm strong enough to get out of bed and join the rest of our little group. And after much pestering on my part, they band together to tell me of the news spreading throughout the camp. I listen carefully as they share their suspicions of another potential attack from the pirates. I'm taken back by the perseverance of the strange new Captain of The Jolly Roger and his fixation on me.

"I'm telling you now, that won't be the last attack," Slightly says, addressing the rest of us.

"Well as long as Wyn remains here, it's safe to say he won't stop," Curly adds.

"I hate to admit it, but Curly's right. But what's so important about Wyn?" Khara asks.

I sit in silence in the small grove near the camp where we've chosen to hold our small meeting. Their discussion deepens, each of them putting their point across until they begin to talk over one another. I drift in and out of the conversation, staring down at the grass as I reach subconsciously for my pendant.

I snap out of my daze as my fingertips claw the air, recalling how the pirates stole it from me upon my arrival. I try to remember what they said to me before all the commotion.

"Who is Kage?" I utter.

The heated discussion between the three of them dies down and they all turn to look at me, each of them wearing an odd look.

Slightly is the first to speak, "What?"

"Well, he's clearly the threat and I'm what he's after. But what if it isn't, what if it was Wendy?"

"Whether he needs Wendy or not, he thinks you *are* her. He's dangerous Wyn," Curly warns, his eyes grave.

"But why? Surely, he's no worse than Hook?"

They glance at each other, hesitating.

"There are rumours that he was the one who drove Peter from Neverland," Slightly explains.

"And that he's possessed Hook's crew with dark magic," Khara says.

"But I thought that magic has ceased to exist?" I question.

"Not quite, but it is pretty scarce around these parts," she replies.

"Magic doesn't just up and vanish, it's gotta go somewhere. Besides how else do you think you got here?" Slightly retorts.

"They say he even has a second ship hidden away in Skull Rock, not that I'd ever go snooping around that place if I could help it. Those that venture there don't come back," he adds as he starts to pick at the grass.

"Where'd you hear that crap? Peter left because he was a coward," Curly grumbles, his words cold.

"Yeah, well it was a long time ago," Slightly says, not meeting Curly's eyes.

"What's got you so interested in Kage anyway? He's dangerous. Hook was no threat compared to this guy," Khara says with a shudder.

"What has he done that's worse than Hook?"

"Drained the poor bastard's life source in front of his entire crew," Slightly replies.

"That's just hearsay," Khara dismisses.

"Even Big Chief is afraid of him," Curly mutters.

"Well when I first arrived, the pirates were going to hand me to him on a silver platter, thinking I was Wendy."

"I can see how," Slightly cuts in.

I give him a pointed look and he holds his hands up for me to continue.

"When they hauled me aboard their ship, before Curly cut in, they snatched my necklace and were about to take me to Kage. I can't help but wonder if I'm tied into Peter's disappearance and Kage's search for Wendy. I mean you did say the tribe was attacked because of me."

I rub the space where the acorn would lay on my chest, my fingertips circling the bare skin, my anger swells at the thought of such a precious gift in the hands of a tyrant.

"I mean, it's possible... but Peter left years back," Curly says with a shrug.

"I do wish they had never got hold of my necklace, it was hers! She never took it off until the day she gave it to me. Such a beautiful thing." I say, rubbing the empty spot at my chest.

I watch as Slightly and Curly share a knowing look, before returning their gaze to me, an urgency in their expressions that makes my chest tighten. Khara notices too and gives them a confused look.

"Yeah you said before. The kiss..." Curly trails off, his slate blue eyes flitting from left to right as he thinks.

"That's what the whisps called it too remember!" I exclaim, thinking that we might be onto something.

Slightly and Curly share another worrying look, while Khara and I sit there, confused.

"You don't think..." Slightly starts, his voice low.

"Would you please tell us what's going on?!" Khara cries in frustration.

Curly turns to face me.

"Did they say anything else? Did they recognise the necklace when they took it from you?"

I think back, trying to recall each moment.

"Yes, I think so. I told them it was a family heirloom and they branded me a liar. They said they knew I was Wendy and that they also knew that Pan had given it to me. Then they began raving about how Kage would be happy to have his Wendy back."

"She can't stay here," Slightly says to Curly.

"It doesn't seem like they'll rest until they have her," Curly adds.

"At this rate, C, it's only a matter of time before they come looking again. Only option really is to find a way to get her home."

"So, you're joining us for that are you?"

"I didn't realise I had to ask permission." Slightly winks in my direction.

"It doesn't matter. The chief said only Pan could help get Wyn home." Curly says.

"Pan's been missing for years, Curly, you know that. How do you think we're gonna find him?"

"Ok, guys slow down. How about including the rest of us in your little discussion? And yes, Curly, Slightly and I are in, we wanna help."

I remain silent again as they bicker and snap at each other, my mind elsewhere. Thoughts of my previous visions creep into my mind as I sit there, my head hanging low as I fiddle with the blades of grass that sway around my legs.

The grass reminds me of the first vision with Shikoba, deep in the forest and I disappear into my own head, reliving the horrors step by step. The serenity, followed by the bodies, followed by the blackened figure with menacing violet eyes, and I visibly shudder.

"W...y...n," a voice whispers, pulling me out of my thoughts.

I look up thinking it was one of the others, but all three of them are locked in a heated discussion.

"W...y...n," the voice repeats softly.

I look all around, until my eyes spot them, through the grove and past the trees, a handful of whisps floating gently in the air.

"*C...o...m...e,*" they call in unison.

I slowly get to my feet and walk through the grove towards them, hundreds of dandelion seeds floating away as my legs brush past the overgrown stems. Curly, Slightly and Khara notice me leaving and watch me, baffled.

"Wyn, what's going on?" Khara calls after me.

"Where are you going?" I hear Curly ask, an edge to his voice.

"I'll just be a moment," I call dreamily over my shoulder to them as I close the gap between the whisps and me.

"*F...o...l...l...o...w,*" they breathe.

"Where are you taking me this time?" I ask, amused as they float towards some overgrown floral bushes.

"Wyn, wait for us!" I hear Slightly shout as he runs up to my side.

"What are you doing?" He asks as he looks from me to the whisps.

"They asked me to follow."

Slightly repeats the gesture with an odd look on his face.

"You're telling me... they spoke to you?"

"Who told who what?" Khara asks as she and Curly join us.

"Wyn, here can apparently talk to the whisps."

"You mean you can't hear them?" I frown.

"They're just balls of fuzz, all they do is float. They're harmless, but annoying." Slightly says, his tone bland.

I look at Khara, but she just shrugs.

"Nothing but pests. Why they're attracted to you I'll never know," Curly scowls.

My heart sinks as I regard them all with disappointment. I watch as they shuffle uncomfortably under my gaze.

"You've all forgotten, haven't you?" I ask sadly.

"Forgotten what exactly?" Curly asks in a defensive tone.

"How to believe in the impossible," I say, before turning and following the whisps down the hidden path.

The winding path snakes to the left then right as I follow the whisps. I hear the others call after me, but I don't look back. The whisps guide me silently and whilst I'm curious to know where they'll lead me this time, I decide not to ask, knowing I'll have my answer soon enough.

I hear the others as they soon catch up to me, falling in line with my steps.

"This is a waste of time," Khara grumbles.

"I agree," says Curly.

"No-one asked you to come and I certainly don't need to be babysat," I snap back at them.

"The siren incident proved otherwise." Curly comments under his breath.

"I heard that!"

"I mean, he does have a point," Slightly reasons with a shrug.

"And what do you know of it?" I demand, my eyes trailing to Curly who shifts uncomfortable under my gaze.

"Enough to know you're quite the damsel in distress," Slightly grins, his dark eyes glinting playfully.

"A point he couldn't have made if I hadn't saved him in time," I retort, a coy smile on my lips as I dare to return my gaze over my shoulder at Curly.

He scrunches his face up as heat rises up his neck. I fight the urge to laugh out of politeness. Slightly, on the other hand, doesn't care about being polite—he bursts into laughter and shakes his head before turning to Curly and slapping him on the shoulder.

"She got you there," he teases.

Eventually, the whisps lead us to a small space in the grove, circled by tall trees whose branches scrape the sky. The sun shines down, casting a halo of light in the centre of the space. In the light, with the sound of chirping birds and the soft breeze, the place looks magical.

"Wow," Khara breathes as she takes it all in.

The whisps beckon me forward and I silently hold my hand out to the others, signalling them to stay where they are. Begrudgingly, they do, and I step forward until I'm basking in the warmth of the sun, its rays pouring over me.

"L...o...o...k," the whisps murmur as they float around me.

"What is it I'm meant to be looking for?" I ask them.

"P...a...t...i...e...n...c...e," they reply, one of them dropping down to my face as I kneel on the grassy floor.

"What are they saying?" Slightly asks, his curiosity piqued.

"Shush!"

I lean back on my legs, watching as the whisps float gently around me, circling my body at an arm's length. The questions grow and multiply in my mind, but I squash them down as I sit waiting for something to happen. I can feel the others growing impatient as they shuffle their feet.

Just as I think I can't wait much longer, I see a flit of wings out of the corner of my eye. I spin in the direction of the movement, but I realise it's gone.

"Did you see that?" I ask the others, my eyes still searching the greenery.

"See what?" Curly asks.

I'm about to reply when I see a little face peek out from behind the bushes and I do my best to bite back my gasp, joy springing to life in my chest. Slowly, so as not to frighten her, I hold my hand out, palm side up and give it a reassuring smile.

"It's ok, come out, we won't harm you," I utter in an attempt to reassure the tiny creature.

After a moment, the creature steps out from behind the mass of leaves and spreads her wings out; she's another fairy. She flutters over to me and lands in my palm, peering up at me through violet eyes.

She chimes like tiny tinkling bells when she speaks, and I return her shy smile with one of my own.

"It's lovely to meet you."

I glance over at the others to find them gawping at me, each of their faces revealing their shock. I frown in confusion at them.

"What?"

"...Is that?" Khara breathes, her voice almost inaudible. "A fairy?"

"It can't be," Curly whispers, his eyes wide.

I'm about to speak when the fairy turns in my hand and flutters her wings so that she's hovering. Her unique sound rings out through the trees for a moment before she settles in my hand once more.

All of a sudden there is a rush of colour and the trees come alive with the sound of beating wings. The flock of fairies fly around me, surrounding me with a beautiful blend of colour, the light filtering through the trees and reflecting off each pair of wings. The little one on my hand takes off and tugs at my fingertips, in a bid for me to stand.

I do as she asks, completely mesmerised as they spin in the air around me. I'm so entranced by the show that the fairies put on, that I hardly notice as they split to let the others through.

"But I thought the fairies died off," Curly murmurs in disbelief, finally breaking the silence.

"F...e...w...O...f...U...s...A...r...e...L...e...f...t," the whisps murmur through the wings of the fae.

"Few in numbers maybe, but not extinct," I answer him, my arm dropping back down to my side.

All three of them stare at me, their eyes wide and their jaws slack.

"You mean, you knew they were here?" Slightly asks incredulously.

"Not right here, no. But I saw them one night in the forest, before Curly and I arrived. The whisps led me to them," I explain, my eyes returning to the green fairy with violet eyes, who hovers in front of my face.

"They must think you're special. No-one has seen a live fairy in years," Khara says as the fae fly above our heads.

Now it's my turn to be shocked and I stare at her with my mouth hanging open.

"What?"

"Neverland is not what it once was. You experienced *that* with the sirens," Curly explains, heat rising up his neck as he quickly averts his eyes.

Slightly looks from me to Curly, his brow furrowed, and I can tell instantly his interest has been aroused.

"What happened with the sirens?"

I look up at the sky pushing back the memory of my lips pressed against Curly's, the fairies dancing through the air as I stare off into the distance.

"They sang a song that my mother used to sing to me as a child," I reply, the memory blossoming in my mind as the pain attached to it rushes through my chest in soft waves.

The melody plays softly in my mind as I recall the words, my voice soft as I start to sing.

'*I know of a place which calls to me,*
A burden that I must bear,
And when my name sounds from her sweet call,
Temptation I cannot fight
Her influence like a siren to men,
A beckoning plea for me,
Answer her call this Darling must do,
Beware should she come for you,
Beware of her call to you.'

The fae swirl around me softly, swaying in time with the melody and the words. I feel the others watching me, but I don't bring myself to look at them until the last notes leaves my trembling lips.

When I finally look away from the bright blue of the sky, I notice the silent tears that spill from my eyes. I touch my wet cheeks in surprise and realise that I could no longer spot the fae anywhere in the air. With a start, I see the others staring at me. And surrounding me from all angles, are the fae. Their tiny faces look up at me, their gaze unrelenting.

"I recognise the tune," Curly comments with a look of puzzlement and wonder.

"Wendy used to sing it to us, before we'd go to bed," Slightly says.

His voice is quiet when he speaks and to my surprise, his posture is humble and small compared to his usual charismatic bravado.

"That's right, I remember," Curly breathes.

"Her mother used to sing it to her, it's a lullaby that's been passed down through my family," I speak softly, smiling fondly at the sweet memories it gives me.

"I suppose it's something we share," I add, looking at each of the young men in turn.

"*W...y...n*," the whisps around me float closer, drawing my attention away from the boys.

I watch as the green fairy resumes her place in front of me, her wings beating rapidly as they keep her body elevated. Her beautiful sound rings through the air as she communicates with the whisps.

"*C...l...o...s...e... I...s... P...e...r...i...l*," the whisps murmur in unison.

A sinking sensation takes over as I think of the overwhelming task ahead.

"I know," I reply.

"*W...e....O...f..f..e...r....A....G...i..f...t*," they continue, their hushed tones increasing in volume.

The green fairy turns to face me, flying so close that I can make out every little detail of her face and body. Her features aren't that dissimilar to the very first fairy I'd met. Her eyes are the brightest shade of violet as she looks into my eyes.

The others look on as she lifts her hand to my face and rests her palm flat against the centre of my forehead, just above my eyes. As soon as she closes her eyes, I do the same. An odd tingling sensation rushes through me as soon as they shut.

It begins softly, but soon an odd pinching takes over, reminding me of pins and needles. As soon as her hand falls away, my body returns to normal, the tingling has vanished.

"What just happened...?" Khara asks warily.

I open my eyes only to cower from the brightness. They ache as I look around and I gasp from the intensity. The world is brighter and so much more vibrant. The air is full of tiny trails of light, each of them leading to a different fairy. The trees and flowers are luminescent as my eyes strain in the brightness, my head beginning to pound from it all, like a deep-rooted headache.

The green fairy smiles at me and bows slightly.

"Wyn, I honour you with this gift. The gift of sight," she says, her voice high yet surprisingly mature.

"I can hear you!"

"There is magic in your blood. As a Seer, you are now one of us," she explains.

Before I can ask her what she means, the rest of the fae join her in bowing at my feet. I spin in a slow circle as I take them all in, each of them surrounded in an aura of colour. Soon after, they take to the air and before I can utter another word, they dart into the trees, each of them taking a different path.

"Wyn, what did she do?" Slightly asks, a wariness in his tone.

I tentatively bring my hands up to my eyes, rubbing them feverishly, but the intenseness of the vibrant colours around me don't fade like I expected.

"My eyes."

I turn to look at the others and their eyes widen in shock. They step forward gingerly, silently gawping at me with an intensity that makes me anxious.

"What is it? What's wrong?" I ask, searching each of their faces.

Curly steps forward and moves closer until he's right in front of me. For a moment he doesn't move, and then he quickly takes my face in his hands, turning it gently from left to right as he examines me, his slate blue irises sharp and unnaturally bright. The sight of them is beautifully alluring and mysterious as I notice the flecks of silver around his pupil. I'm mesmerised by his ocean eyes; two deep pools of water, and I find myself getting slightly hot and flustered under his intense gaze.

"What is it? Tell me!"

"What did they tell you?" Khara asks, an edge to her voice.

"Your eyes, Wyn," Curly interrupts. "They're violet."

"They're *what*?!"

"It's the most common sign of magic," he continues, his voice empty.

Curly lets go of my face and steps back, giving me some room. My mind spins as I think back to my dreams and the entity that haunts them. His cruel laugh echoes through my ears and his luminous violet eyes burn brightly in my mind.

After a copious amount of silence, Khara speaks up once more and draws me from my dark thoughts.

"Wyn, *what* did they tell you?"

"That I have magic in my blood, that she has granted me the gift of sight," I answer breathlessly, not even sure what that means.

All three of them share a look, a mixture of surprise and thoughtfulness. They mutter amongst themselves and I only manage to pick out parts of their conversation.

"Would you care to share with me, what on earth you're all mumbling about?" I cut in.

"There's only one other person that we know about who was given the eyes of a Seer by the fairies," Curly explains to me.

"And I'm sure you can guess who *that* was," Slightly adds, his face set in a serious tone.

As I think of their words, the realisation dawns on me and my mouth drops open.

"Peter," I breathe.

XIV

Later that day, I return to my teepee, staring at my eyes in the mirror that was gifted to me by the princess. I peer at my green irises with relief as Curly watches on. Khara and Slightly have disappeared, probably hanging around the camp somewhere, contemplating our next steps.

"I don't see any purple... it seems normal again to me. Maybe it wore off," I suggest to Curly as I pull away from my reflection, tucking some loose strands behind my ear.

"That's not how it works, Wyn," he says in an amused tone.

I glance over to him as his thick arms are folded over his broad chest. There's a smug grin plastered across his face as he watches me and I know he's belittling me, however I'm unsure whether he's being playful or whether he's reminding me that he knows more about Neverland than me.

"Oh, because you're the expert," I retort as I glide past him.

"No. I'm just telling you that's not how fairy magic works. If they bestowed a hidden power upon you then it wouldn't just wear off. This isn't just some parlour trick, this is powerful magic," he warns me, his eyes following me around the room.

"Don't you have a date with the princess?" I tease, throwing a smirk over my shoulder.

The question catches him off guard and he averts his eyes, his ears turning red as a bout of laughter escapes me. He sends a sharp look my way as he awkwardly scratches the back of his head, his feet shifting uncomfortably beneath him. I abruptly bite back my laughter as my stomach twists and I turn to face him.

My stomach twists at the thought of him with Princess Tiger Lily. I brush the feeling aside and gather myself. Closing the gap between us, I put a friendly hand on his shoulder and give him a warm smile.

"Go, you'll be late."

Curly gives me a curt nod and quickly leaves, the fabric at the opening flapping shut behind him as he disappears out of sight.

I quietly leave the camp, nodding to the two men on guard duty as I wrap each of my hands with long strips of cloth. Heading down the slope, I slip between the tall pines and into the cool shadows.

As I weave my way along the narrow woodland path, I tie up the loose ends of the fabric and keep walking until the grove clears to create a beautiful open space. Khara is already there, shooting arrows at invisible targets, her aim precise and lethal.

She drops her bow and quiver as she turns to face me, holding her hand over her eyes to shield them from the sun.

"Figured you'd show up sooner or later," she calls over.

"I have a lot left to learn," I shrug.

"Well then I guess we'd better get started."

I reach up and tie my hair back, my three braids falling loose over my shoulders as Khara rolls her neck and shoulders in a bid to warm up. As soon as my arms drop back down to my sides, she squints and she lunges at me.

I lurch back just as her fist swings past my face. She pushes on, taking another few shots at me. I bring my arms up to deflect them before swinging my hips around and kicking my leg out toward her unguarded waist. The force of it knocks her to one side and I smile smugly at my accomplishment.

She stumbles back and a chuckle bubbles up out of her mouth as her fist flies toward my face. This time, I'm not quick enough to deflect it and her knuckles catch my jaw with a painful *crunch*. I sprawl back as the coppery taste of blood fills my mouth. I wipe away the beads of sweat that coat my forehead with the back of my hand. The adrenaline kicks in as I jump up to go again. I spit out a mouthful of blood and look up, ready to attack, just as she spins into a roundhouse kick.

As Khara's leg comes rushing towards me, my vision suddenly changes. The colours around me become unnaturally vibrant, and Khara's movements are slow enough for me to react in time, and to predict the next one. I duck and roll away from her as her foot continues its path, missing its target by a long way. She grunts as her boot slams to the ground, bouncing the first fallen leaves back into the air for a few moments.

Though the light sifting through the trees is poor, I can see everything with utter clarity.

"I see you're making the most of The Sight," she comments, breaking the mutual silence.

"How about we make this interesting?" she suggests through heavy breaths.

She pulls her twin daggers out from behind her, and grip them tightly in her hands, a playful smirk on her face. Her amber eyes glow with my now heightened vision. I spin around and crouch down, pulling two sharpened arrows from Khara's quiver before I turn back to face her.

She glances down at the arrows as I spin them around with my fingertips, and she raises a brow.

"An interesting choice of weapon," she comments as she steps forward towards me.

There is a purpose in the way she moves, a fluidity to her movements and yet I find myself feeling confident, the adrenaline pumping through my veins as I prepare for her attack. I'm surprised to realise the suspense causes nothing but excitement as we circle each other, waiting for the other to make the first move in this violent dance.

This time it's me who breaks the circle and dives towards her, the sound of metal clashing as our blades connect. I refuse to let up, throwing blow after blow left and right. I'm relentless in my efforts, until I see a gap in her rhythm and strike, the tip of the arrowhead slicing through her upper arm and leaving her with a small, superficial cut.

"Well someone's learning to play dirty," Khara teases.

"Learning from the best," I respond, opening my arms in a welcoming gesture.

A determined look crosses her face as she flies towards me, kicking and slashing at me with newfound energy. Even with my heightened sight, I'm unable to deflect every blow, and eventually I feel the cool steel of the dagger slice through the skin on my forearm.

I back up as blood wells to the surface, trickling down my arm. I look from the cut, to her eyes, an amused smile on my lips.

"I suppose now we're even," I say, my chest rising and falling with exertion.

Khara drops her chin in a quick nod and sheaths her weapons, before walking over to me, holding her hand out.

"I think that's enough training for one day. You're improving. And as for your choice of weaponry and handling of my arrows... well, I'm impressed."

I hand her the arrows and smile at her, before following her over to her bow and quiver. She crouches down to return the arrows to the quiver.

"You know I still don't really get why you want to learn to fight," she says, looking up at me.

In my mind's eye, I see her lifeless body and the way that the wind brushes past her pale face and dead eyes. With a shiver, I bury the thought before I can envision the rest of them.

"If I'm going to be here for the foreseeable, which it looks like I will be, then it's essential. Getting home won't be anytime soon," I reply.

"You have me, Slightly, and Curly. Between the three of us, we'll keep you safe."

My heart slows in my chest as a shadow passes over my face. My heightened sight fades and dulls as my eyes return to normal. I think back to the Shaman's warnings, and the visions that plague my thoughts, asleep or awake.

"And what happens when you can't?" I ask as my eyes dart to her face.

"What do you mean?" she asks as she watches me closely.

I consider telling her the truth, about the visions and what they show me. The pressing warning of what is to come, what I have to stop from happening. I think of her lifeless body in the forest, and the other one, frozen in the high snowy trails of the mountains. I decide not to tell her.

"Nothing," I reply, putting pressure on my wound.

The day has fallen into night as I stare up at the pinched ceiling of my teepee, my body wrapped up layers of thick blankets. My mind is loud and awake, and the thought of slumber feels so far away, even at this late hour. With a heavy sigh, I give in trying to sleep and slide out of bed.

As I leave my teepee, I listen to the surrounding silence and breathe in, filling my lungs with the rich night air. The camp is dimly-lit but I manage to stumble my way through the maze of tents. Other than the occasional tribesman patrolling the area, the camp is empty, everyone is sound asleep in their beds. Deep down I envy their beautiful dreams.

Silently, I slip away from the compounds of the camp and make my way over to the cliff edge once again. I seat myself down and stare up at the cloudless night sky with its millions of stars and three large full moons. One hangs above the horizon, the second is dipped low, halfway into the sea, and the final and largest of the three, rests high above the others.

I watch the reflection of the moons in the rippling waves of the ocean, its deep blue hues now a murky black. I lose myself in the scenery, enjoying the sound of the crickets and the glow of fireflies hidden away between the trees.

I'm pulled out of my serene solitude when I hear footsteps treading softly towards me. I look up as Curly seats himself beside me, swinging his legs over the edge and looking out at the horizon, the light of the moon reflecting in his eyes.

"Can't sleep?" he asks casually, his eyes not leaving the view.

"No, you?" I reply with a small sigh, my eyes still trained on him.

"No."

We fall into a comfortable silence, and I pull my eyes away from his face to join him in basking in the incredible view.

"I never thanked you," he speaks up after a long pause.

"It's fine," I reply quietly.

"No," his voice is stronger this time.

His eyes meet mine as I turn to look at him, an earnest expression softens his features.

"You saved my life, Wyn," Curly says, his voice husky with emotion and gratitude.

"Yes, and you also saved mine," I reply, giving him a small smile.

He looks taken aback. I can tell he doesn't know how to respond and so I turn my attention back toward the horizon to save him from my stare.

"The way I see it, we're even," I shrug.

"...I suppose."

"How did it go with the princess?" I ask after a few moments, my stomach tightening.

"What's it to you?" he snaps.

Laughter bubbles up in my throat and rings through the night. I shake my head slightly and glance over to find that he's already watching me.

"What?" he asks.

"Nothing. She's strong, she's beautiful. Like I told you before, I see the appeal. You should tell her how you feel though."

He looks away and even in the dark I can tell his neck and ears are tinged red with embarrassment; the heat rolls off him in waves.

"You know, it's alright to admit you care for her," I say as I continue to watch him.

"No use in that, her heart is Pan's. Always has been, always will be," he replies, his tone set.

"Well it would seem she isn't alone there," I reply, my eyes lifting to the stars.

"What do you mean?" he asks.

"Grandmamma Wendy loved Peter, even after she married and had children, and her children had children. Deep down her heart always belonged to him," I explain.

"And what about you?"

I give him a pointed look and he looks away with a smile.

"There's no-one. My heart is my own," I tell him.

'*Liar.*'

"You must have someone waiting for you back in London," he comments.

"Would it be so terrible if I didn't?" I ask, more curious than defensive.

He pauses, and out of the corner of my eye I see him regarding me carefully.

"It's so beautiful here," I say, quickly changing the topic, suddenly afraid of Curly's answer.

"It can be."

"Even in the dark of night, the water looks so enticing," I sigh, staring out at the soft waves.

Curly falls silent for a moment before he suddenly gets to his feet. I watch him in confusion as he holds out his hand.

"Come with me," he says.

Hesitantly, I take his hand and get to my feet, the warmth of his palm burning my cold hand. He leads me downhill, stopping where the cliff collides into the jagged rocks below. He glances over his shoulder at me, grinning a lopsided grin that makes his eyes crinkle at the corners. The moon glimmers in his eyes and the way he looks steals my breath away.

"Careful of your step," he tells me.

Clearing my head, I watch how he pushes himself off the edge and begins to descend the rock, until he reaches the bottom and calls up to me.

"Your turn!"

I hesitate for a moment, the height causing me slight unease as I shuffle toward the edge, sitting down whilst I get a good hold on the rock. I ease my feet into the uneven holes as I slowly make my way down to Curly.

When I reach the bottom, I realise that the high walls curve into a small cove with its own tiny beach. I stare at Curly with my mouth hanging open before I kick off my boots and rush over to the water's edge, the waves lapping at my feet.

As I turn to speak to Curly, I'm stunned to silence; he removes his belt and shirt in one swift movement, his skin shining under the moons' light. As he turns, I notice his scar. In the blue light it no longer looks angry and painful, but soft and smooth. Something stirs within me at the sight, as I'm filled with an aching desire to trace the puckered skin.

I watch in silence as he walks toward me and then past me, wading into the water before diving under the soft waves before resurfacing a few yards out.

"Wyn, you coming or what?" he calls to me as he shakes his head free of water.

My heart picks up as a warmth spreads through me at his beckoning. I waste no time in undressing, dropping my clothes with his, just before I dive into the ocean. I gasp as I break the surface, surprised at how warm the water is. Curly waits for me to swim over to him before pushing his palms through the water, the tiny wave rolling over my head.

Laughter spills from my lips as I return the gesture. We keep going until we've created a full-blown splashing war. Our playful shouts and giggles echoing through the stillness of the night. For the first time since I arrived, I feel young and carefree. The feeling is liberating.

I dip down in the water, the surface kissing my chin as I swim around Curly. I turn onto my back to stare up at the skies, still amazed at the beauty of the thousands of stars shining above. I stretch my hand up and out of the water, my fingertips are so close and yet so far, desperate to graze the sky.

"To soar amongst the stars would be an awfully big adventure," I murmur to myself.

"You come out with the strangest things," Curly says, his voice thoughtful.

"I didn't realise you could hear me," I reply, blushing a little.

I hear him shift in the water and swim over to where I'm floating. I tear my eyes away from the sky, twisting in the water until I'm upright, my feet scraping the sandy seabed as Curly closes the gap between us. Seawater drips from his wet curls as he stands up in the water, looking down at me.

The soft waves crash into us as we stand centimetres apart, our eyes locked in a deep gaze.

"What is it?" I ask, searching his eyes as he watches me.

For a moment he says nothing, his blue eyes focused on me, his gaze pointed and so direct that I find myself getting warm.

"You're just... full of surprises, Wyn," he comments, his voice husky and quiet.

He leans closer, his eyes still on me and my heart begins to hammer in my chest as I realise his intention is to kiss me. My stomach drops. The blood pounds in my ears and when he's close enough for me to feel the warmth of his breath on my skin, it's as though a switch has been flipped, and the world around me comes to life with colour. The rippling water is suddenly a sea of diamonds, reflecting those that sparkle above us. The moons' rays are so bright that I can't bring myself to look directly at them.

Curly pulls away, his softened expression now masked with a guarded one. I'm unable to read much from him other than a desperateness his eyes try to hide. He breaks eye contact turning his head to one side as he contemplates something. My heart continues to pound as I wait for him to speak.

"It's late and we leave at first light tomorrow," he says eventually. "We should head back and get some rest."

Before I can argue or muster any sort of response, he turns and swims for shore, leaving me lost and confused, with an odd feeling in the pit of my stomach.

XV

The light of dawn has barely crept over the horizon when Khara comes to wake me. She strolls in, expecting me to be still lost in slumber, instead she finds me awake, dressed, and alert. Her face registers a hint of surprise as my eyes sweep over to her.

"Didn't expect you to be awake yet," she says as she watches me.

"Didn't sleep much," I reply with a shrug as I get to my feet.

"Bad night then?"

"You could say that."

My thoughts drift back to last night. I think of Curly's face so close to mine, how far away he seemed as we headed back to camp dripping wet from our midnight swim, and the long hours after I stayed awake unable to fall asleep. Here I am, still wondering how the moment had shifted so quickly.

"The others are waiting at the gate with Big Chief and Tiger Lily," she informs me.

I nod distractedly, glancing around the small space in a daze while Khara watches me patiently. My mind is fuzzy, my body heavy with fatigue as I walk over to her, running a hand through my long waves.

"Time to go," I breathe.

I'm quiet as we leave the teepee, my mood sullen as we make our way through the campsite. We reach the gate in no time and I look up to see Slightly and Curly standing with Big Chief and Princess Tiger Lily just as Khara had said. My stomach twists as my eyes fall on Curly, his attention on Tiger Lily as they converse amongst themselves and I force myself to look away.

Slightly notices us as we get closer, his usual cheeky grin broadening as we stroll over.

"Good morning ladies," he says with a wink.

"Someone's spritely this morning," Khara comments, sending a sideward glance in my direction.

Curly looks up as Slightly speaks, his gaze falling on me as his conversation with the princess dies in his mouth. I look away before he can say anything, my eyes fixed on the dusty ground instead.

A hand falls on my shoulder and I look up to the kind face of the chief.

"Good luck on your travels, Shenandoah, may you find your way to Little Flying Eagle and follow his flight home."

"Thank you, Big Chief," I reply, bowing my head.

He steps to one side, allowing his daughter to pass through. She smiles at me as she hands me a moderately heavy sack, watching silently as I take it, gratefully, lifting the loose straps over my shoulders.

"Supplies for your travels as promised," she comments, nodding to the sack. "And a gift," she adds as she hands me a leather pouch.

I glance at her as I undo the neatly tied string and unveil a newly sharpened blade, the hilt wrapped tightly with animal hide for better grip, the blade pearly white and made of what looks like bone.

"That's a beauty," Slightly whistles as he peers over my shoulder.

"Carved from the fang of the Nymbeast," the princess explains as I wrap it back in its leather pouch and fit it to my belt.

I grab her hands in mine and meet her gaze with a warm smile.

"Thank you, for all that you've done."

"There will always be a home for you here, Shenandoah," she tells me, her voice kind as she steps back to stand with her father.

"Time to go," Curly states as he walks away, a purpose in his movements.

I glance over my shoulder at Big Chief and Princess Tiger Lily as I fall in step with Slightly. Their faces grow smaller and their bodies shrink with each step away from the high gates, until eventually, our small group merges into the trees and I lose sight of them altogether.

It's around noon when we finally stop to rest. The day is warm and even with the protective shade of the trees, the heat clings to my skin, making it clammy and hot. Slightly and Curly have decided that we should start our search for Peter in the last place they saw him: their old hideout in Hangman's Tree. I listen as they talk amongst themselves, bickering as they discuss the best route through the vast wildlands of Neverwood.

I seat myself a little way off from them, leaning back against the thick trunk of a giant sycamore as I gaze at the pretty clusters of flowers dotted across the woodland floor. Though they range in colour, the combination of vibrancy and scent makes them all equally as lovely to look at, as they are to inhale.

I sit and enjoy the peace around me for a moment. The bees fly from flower to flower, birdsong twitters in the high branches above, all walks of wildlife living in a natural balance and harmony.

This is something I'd never be able to see back in London. The busy streets full of motorcars and their fumes, the smog in the sky from the working factories. Even Hyde Park, though a lovely splash of nature in the middle of the grey, is nothing compared to the sheer wildness of Neverland. The thought of leaving it behind saddens me.

I turn my focus to my lap as I open the sack that Princess Tiger Lily had given me. Inside I find necessities such as strips of cloth for bandages, as well as plenty of food preserved in animal hide. At the bottom, I find a pouch similar to Curly's, full of fresh, cool water. I allow myself a few gulps before placing it back in the small sack, unsure when the next source of fresh water will be available. As I place it back, I feel a slight discomfort as the Princess' gift digs into my leg and draw it from my belt

Khara wanders over to me and sits down next to me. For a few moments she's quiet, glancing over at Curly and Slightly, as the two of them squabble. Eventually she turns to me, a thoughtful look on her face.

"Wyn, what's going on?"

"Hm?"

I look up from studying my blade and meet her eyes.

"You've been pretty quiet all morning," she points out.

Without meaning to, my eyes drift over to Curly. Khara notices immediately. She follows my gaze and frowns as she tries to connect the dots.

"I'm fine," I reply curtly.

"Has something happened?" she asks coyly, a playful smile tugging at her lips.

I pause for a moment, before I shake my head.

"No," is all I reply, before my eyes fall back to the sharpened blade in my hands.

I brush my fingertips along the smooth surface of the blade, balancing it between my fingers as I examine it more closely.

"May I?" Khara asks as she holds her hand out to me.

I pause for a moment before reluctantly handing it over. She takes it in her hands and twists it around a few times, grabbing the hilt in different stances before admiring the carved blade.

"It's beautiful," Khara breathes as she hands it back to me. "Rare too," she adds.

"Really?" I ask, surprised as I wrap it back up in its leather pouch and store it away.

"Yes, defeating a Nymbeast is incredibly hard, not to mention dangerous," she explains.

"Girls, come here a moment," Slightly calls over with a wave of his hand, interrupting us and cutting our conversation short.

Khara and I share a look before getting to our feet and walking over to where the boys are sat, a map spread out between them. The map is old and worn, the artwork faded and dull in sections, and the corners are ripped and curled.

Slightly points at a section of the map as we crouch down to their level, our eyes following his finger.

"At the moment we're here, in this part of Neverwood, getting to Hangman's Tree is two days' travel and we don't know what we'll find when we arrive."

"There could be an ambush," Curly cuts in.

Slightly gives him a pointed look before returning his attention to the map.

"You thinking about stopping at the den before making our way up to Hangman's Tree? Might be an idea," Khara considers.

"Exactly!"

He pulls his finger along the illustration of trees, stopping at the edge of Neverpeak Mountains.

"Hidden along the base of these mountains, is our hideout, Stone-shaw," he explains, lifting his eyes to mine, then to each of the others. "It's only a day's travel and we can eat and rest, then head straight for Hangman's Tree first thing tomorrow."

Curly shakes his head.

"I don't like it. We'll be heading away from where we need to go and wasting time. If we keep to the coast, we'll get there by tomorrow noon, that's if we don't stop too many times on the way."

"And we'll be tired, hungry, and in no shape for combat should we need to fight our way out of there," Khara argues, looking to Slightly and me for backup.

"Yeah... I dunno, C, seems a bit too risky to charge in like that. We need to scope the area, god knows what's happened to the place since we left all that time ago," Slightly reasons.

Curly frowns and mutters something under his breath, before his eyes dart up and meet mine. For a moment our eyes lock, though as I avert my gaze his words cut through the air between us.

"Wyn, what do you think?"

The question takes me by surprise and I'm equally astonished when

I look around at each of their expectant faces and I realise... they actually *want* to hear what I have to say.

"Well..." I trail off, my eyes dropping to the map. "I mean tactically speaking, what Slightly suggested makes sense. It just seems too risky to rush into unknown territory unprepared."

"I guess that's it then, to Stoneshaw it is!" Slightly shouts as he rolls the map up, returning it to his makeshift rucksack.

Curly grunts as he gets to his feet, storming off into the trees as I watch silently, guilt drawing my chest into a tight knot.

"There's always one. You would've thought he'd have grown up by now!" Khara scoffs as she rolls her eyes.

I remain silent, my eyes drawn back to the spot in the trees where Curly disappeared.

"He'll be fine, just give him some time to cool off. He's not used to working as a team, that's all," Slightly tells me with a reassuring smile as he ties his sack.

I nod before getting to my feet and walking over to collect my own belongings. It was time to go.

Slightly leads us through the trees for hours before we reach the foot of the mountain. Khara walks beside him, Curly behind and me taking up the rear. The late afternoon is dipping into early evening and clusters of small flies buzz through the trees in the summer heat.

"We aren't far now. Curly, Wyn, keep close," Slightly calls to us over his shoulder.

I glance up, nodding absentmindedly as I'm drawn away from my thoughts. Looking in front, I see Curly do the same. I watch how Slightly keeps us close to the base of the mountain with the rock looming high into the clouds to our right. He lets his hand trail along the rough stone, as though searching for something.

We follow closely behind as Slightly guides us along the path until he stops abruptly and signals for Khara. Curly and I watch as they pull away the snapped tree branches and leaves, throwing them to one side, before pushing at the oval-shaped boulder. They pushed until there was just enough of an opening to climb through.

Slightly gestures for us to go first, but Curly stops and gives him a look, though from where I'm standing, I'm unable to see it. I can only imagine how unimpressed he looks.

"Would you just trust me?" Slightly asks.

With a sigh, Curly steps forward and climbs through the gap in the rock, disappearing into the darkness on the other side. Khara follows quickly behind, as Slightly turns to me with an expectant look on his face as he leans against the boulder, one of his usual playful smirks on his face.

"Well in you go, love," he teases with a wink.

I roll my eyes at him and punch his shoulder playfully, causing him to laugh before I follow after the others. Once inside, everything is shrouded in shadow, until I see a flicker of light. I turn to the sound of flint and steel as it sparks. I watch as Khara lights the prepared fire pit before pulling a burning branch from the flames to light the lanterns dotted about the cave walls.

In the light, it seems to be a well-established and cleverly disguised base.

"The cave goes deep into the side of the mountain so this is where we store most of our food and supplies, but we've made up rooms further down that way," Khara explains, pointing to a darkened pathway leading further into the rock.

"What's down there?" Curly asks, facing the other side of the room, lazily lifting his hand to point at what looks to be another passageway.

"A dead end," Slightly answers as he climbs through the entrance.

"There's a freshwater stream that comes through an opening in the rock. We use it to drink and bathe," Khara adds.

"We'll stay here for the night and then tomorrow at first light, we'll make our way over to Hangman's Tree as planned," Slightly tells us as he plonks himself down by the fire.

"Where will we sleep?" I ask as I kick at the uneven, rocky ground.

"I'm glad you asked," Slightly says with a wink as he claps his hands together.

"Oh, grow up Slightly. Wyn, you'll bunk with me, Curly can bunk with Captain Flirt over there," Khara speaks out, looking at each of us as she speaks.

"If it's all the same to you, I'll just stay out here. With the threat of pirates, one of us will have to keep guard anyway," Curly reasons, his voice gruff.

Slightly glances over at him before returning his gaze to the dancing flames and shrugs indifferently.

"Suit yourself."

An hour or so later, I find myself wandering into the forest, relishing the solitude as the tension I felt from being near Curly, and his unsettling silence, fades away.

I pull my dagger out from my belt as I step forward, twisting it quickly in my hands as I get a feel for it. As I watch my own hand movements, I feel myself mentally take a step back.

I let my body move fluidly through the motions that Khara had taught me, putting them into practise. My mind, however, is separate from my body. I consider the girl I was and put her next to the one that I feel myself becoming. As I swing my body around in a strong kick, I wonder to myself... after everything that I have experienced until now, and everything that I have yet to go through, will the thought of London be as welcoming as when I first arrived.

'What will happen when I make it home?'

The Wyn that arrived in Neverland all those weeks ago, is not me anymore. Not entirely. And the thought of returning home to become the daughter of an Aristocrat once more, with a hidden shame upon her family, causes an uneasiness within me that I can't explain.

A rustling in the trees behind me pulls me back into my body and I swivel around, launching my dagger through the air. The blade embeds itself into the tree trunk as Curly emerges, a hint of amusement in his eyes as he looks from the dagger to me.

"You could've hit me," he comments as he grabs the hilt and tugs, releasing the blade.

"But I didn't," I retort, folding my arms.

He approaches me slowly, twisting the dagger between his fingers, his eyes directly on me.

"Were you trying to?"

"Maybe if you hadn't been so busy trying to snoop, I would've realised you weren't a threat," I point out.

At my snarky reply, he throws his head back and laughs, the sound catching as it resonates through the trees. He looks down at me and hands me the knife. I hesitate for a moment before I take it, flipping it upwards in my hand as it falls to my side, the blade tucked up against my wrist.

"You really are a Darling, aren't you?" he chuckles as he shakes his head.

"What do you mean by that?" I ask, but he shakes his head.

"I will say though, that was impressive. We'll make a warrior out of you yet," he says candidly.

When I don't reply, he lets the silence simmer between us for a moment before he lets out a long sigh and faces me.

"We should head back to the others; they're probably wondering where we got to."

I stare at him in disbelief and shake my head, frustration leaking from my pores. Confusion washes over his face as he regards my expression.

"What?"

"You barely acknowledge me, or speak to me today after whatever *that* was last night. I got no explanation from you. You sulk like a child when I agree with the others *and then* think you can wander out here and act as though none of that has happened?!" I yell, anger surging through me.

I drop my dagger and before I realise what I'm doing, my hands are firmly against his chest, shoving him hard. He stumbles back a few paces, a stunned expression on his face. Angry tears blur my vision and threaten to spill over onto my cheeks as I look up at him.

"So far, you have been my only constant in all of this," I begin my voice shaky as I throw my hands up at our surroundings.

"And deep down the truth is, I'm alone in a foreign place with no way home," I continue, roughly wiping the tears away as they fall.

Curly just stares at me speechless as I carry on. His eyes pierce me as I trip through my words, my emotions getting the better of me.

"I feel lost enough as it is. And I would thank you kindly if you didn't make that any more difficult than it already is," I finish, the lump in my throat blocking any possibility of any further words.

I bend down and collect the dagger from the grass and slip it into my belt. Curly looks as though he's about to speak, but out of anger and pride, I find that I can't bear to hear anything he has to say. I brush past him as I surge forward through the trees and back to the others.

XVI

I gasp as I bolt upright in my makeshift bed, my breaths shaky and uneven as I'm thrust back into the land of the conscious. My eyes adjust to the gloom of the cave and I calm a little when I remember where I am. The remnants of last night's dream cling to me as I wipe the beads of sweat from my brow with a shaking hand. Since my arrival at the Indian camp and every day since those first visions, the same dream haunts me every night. Or rather... nightmare. Every time I close my eyes and drift off, it's lurking, waiting for me with its piercing violet eyes and malicious laugh.

I look down at the sheets tangled around my body, before glancing over at Khara's sleeping form across the room. She snores gently from under her covers, curled up in a ball, still deep in slumber. Untangling myself from the folds of blankets, I pad out of the room trying not to wake Khara.

'I wonder what time it is...'

I trace the cave walls with my left hand, feeling my way through the dark passageway, past a room filled with Slightly's loud snoring, and out into the main area of the cave. The morning light trickles in through the entrance, illuminating the cold fire pit from last night. I glance over to see a handful of sheets strewn to one side and an empty space where Curly should be.

I feel relieved that I don't have to face him just yet. The memory of yesterday plays in my mind as I walk across the room and down the pathway that Khara had pointed out—the one that leads to a natural fountain of water. I contemplate what I'll say to him when I see him, unsure how he'll react when I see him.

I come to the end of the passage, my hand dropping back down to my side as I peer through the gloom toward the small opening between two stone walls. Trickling water sounds through the stone and a satisfactory smile reaches my lips.

Stepping forward, I slip through the gap. The sound of rushing water is much more than a trickle now, looking around the small dimly-lit area. A natural shower of water rushes down from a gap in the ceiling and spouts down, draining through a gap in the rock below.

The walls are slick and damp as I lean on them to take off my boots and place them to one side, out of the water's reach. Tentatively, I hold my hand out and to my surprise, the stream of water is mildly warm considering the early hour. As I step back and begin to undress, undoing the tightly woven belt from my waist, I hear something behind me and spin on my heels.

My lips part in surprise as Curly steps toward me. In the dim light I notice the calmness in his expression, the light in his dark blue eyes as he studies me.

I'm alert, ready for him to give some kind of a warning, but he remains silent. I contemplate his stature and closed expression.

'What is he doing?'

"Is something wrong? Are we in danger?" I ask, my voice cutting through the sound of rushing water.

Curly doesn't say anything for a moment, flexing his hands as he stands across from me. By the look in his eye I can tell that something is on his mind, but he seems hesitant to share.

"No... I—It's not that."

"What is it?" I ask, my tone softer.

I take a step forward as he moves closer to me, his hands finding my hips as he pulls me in. I'm surprised at his touch and find myself welcoming it.

I breathe in his musky scent; the fresh odour of the woods clings to his skin. The heady combination of his smell and proximity causes my stomach to uncoil and heat up, my head is almost delirious. My heart lurches in surprise as his lips close in and press against mine.

I'm breathless as he pushes against me, the both of us stumbling back until I hit the wet cave wall, the cascading water from above just catching us as he tightens his grip on me. I can feel the uneven thumping of his heart as he presses his chest to mine. His days old stubble scratches against my chin as he deepens the kiss, his tongue pushing past my teeth and teasing my own.

The sensation ignites a fire in the pit of my stomach, my heart hammering and my head reeling from this new sensation, my body encouraging his touch as he brings a hand up to my face, brushing over one of my breasts before cradling my cheek as he kisses me.

In the midst of this, I tease his bottom lip with my teeth and hear him groan softly as he deepens the kiss. As he presses his body against mine, I can feel how he's fighting against his body's desire and it draws me in further, making me want more.

My lungs feel as though they're going to explode from the lack of oxygen when he finally pulls away, taking a step back. We stand facing each other, our chests heaving and our eyes locked.

My head is reeling from the kiss as the heat in my stomach spreads across my torso. I realise in amazement that we're both drenched by the waterfall. *How didn't we notice?* For a moment he looks as though he's torn between saying something or resuming the kiss and I watch breathlessly as he struggles with his thoughts. I take a step toward him, my legs a little wobbly. But before I can reach him, he turns and leaves, disappearing through the gap in the rock. He leaves me alone, my heart throbbing from his touch and my lips swollen from his kiss.

"You aren't alone," his voice resonates across the empty space.

The words replay in my mind as I find myself alone once again, leaving me to wonder if he had even said them at all.

Once I've gathered myself, I peel off my sodden clothes and do my best to wring as much of the water from them as possible before I step under the flow of water, untangling my braids as I do so. As I clean my body, I try to wash away Curly's touch, but to no avail. As soon as I close my eyes and let the water run over my face, the places he's touched burn hot.

Khara gives me an odd look when I return to the room that we'd shared the night before, my clothes soaked through and my hair dripping wet. Before I can utter a word, she marches over to a darkened corner and I listen as she rummages through a bag before returning to me, holding out a pile of new clothes, a bemused grin on her face.

"You know, you're meant to bathe without clothes, right?"

"I slipped," I mutter, rushing through my excuse as I gratefully take the clothes that she hands me.

She gives me a funny look and shrugs before turning around and busying herself with something else. At that moment, I'm glad for the dim light that hides the blush that creeps up my neck. I wander over to my bedding and peel off the clothes, drying myself down with one of the sheets before I pull on my new attire. The leathery trousers are tight, clinging to my thighs and emphasising the curve of my hips. I pull a grey shirt over my head and down over my torso, the fabric clinging to my shape, the long sleeves cutting off at my wrists. I look down at the ensemble, feeling far more exposed than I did in my old clothes.

"Khara, you don't have anything a little less fitting, by any chance, do you?" I call over, as I look down at myself with a frown.

Khara glances over, before getting to her feet and returning to the corner once more.

"Here, try this over the top," she calls over her shoulder as she flings a piece of fabric in my direction.

I catch it and hold it out. It's soft to the touch and I can just about see the navy blue colour of it. It feels light and loose in my hands and I quickly slip it on and over the grey shirt. At least this is looser—and not so revealing. I drape my belt around my waist and tighten it, satisfied as I look down at my appearance.

The sound of Slightly's voice echoes down the passage as he calls out to us, impatient. I glance over at Khara as I braid my damp waves into a loose plait, her eyes meeting mine as she jerks her chin toward the open doorway.

"He probably wants to head out. You go, I'll be right behind you."

I nod and reach down to collect my sack, slinging it over my shoulder as I stand up. Without a word I leave the room and walk along the rocky path, the sunlight floods the previously gloomy hall.

As I make my way into the large space, I find Curly and Slightly waiting somewhat impatiently. They look up from their seats as I walk in, Curly's eyes wander up and down my body as I come to a stop.

"Those look familiar," Slightly comments with a smug look.

"Khara gave them to me," I reply as I glance down at my attire once more, the navy shirt is much more vibrant in the light.

"What happened to your other clothes?" he asks, feigning a casual tone.

My eyes flit over to Curly and for a second our eyes meet. Heat rises up my neck as I shy away, thinking back to this morning.

"They got wet," I say curtly.

"Right, what's the plan?" Khara asks, unaware of our conversation as she emerges behind me.

"You took your time," Slightly huffs, his usual playfulness clear in his mannerisms.

"I'm here, aren't I?" Khara retorts as she stops beside me.

"We need to be prepared for a possible ambush, we don't know what's out there," Curly cuts in, changing the subject.

The playful mood turns serious as Khara and I move closer and the three of them begin to form a strategy for our arrival at Hangman's Tree. I watch on as they settle on a plan.

"When we get a few yards before the tree, I think we should split up. Two of us scout around to the back while the other two scout the front and we'll meet in the middle," Slightly suggests as he points to the area surrounding the outpost in the map.

"And if we spot anything out of the ordinary, we signal," Curly says, leaning in.

"Someone can keep a lookout, while the others search inside. It's safer than all of us going in and getting trapped."

"Good idea, Khara. That way, if anyone does show up, we'll be ready for them."

"And if for any reason we're separated, head back to Stoneshaw and we'll regroup there," Curly says, his voice stern as he looks at each of us in turn, his eyes lingering on mine a little longer than the others.

"There is a high chance that the place has been ransacked," Khara points out.

"There could be dwellers."

"And what if we find nothing?" I ask, cutting into their stream of conversation.

They turn to look at me, before glancing at one another. They hadn't thought of that. Slightly slumps back, his eyes shifting from left to right as he thinks. Both Curly and Khara are silent for a moment before Khara speaks up.

"Then we'll have to figure out a new approach. If he's the only way of getting you home, then we don't have much choice."

"As of the moment, our old hideout is the only lead we got."

Despite my unease, I realise Slightly is right and nod silently.

The air is mild as we tread through the clustered trees, a swirling mist spreading around us, hindering our ability to see ahead.

I follow closely behind the others as both Slightly and Curly navigate their way through the mist, both quiet as they focus on the path ahead. The area looks dark and uninviting as shadows loom behind the trees. The air is deathly quiet; Neverwood is void of birds and little furry creatures that skulk through the tall grass in search of food. The silence makes me uneasy and my stomach flips.

By the time we've reached the hideout, the forest has become a dark and hostile looking place. The sun is trapped behind the thick clouds looming above, they threaten a downpour.

Curly holds his hand up and stops us from walking any further. He's quiet for a moment as he scours the trees, before his attention turns to the rest of us.

"This is it. Hangman's Tree is just through this cluster of pine trees."

"Right, time to split up," Slightly comments, glancing from Khara to me.

"I'll go in with someone, perhaps I'll find something useful," I offer.

"Then Khara and I will head around the back, while you and Curly aim for the front," he continues, turning to Curly as he speaks.

Curly gives him a curt nod and then they're gone, disappearing through the undergrowth. I watch as they leave, the greenery rustling with their movements. When we're finally alone, Curly turns to look at me, his eyes lingering for a little too long before he nods in the direction of the trees. I nod in response, grateful for my dagger as we cross through the trees and out into the open.

I follow Curly, both of us scanning the area for movement as we make our way over to Hangman's Tree. The sight of it is eerie in the mist with the overgrown dead tree twisting up towards the sky. He stops, gesturing for me to wait as he treads silently over to the large, round opening in the tree and peers in.

When he's satisfied, he waves me over. Before he can stop me, I climb in, lowering myself into the hole in the trunk and let go, expecting to drop. I gasp in surprise as I slide down a winding tube, stumbling forward as my heels hit the ground.

I'm picking myself up and dusting myself off as Curly comes flying down the shoot, falling forward and crashing into me. We land in a heap in the corner of the room with Curly on top of me. His face is flushed as he quickly lifts himself off of me before holding out his hand.

"What were you thinking?" he whispers harshly.

"I want to help, so let me."

"There could've been an ambush waiting."

"Well there wasn't, was there?" I retort, swiping his hand away and getting to my feet.

I distract myself by looking around the room. There is a staleness to the aroma as I take in the dusty cushions and blankets strewn across the dirt floor.

"It doesn't look like anyone has been here for years," I murmur as I step across the room.

I crouch down as I sift through the dusty blankets, picking up a slingshot from under them. The handle is smooth from constant use, the rubber band thin and weak. I feel Curly's presence beside me as I stand up, still regarding the child's toy.

"That used to belong to Nibs," Curly comments quietly.

"Do you know what happened to him?" I ask softly, breaking my gaze away to look at him.

He shakes his head and shrugs.

"My guess is as good as yours. Probably went off to do his own thing like the rest of us," he says, before walking away.

I move over to the ladder leading deeper into the den. I stick my chin out, leaning over the edge of the hole as I glance down into the gloom.

"What's down here?" I call over to Curly.

Curly stops what he's doing and glances over his shoulder to where I'm standing—leant over a large hole in the ground.

"Wendy's room, amongst other things," he says before turning to examine something in his hand that I can't quite make out.

I glance down into the gloom, my curiosity getting the better of me. Before Curly can protest, I'm climbing down into the darkness, jumping down the last few steps. My boots kick up debris as they hit the floor. I cough and splutter as the dust clears and my eyes adjust to the lack of light. The room is just as dishevelled as upstairs, with a heavy layer of dust covering everything I can see. The stale scent smells stronger down here as I wander around the room. Blankets and clothes litter the floor, a hammock swings in the corner of the room as the air shifts around my movements.

I take in the small beds fitted into every nook and cranny, fluffed pillows that are now grey and filthy, handmade mattresses torn open and worn down by the elements. The sight is as eerie as it is sad. I imagine my great grandmother as she sat here surrounded by the Lost Boys and Peter Pan, her brothers sat amongst them as she told them wonderful tales of far off places and magical lands.

As I dip into the connecting room, a similar sight greets me, nothing stands out. All I see is an abandoned home. With a sigh, I make my way through the rooms and back to the ladder, trudging back upstairs to Curly.

I find him sifting through the shelves that are carved into the mud walls. I watch, intrigued, as he pulls out little trinkets and studies them carefully, drawing each one out and returning it.

"Have you found anything?"

He turns to me startled, his posture relaxing as he realises it's me. He places the object in his hand back on the shelf and shakes his head.

"Nothing of any use to us," he says sombrely.

I'm about to suggest that we wait for the others, when the hairs on the back of my neck stand on end. I immediately sense someone behind us and realise there is no time to warn Curly. Before he has a chance to reach for his weapon, I lunge forward, my hands already grasped firmly around the hilt. With all my strength I unsheathe Curly's sword and swing it around on the intruder, the blade cutting through the air with an audible hiss.

"Woah there, little lady!" Slightly cries, jumping back from the sword at his throat.

Curly turns as the tip of the blade hits the floor with a loud clang.

"Oh for—Jesus, Slightly!" I yell, pressing one hand to my forehead as my other goes slack.

"It's not like you'd have actually hit me," he replies mockingly.

"Next time, I'll make sure not to miss," I comment dryly as I hand Curly his sword back, noticing the amused smile on his face.

"Really starting to let your spunk show now aren't ya, darling?" Slightly teases as he steps forward.

I scowl at him and turn away in a huff, irritated by his smart idea to sneak up on us. He ignores me and turns to Curly.

"Find anything useful?"

"Not yet."

"What about down on the second level?" he asks, pointing toward the ladder.

"I've already had a look, there's nothing down there but dust," I inform him.

Curly and I watch as he frowns, his eyes dropping to the ground.

"I know that look, what are you thinking?" Curly asks, his eyes trained on Slightly.

"Something just ain't right, there's no way he would've just left this place without leaving us some type of clue to find him," he comments, his eyes lifting to meet Curly's.

"He left us, remember?" Curly points out.

"Yeah and it wasn't the first time either, but he'd always come back... eventually. Maybe he just came back after we'd all left," Slightly reasons.

"But this is getting us nowhere, there's nothing here but dust and children's toys. Anything of any value was taken when we left, or it's broken and rotting away with the rest of this place," Curly spits as he steps towards Slightly, rage evident in his voice.

"Maybe you're so hung up on the past that you can't see what's in front of you!"

"That doesn't even make any sense! Pan left nothing here for us, no clues, no notes, nothing! He left us here and he never came back and that's the hard truth!"

Before the conversation can get any more heated, I step between the two of them, holding my arms out to keep them separated. I give each of them a long, hard look as I speak.

"This is not helping anyone. Your childish bickering is getting us nowhere and it's wasting time. So, I suggest that you either learn to set aside your differences, or you keep your opinions to yourself!" I snap, sending a hard look at each of them.

Both of them fall silent and look away, each of them turning away from the other and storming off in opposite directions of the den. I watch as they walk away, seeing two broken adolescent boys in place of the two young men I've come to know, and an unexplainable heaviness settles in my chest.

XVII

After a few silent moments alone, I decide it best to check on Khara and update her, regardless of how disappointing it is. I decide to leave Curly and Slightly to themselves, allowing them space to cool down before I go searching for either of them.

As I pull myself up and out of the narrow entrance into the open, I scour the trees searching for any sound or movement. I wander around to the back of the large tree, searching for Khara as cautiously as I can. My heart lurches in my chest when my eyes fall on her crumpled body, tied up and gagged.

"Help!" I scream as a rough hand covers my mouth.

"Now I wouldn't go doin' that, darling," a voice sneers into my ear.

My eyes widen as a number of silhouettes emerge from the mist and into the clearing. The pirates watch me with twisted grins and hungry, malicious eyes. Even with Hangman's Tree obstructing my vision, I can tell they have the area surrounded.

"You're gonna be comin' with us nice and quietly now missy, d'ya here?" the voice murmurs into my ear, his rancid breath creeping up my nostrils.

"What about this one, and the others?" one of the pirates call, lazily pointing his blade at Khara's unconscious form.

"Leave 'em, we have what we came fer," orders the one restraining my arms with one hand and covering my mouth with the other.

In a moment of panic, I try as hard as I can to loosen myself from his grip, but that only tightens his hold on me. He drags me into the depths of the trees, kicking and screaming, with his handymen not far behind. A sinking feeling washes over me as I'm dragged further and further from the others.

As I continue to kick and claw at my captors, I'm hit over the head with something hard and I crumple, slipping into unconsciousness.

My mind is swimming as I feel my body being dragged along by someone with a hefty grip. I hear voices, but the words escape me as my hearing is muffled.

The air is cold and damp as we move, my slack body creating a grooved path in the earth with my boots as I'm half carried, half dragged. I try to clear my mind as I fully come to, blinking my eyes rapidly as they focus.

My eyes flit from left to right as I take in the clustered trees that span for miles. The smell of damp earth and moist leaves fill my nostrils as I stare through the swirls of mist. The light of the day is bleak and barely filters through the canopy above. As I become more alert, I notice the cloth tied tightly around my mouth stuffed between my teeth in a bid to silence me. I try to move my arms and soon realise that they're bound in front of me, taunting me. A bulky and brutish-looking arm lugs me along.

At the end of the arm, I find a face that matches the thuggish limb. I let out a strangled scream. Panic explodes in my chest as I recall the ambush, the pirates, and the fact that I'm alone.

"Ooh lookie 'ere lads, it would seem our sleeping beauty has woken from her nap," another one says. I recognise his voice from before.

My eyes flick over to a greasy, shrivelled up man. His face is shiny from oil and sweat, his uneven skin patchy and grimy as he squints at me through his cracked spectacles.

I squirm and try my best to free myself, but my bonds are too tight and as I look around at the band of pirates, I realise, with a sinking heart, that I'm heavily outnumbered. Even if I managed to escape, I'd be lost in the depths of the Tiki Forest in a heartbeat.

"Oh, don't ya worry Wendy m'dear, we'll be taking good care of you. Cap'n is real eager to see your pretty face," he breathes on me, the stench of rotting teeth and strong liquor heavy on his breath.

He steps closer and grabs my chin between his thumb and forefinger. I shake my head roughly to be free of his touch but as soon as I'm free of him, he grabs me once more and forcefully presses his scabbed mouth against the cloth over my lips. Out of disgust, I headbutt him as hard as I can. He's sent sprawling backward while my own head reels from the impact.

I feel the pirate's grip tighten as the giant man holding me growls at me.

"Vance, y'okay?" his voice bellows, unnaturally deep.

My eyes fall back on Vance as he quickly shakes his head, fury burning in his eyes. Fear runs through me, though it's quelled slightly by the red mark forming on his head.

"You little wench!" He screeches at me.

He flies towards me, his fist connecting with my cheekbone before I have a second to prepare myself. His knuckles crunch into my cheek and my head whips around from the force of the blow. I feel the lump form in my throat and try my best to blink away the tears that are forming.

"Vance, cut it out. Cap'n wants her in one piece and *unharmed*," the giant argues, drawing me away from the enraged man.

Vance glares at me and grinds his teeth, before letting out a short and irritated sigh. He takes a step closer to me, a menacing grin growing on his cracked lips as he holds my gaze.

"I may have my orders, but don't think for a second that I won't come looking fer ya once the Cap'n's finished with ya, *Wendy*."

And with that, he saunters away back to the front of the group. My heart beats loud in my chest as the group moves on through the trees, my eyes shifting as my seer power takes over my trembling frame.

"Right boys, let's head back to the good ol' Jolly Roger. I bet Scully and thems are bored of waitin' fer us!" Vance hollers at the others.

As the band continue down to the shores, I wonder where the others could be and pray that they follow the trail.

Even with the gift of sight, I see nothing but vibrant colours and small creatures shifting through the mist and I can't help the small whimper that escapes as I'm dragged through the Tiki Forest toward my uncertain fate.

Night has drawn in when we finally arrive on the water's edge where wild waves chop through the air as a heavy storm rolls in. My wrists ache from the rope, but I remain mute as I'm shoved forward by the giant toward a couple of rowboats that have been dragged onto the wet sand, just out of reach of the tide.

Before I can climb in, I feel a pair of oversized, rough hands grab a hold of me under my armpits and lift me into the rowboat, dropping me so abruptly that I lose my balance and fall into my seat with a thud.

I glare at the overgrown oaf, but he ignores my gaze as he climbs in after me, a bored expression on his gruesome face. The other men laugh and chat amongst themselves as the two rowboats are pushed off the sandy floor and pulled into the strong current. As they jump back into the boat, I lift my bound hands and gently touch my cheek, wincing as my face throbs with pain. It's hot to the touch and I realise it has begun to swell.

I glance briefly over at the other boat, and my eyes fall on Vance whose vulture-like eyes are already honed in on me. A shiver runs down my spine and I quickly turn away, dropping my gaze to my feet as I frantically try to come up with a way to escape.

Just as I'm considering throwing myself overboard, the sharp pointed edge of a sword cuts through the air, aimed at my throat. My eyes flit up to the giant, my breath shaky as he regards me, slowly shaking his head.

"I wouldn't even think about it, missy," he warns, as if reading my mind. "If the current don't kill ya, those blasted sirens will."

I try to swallow, but I struggle with the cloth stretching my mouth open. Turning my gaze from him, I stare longingly at the rough waves, wishing they could whisk me away. The clouds break above as the storm progresses, the rain beginning to fall in heavy bouts.

When we reach The Jolly Roger, I'm dragged onboard in a soaking, crumpled mess. Orders are shouted as the storm ensues, thunder and lightning rolls through the clouds as I'm taken below deck by the giant. He leads me down narrow corridors and down countless stairs until we reach the brig.

The stale stench of urine, damp, and rotting straw makes my stomach turn. My eyes water as I try to fight back my urge to vomit. He rags the bonds down from my mouth, my jaw instantly relieved of the pressure. Before I can utter a word, he shoves me into an empty cell and slams the metal frame shut with an echoing clang. He ties his end of the rope in a tight knot around one of the metal loops just outside my reach. I crash into the wall and fall to the ground, unable to get my balance with my wrists still tied. My eyes flicker to him as he grins wickedly through the bars at me.

"Welcome to yer room, we hope you enjoy yer stay. And don't ya worry yer pretty little head, beastie here will keep you company until we reach the Cap'n."

With a throaty chuckle he leaves, and I hear the deep, rumbling growl of a large animal. My heart picks up speed in my chest as I slowly turn my attention to the neighbouring cell. In the dimness of the room, a pair of large, opal eyes stare out at me and I bite back a gasp.

The beast's rumbling grows louder until all of a sudden it rams against the metal bars separating our cells, baring its oversized fangs at me as I scream, backing away into the furthest corner.

Up close, I can truly see the creature; its huge frame and broad back is covered in thick forest green fur, its paws are widespread and hand-like, equipped with vicious claws. Its face is wolf-like yet its snout much shorter than that of a canine, with large fangs protruding from its jaws as it snarls at me. When I don't move, it changes its stance and sits back on its haunches, regarding me warily as it flicks its long, thick tail around itself.

The lightning flashes through the sky and shines its light momentarily through the tiny porthole in my cell. As the light shines through, I see the metal contraption secured around the creature's jaws and the matching pair around its wrists. Thick, heavy chains connect the creature to the wall. My fear subsides a fraction as sympathy edges its way in.

"What are you?" I breathe shakily as I sit up straight.

The beast notices my subtle moment and immediately moves into a defensive stance, baring its fangs at me through the metal muzzle.

Suddenly we're both thrown across our cells as The Jolly Roger battles the angry waves outside. The beast crashes into the wall whilst I find myself pressed against the metal bars that separate us—the bruised and swollen side of my face smacks against the metal, leaving me reeling. As the boat steadies and I try my best to push myself away from the creature, it's already gotten to its feet and is prowling towards me with a low growl in its throat.

In my frightened state, I lift my bound hands in front of my face as I cower behind them. I try to speak, but all that escapes my lips is a light whimper. The creature moves closer, its claws unsheathed, when all of a sudden it stares me straight in the eye, my gift of sight springing to action.

The growl dies in its throat and it peers at me unblinking, tilting its head in confusion. My heart hammers so hard in my chest that it feels as though it might burst free. I don't dare move or even breathe as I return its gaze. I watch the creature lower itself down into a relaxed position, crossing one paw over the other as it watches me silently.

Eventually, I lower my hands and manage to shuffle back until I feel

I'm at a safe distance, though the creature doesn't seem to show any aggressive signs. As I lean back, my blade falls loose from where I'd hidden it under my shirt.

I stare at it in wonder. It had completely slipped my mind that I carried it and a surge of hope rushes through me. My surprise turns into joy as I scramble for it and try to cut through my bonds as the boat sways to and fro, the sea water crashes against my small window. I quickly stop, coming to my senses as I experience a moment of clarity, securing the blade in the waistband of my trousers and pulling my tunic back over it, hoping it won't tumble out again.

I glance up at my fellow prisoner and it blinks once, its attention focused on me. Once more, I take in the chains and muzzle, its large size and then the size of the tight space of the metal cage holding it. I let out a heavy sigh as I make up my mind.

"I must be crazy," I breathe, "but when the time is right, I'll get us out of here."

XVIII

Minutes melt into hours, the hours into long days, and the long days into even longer nights.

My body is sore and stiff from sleeping curled-up on the hard floor amongst the rotting straw, my wrists are bruised and my skin is chafing from the tightness of the bonds. My mind is fuzzy from too many sleepless nights filled with shadow creatures and bloody nightmares.

The creature in the neighbouring cell is quiet and seldom does anything but lie quietly in its cage, either watching me with its wide eyes or curled up, seemingly asleep. It's only when the pirates come down to taunt us, that the creature's demeanour changes and its passive nature shifts into something feral and deadly. Though this only amuses our captors.

I lick my cracked, bleeding lips as I wait for the giant—I now know as Kram—to come down the crooked steps with my daily meagre cup of warm water, soiled fruit, and hardened bread. It's through this alone that I've been able to count the four days I've been kept as a prisoner on this ship, five if I count the day that I was abducted.

'Curly'

I think of his face and wonder where he is. Despite myself, I think back to the cave and the kiss, and the growling hunger in the pit of my stomach is replaced with a longing for something else. Knowing they couldn't have given up on me, I wonder if Curly and the others are looking for me, or whether they've holed up in Stoneshaw hoping for me to regroup with them. I crave nothing more than the comfort of their company and fight back the daily urge to pull out my knife, free myself from my bonds and try to escape.

But I'm quickly reminded of the metal bars caging me and the ruthless waves outside of them, with far worse creatures hidden beneath the ocean surface than those clomping around on the higher decks of The Jolly Roger.

As I sit daydreaming, swaying with the ship's movements, the creature suddenly lifts its large head and lets out a low growl. Right on cue, I hear the heavy footsteps of Kram as he climbs down the steps and into the room with a handful of red material bunched up in one hand and in the other, a small cup of water that sloshes over the sides as he moves.

"No food today, Cap'n's orders. Says he wants ya in his quarters fer a feast, and ya gotta dress proper fer it," he tells me as he unlocks my cell, throwing the garment at me.

"And you do everything the brute says?" I counter.

"Cap'n Kage makes the orders, I follow."

"And how do you expect me to change?" I rasp as I hold up my tied wrists, the wounds on my dry lips reopen and pool with blood as I speak.

He hands me the cup and I grasp it between my hands, gulping down the water and gasping once the last drop has trickled down my throat. Before I can react, Kram whips out a jagged dagger and saws through the rope, catching me as the last strand is cut. As soon as I'm free I rub my aching, blistered wrists and glance at the open cell door.

"Wouldn't even think about it, Miss Wendy," he says, bringing the knife to my throat.

"I've told you that I'm not Wendy!" I retort as I glare at him.

He chortles to himself as he lowers the blade from my throat and walks out of the cell, leaving it slightly ajar as he turns to face me, regarding me with a malicious grin.

"Well get on with it. Cap'n's waiting fer ya."

I WATCH IN DISGUST AS HIS GREEDY EYES TRAVEL THE LENGTH OF MY body as I get to my feet. I stride the small space and spit at him through the bars, glowering at him in anger. As anger ignites within me, it flicks a switch, initiating my eyes to change.

Kram is somewhat taken aback by my boldness and after a moment or two, he turns to the steps leading back into the higher decks.

"I'll be right at the top of them stairs. If yer not dressed in five minutes, I'll drag ya to the Cap'n in nothing but the skin on yer bones!" he warns before stomping stroppily up the stairs and out of sight.

Once I'm sure he's not coming back, I glance down at the crimson fabric. It doesn't take me long to change into the velvet dress, making sure to slip my blade into the folds of the inner skirts. Unsurprisingly, the garment fits like a glove and is more than moderately revealing with sleeves that drape over my shoulders, and a sultry sweetheart neckline that barely covers my bust.

I draw my attention away from the ghastly dress, and glance over at the creature once more before my eyes dart to the stairs. I decide to risk it and make my move. Quickly.

I shakily pull a pin from my tangled hair and slip out of my cell, moving over to the creature's cell beside it. Glancing over my shoulder, I quickly fashion it into a lockpick and unlock the door. Despite my fear of being torn apart, I move into the creature's space and unlock the chains, slipping out of the cell just as I hear the heavy clumping sound of the Kram's footsteps as he returns.

"Go," I mouth to the beast as it stares at me motionless.

I make it over to the door of my cell, dropping the hairpin and kicking it away with my boot just as he walks back in, his expression instantly suspicious as he notices me outside of my cell.

He lifts the dagger to my throat as he quickly scans the room.

"What do ya think yer doing?" he asks distractedly, searching the room for any change.

"I'm dressed. So, lead the way," I answer quickly, extending my arm toward the stairs.

"I don't know what yer up to, but don't be getting any funny ideas," he growls, pointing the dagger at me, his eyes wandering south as soon as they fall on me.

I swallow silently, disgusted at his greedy gaze, but hoping that I've distracted his attention away from the cells. He soon withdraws the knife from my throat and reties my wrists. I wince as the rough rope tightens around my blistered skin.

"Stop yer whining and move," Kram barks at me, shoving me toward the narrow staircase.

I fall forward before quickly regaining my balance. I glance over my shoulder at the creature, climbing the narrow steps until it's out of sight.

I have to shield my eyes from the sudden brightness after being locked up in the underbelly of the ship. I'm shoved forward onto the upper decks, stumbling as I hear the whistling and jeers from the crew, their leery eyes exploring me.

As my eyes adjust, I realise the brightness isn't coming from the sky at all, but from the array of lanterns hung around the ship. The weather in fact is gloomy; grey skies and a chill to the air that raises goosebumps on my bare skin.

The water is silent and eerily still as the ship glides through it, curving around the long, jagged rocks scattered through the waters.

I recognise the place immediately through Grandmamma Wendy's tales as we drift closer to the largest of the rocky islands.

"Skull Rock," I breathe, staring at the eye holes and mouth of the rock, open wide as though the cave's jaws are going to swallow us whole.

"The very same," Kram comments as he comes up behind me, the dagger pressed into the small of my back.

Men hustle around me, following the orders barked at them from Scully, high up on the stern, behind the ship's wheel. I watch on as the ship coasts peacefully through the lagoon, sailing straight towards the open mouth of Skull Rock. Droplets of water splash onto the deck and into the water, creating a ripple effect as the sound echoes through the cave.

As The Jolly Roger turns down another twisting bend within the cave, another ship comes into view, with rugged red sails and an abandoned deck. A shiver rushes down my spine as I take in the magnificence of the ghost ship. Its size heavily outweighs that of The Jolly Roger, with several cannons on either side of its bulky body, and an intricately carved skeleton wearing a pirate captain's hat, hanging proudly as the ship's figurehead.

When we slow to a stop beside the beastly ship, a gangplank is lowered across the gap. Kram propels me toward it, and a small group of pirates cluster around the plank, watching me with wide smiles, their mouths full of grey and gold rotting teeth.

I do my best to ignore them, holding my head high as I gingerly climb onto the flimsy looking walkway. For a split moment, I allow myself to glimpse down at the dark waters flowing between the ships, the surface twisting and bubbling as it slips along the narrow passage to freedom. I watch on with a deep longing.

"If I were ya, I'd keep moving missy," Kram growls as he shoves me forward.

He knocks me off balance as I totter precariously near the edge of the walkway before falling onto the deck of the other ship. I glower at Kram as I push myself up with my bound hands. He barely glances at me before opening his arms and grinning proudly, his eyes virulent and glassy as they return my gaze.

"Welcome aboard The Redbreast, Miss Wendy. The Cap'n and his crew are honoured you took him up on his invitation," he sneers.

Before I can answer, he grabs me under my arm and drags me to my feet, his grip tightening as he leads me down the steps and through the narrow corridors toward the back of the ship. We reach a large door with a trim of flaking gold paint and come to a short stop.

Kram unhands me and loosens the rope before opening the door and shoving me in. I trip over my skirts, landing in a heap on the floor and turn my head to glower at the giant oaf.

"You know, you don't have to constantly throw me about like a ragdoll!" I growl at him.

"The Cap'n will be in shortly and I'll be right outside this door until then, so no funny business missy!" he replies, slamming the door shut, a soft *click* sounds as the key turns in the lock.

I huff as I get to my feet, my hidden blade falling out of its hiding place with a thump. I quickly stuff it back in my dress before I take in my surroundings. The space is large, open, and mostly shrouded in shadow, with huge paned windows that stretch from one side of the room to the other.

I try to peer out of them but find myself unable to see past the grime and muck coating the glass. In front of the window is an impressive desk, piled high with scrolls and notebooks. Three lit candles flicker dangerously close to the stacks of paper.

As I walk round to the front of the desk, I notice the large map of Neverland spread out on the table, splodges of ink and large messy crosses scribbled across the different locations.

"What are you looking for?" I mutter as I take in the cluster of crosses overtaking the map.

As I'm scanning the map, I notice a small and worn looking notebook to one side of the stack of books and scrolls, the red leather fading and curled with age and use. I read the fading inscription on the cover, mouthing the words.

"Captain's Log."

I open the cover and read the first page aloud to myself, all thoughts of escape temporarily banished as curiosity takes over.

'I, *Captain James Hook, do solemnly swear to notate all of my findings and Captainly duties to this log, with the intent of sharing my knowledge with fellow Captains. Should I fail my task, and my title be stripped and given to another, he should respectfully continue this log with dignity and discretion.*'

I gasp, my eyes widening as I reread the words.

"Hook's logbook," I breathe.

With a trembling hand, I flick through the pages as I greedily scour the entries, my hand stopping suddenly as I come to the twelfth entry. In my eagerness, I knock over a few scrolls, sending them rolling over the edge of the desk and sprawling across the floor. I'm about to pick them up when a glimmer on the desk catches my eye.

I turn to see Grandmamma Wendy's pendant, hidden just under one of the corners of the map. I swipe it off the desk and shove it down into my bodice, relieved to be reunited with it once more. I grab the scrolls and dump them back on the desk, distracted by Hook's logbook. Wasting no more time, I turn back to it and continue reading.

CAPTAIN'S LOG: ENTRY 12.

I stumbled across the most beautiful creature this past day; she revealed her name to be Mary. I have never met a soul like her; she is simply breathtaking.

She tells me she is a distant traveller. She escapes the clutches of her mundane world to explore those in her dreams. I did my best to explain this place of her so-called dreams is one true to life, but her acceptance was more a dismissal and a tuneful laugh. She tells me she will return again soon, though I have yet to see her again.

I have yet to meet a young lady like her, she intrigues me so.

"Who is Mary?" I ask out loud.

As I try to make sense of the words, I hear the key turn in the lock. My breath hitches in my throat and I quickly shut the book and stuff it into the folds of my skirts, slipping it silently between the fabric. I step away from the desk just as the door opens and a sudden gust of wind kills the flickering light from the candles.

"Now aren't you a sight for sore eyes, Wendy dearest."

The voice is raspy and hollow. The sound echoes through my ears as it travels over the space between us. My eyes lift to the person, or rather being, that I find myself staring at.

He shrouds himself in the shadows as the door clicks shut behind him. Past his fancy buttoned waistcoat and vibrant red coat, I notice the way his body shifts and vibrates. His skin is not of any regular complexion; it's smoky black, and as my eyes reach his face, my blood runs cold. Bright violet eyes pierce through me and I edge away until my back is pressed up to the window, almost knocking a clock off of a small table to my right.

"You're the one in my premonitions," I gasp.

"Careful, we wouldn't want to break that. That clock is a very dear keepsake, retrieved from the tail of the biggest crocodile that lurked in these waters. Be a pity if it broke from your carelessness."

"You... you aren't human," I murmur, stunned.

"Well that is a matter of opinion, my dear," he replies, moving toward the desk.

"I appreciate that you've dressed appropriately for the occasion," he comments, his glowing eyes drifting lower.

"I didn't realise it was an occasion to begin with. Besides, you hardly gave me a choice," I retort.

"As clever and quick as always, Wendy," he chuckles, the sound eerie and echoey.

"I'm not who you think I am," I explain.

"Oh, but you are. The same wide eyes and mousey blonde hair. Same bold nature behind that pretty face. I could never forget a face like yours, Wendy, no matter how swollen or bruised."

As he turns the desk and wanders closer, I realise I have nowhere to go. He has me cornered. His violet eyes take me in, picking out every detail as he pulls my loose and ratty braid around from behind me and places it gently over my shoulder. I decide to play along, hoping that this will buy me time to make my escape.

"Well I'm sorry, but I certainly don't remember you."

He brings his blackened hand to his chest in mock pain, before turning back to me, lowering his large hat from atop his head, the black silhouette vibrating and shifting unnaturally with each movement.

"Your words wound me, my dear, but I shall forgive you. It has been a while since we last saw one another, and I've changed much about myself in that time, including my name."

"Kage."

"Well it would seem you've learnt a little about me at least," he comments as he regards me intently.

"What do you want with me?" the tremor in my voice betrays me.

"Isn't it obvious?"

When I don't answer, he shakes his head and chuckles once more. The sound rings through my ears as another shiver runs the length of my spine.

"I want Pan, and you're going to help me find him. For too long I have lived in his shadow."

"I don't know where he is," I argue, my voice faltering as he bridges the gap between us.

"I don't appreciate you lying to me, Wendy," his voice catches, rage simmering beneath his words.

"I'm telling the truth," I reply, backing further up against the window.

"I'm disappointed in you, Wendy. For too long I have lived in Pan's shadow, and if you won't tell me willingly, then I will just have to use force," he growls as he grabs hold of my arm.

"You *will* help me, or you will die."

As soon as his hand touches my skin, an icy, excruciating pain spreads up my arm and over my body as a deafening scream erupts from my mouth. Black veins begin to spread like twisting tendrils from Kage's grip. They move through my arm, visible under my pale skin.

The white-hot pain renders me immobile as I writhe and scream in his grip, unable to pull myself free.

"Stop, please!" I manage.

"Not until you have given me what I *want*," he growls, his eyes growing brighter as he tightens his grip. "Where. Is. Pan?" anger emanates from him in waves.

He pushes me past my pain tolerance and the scream that escapes me is unearthly and resonates around the room. His touch is unbearable. As I feel myself weaken under his strengthening grasp, I barely register the shouts and the sound of rushed steps along the upper decks. Kage must hear it too and is momentarily distracted, his grasp on my forearm loosening.

As the pain clears, so does my mind. I switch to survival mode; the pain had made me into someone wild and dangerous. In the second that he's distracted, I pull my dagger out from the folds of my skirts and with a force I didn't know I had, I slice open Kage's chest, popping the brass buttons as the blade leaves its mark. An inhuman roar of pain cuts through the air as hot, sticky, black blood spurts out from the wound.

He stumbles back, his already vibrating silhouette shaking all the more violently. He grabs a handful of my hair and throws me to the floor, his boot flying into my stomach before I have a chance to deflect the blow. I gasp and groan as I writhe around on the floor for a few moments. As he looks down at his bleeding chest, I manage to scramble to my feet.

I sway slightly as I grab hold of my dress and kick him, sending him sprawling into the wall before I dart around the desk and fumble with the door handle in a panic to escape.

I hear a menacing roar from behind me and my stomach drops as I fight with the door.

"Dammit, open!"

After endless wiggling and pulling, I finally fling the door open, relieved to find Kram's post and the corridor empty. Without a moment's hesitation I slam the door shut behind me before Kage can reach me, shakily twisting the key in the lock.

I back away from the door, my heart pounding in my chest as the adrenaline kicks in. I let out a shaky breath and try my best to steel myself for what will come. Turning away from the captain's quarters, I pick up pace and run down the corridor toward the commotion on the upper deck.

XIX

The upper deck is in absolute chaos as I creep up the steps and peer over the lip onto the main deck. Shouting and screams echo through the misty waters as swarms of pirates run all over the place in blind panic. Despite all the commotion, I'll immediately be spotted by a pirate and recaptured if I'm not careful, so I keep my dagger close to my chest.

I emerge from the staircase and out onto the main deck, gaining attention almost immediately. Most of the pirates are gathered in a tight cluster fighting something I can't quite make out. However, as soon as I'm out in the open a few of them break away from the group and rush over, swords raised.

I slow my breathing and The Sight materialises as they surge toward me. The Sight slows down their movements just enough for me to anticipate their next moves. I dodge one of the blades and trip the swordsman, only to then feel the other slice my side. As I gasp in pain, I thrust my blade forward without realising; a knee-jerk reaction. The squelching, crunching sound that follows as my dagger cuts through flesh turns my stomach, and I turn to see the face of a young lad grasping at his stomach as I pull back the blade.

Blood wells around the open wound as the colour drains from his face and he stumbles back, falling against the handrails. The blood stains his hands as he tries to put pressure on the wound, but his clothes soak up the crimson liquid, until the beige tunic is dark and heavy. I spin and vomit what little was left in my stomach as I reel at the sight. I try to gather myself, staring at my shaking hands splattered with blood before I look back at the dying pirate.

Before I can decide what to do next, a number of pirates notice me and head in my direction. I shove my dagger back into the folds of my dress and grab the young pirate's sword, the weapon heavy and clunky in my hands. I have no time to second guess myself. The first pirate swings his sword at me, and I quickly lift mine to meet it. The clashing sound of colliding metal fills the air as I try my best to throw my full weight behind my sword.

As the blows rain down, I feel my strength waning. As another strike comes my way, a fist flies toward me and sends me sprawling backwards. My back and head crash into a wall, sending me reeling as they close in on me. In a desperate plea to keep myself alive, I throw as many kicks and punches as the space allows, but between the three of them they manage to get the better of me. I feel one of them grab my arm roughly while another tries to hold me down. Suddenly a cry escapes my lips as I feel the cool metal of a dagger being plunged into my side, cutting through bruised flesh.

With my last ounce of strength, I pull my arms together and the two pirates restraining me collide. Their heads connect with a satis-fying crunch before they crumple to the floor. I move before the third can react, groaning loudly as I pull the blade from between my ribs. Blood is already spurting from the open wound. The filthy man swipes at me for the blade but just misses as I jab it into his chest as hard as I can, unable to stomach the sickening pop and familiar squelching sound of muscle and flesh ripping. I vomit bile, my eyes streaming as he falls back lifelessly onto the deck.

I grimace at the pool of my stomach contents as I wipe a trem-bling hand across my mouth, traces of blood smear the back of my hand. Making sure to keep pressure on my wound, I turn my attention to the cluster of pirates still surrounding something as I limp toward the gangplank.

While no-one is watching, I lower the rowboat into the water and chuck away the ropes. It's then that I notice the familiar growls of my cellmate and whip my head around to see the large, green creature snarling and swiping at the barrage of angry pirates surrounding it.

I notice the blood staining its fur from multiple wounds and instead of a dangerous animal, I hear the cries of a cornered and frightened creature. To make matters worse it's still wearing the thick metal muzzle, unable to free its fangs and defend itself.

My heart pounds in my chest as I plan what I'm about to do. With a shaky breath I bring my trembling hands to my lips and let out a long and loud whistle. The pirates all turn one after the other, their attention diverted, until all of their beady eyes are on me.

"Get her!" one of them bellows.

I watch on as they all scramble across the upper deck of The Redbreast, the beast skulking away before turning and meeting my eye. All of a sudden it turns and runs across the deck, jumping the gap between the ships easily and landing with a skid.

The pirates aren't far behind, but the beast doesn't stop when it lands and I barely let out the scream that escapes my lungs as the beast barrels into me and sends us both overboard, into the dark waters below.

I thrash about in the water as the current sucks me under. My bruised and broken body is no match for the rough waves that spin me about and leave me disorientated. The stab wound stings ferociously from the salty waters, clouds of crimson billowing out before me as I slowly bleed out. My lungs burn from the lack of oxygen as air bubbles escape my nostrils and ripple up towards the surface. White noise rings in my ears and my head goes fuzzy as the weight of the waterlogged dress drags me further under. My chances of surfacing for air diminish with every inch that I sink.

Just as I think my lungs are going to give out under the pressure, my conscious state begins to fade. I think of Curly, Slightly, and Khara, and how I'll never see them again. But be it shock, or my fuzzy head, I feel calm. As I sink silently through the dense waters, my eyes pick out moving shadows in the ocean's depths and as I think they're coming closer, I pass out, surrendering to my fate.

My eyes fly open to the sound of the sea kissing the shore, grit and sand plastered to my swollen cheek. I cough up water, blood, and bile as I retch into the wet sand, my breathing ragged as I realise, to my surprise, I'm still alive. Eventually, I manage to sit up, a painful groan escaping my cracked and split lips. A splitting ache ripples through my head as the world spins for a few moments and the nauseating pain ebbs through my battered body.

Gently placing my fingertips against my ringing ears, I draw them back to see the blood dyeing my skin red. My mind goes back to the events before I was catapulted overboard.

Kage and his crew. A shiver runs through me as I recall the ones that I'd killed, their faces resurfacing in my mind, the sound of my blade cutting through their flesh.

"I killed them," I barely register my own voice, as I choke on the growing lump in my throat.

I do my best to shake the thoughts as they flash through my mind, but they ring loud in my head as I recollect each moment. Instead, to distract myself, I attempt to ground myself and take in my surroundings. Whilst watching the sun glint on the rippling waves, I remember my pendant and frantically feeling for it inside my bodice. A huge sigh of relief escapes my mouth when I pull it out and fasten it safely around my neck.

I surmise that I'm far enough from Skull Rock to be safe. Feeling calmer now, I stare out to the sea before drawing my gaze across to the lush greenery of the forest behind me. The water clings to the heavy fabric of my dress as I force myself to my feet.

I tentatively move forward and my ribs scream with every expansion of my lungs, causing tears to well in my eyes. Tears I refuse to let fall. I look through the thick depths of the forest at the three high mountain peaks with Curly's words ringing in my head.

"If for any reason we're separated, head back to Stoneshaw and we'll regroup there."

My hand lifts to where the dagger entered my body and I suddenly notice the burn mark in the shape of a hand wrapped around my forearm. This skin is blackened and bruised with black veins that spread up to my elbow. The marks left in his wake are a reminder that I don't need.

As the ringing in my head subsides, I hear rustling in the trees ahead and my heart stops, fearing the worst. I'm stunned when out from the trees emerges the beast, its damp green fur a perfect camouflage amongst the foliage. I stand still as it moves towards me, its body language screaming uncertainty and fear.

"Did you bring me here?" I ask quietly as it comes closer.

As I make a move towards it, it bares its teeth through the muzzle, its hackles raised. As a gesture of peace, I hold up my hands.

"I'm not going to hurt you," I say softly.

I move closer, keeping my hands where the creature can see them until I'm standing right in front of it. Out of its cell, I can see how colossal the creature really is.

'It must be at least the size of a grown bear.'

I gaze into its opal eyes and reach out, my heart pounding as my fingers slip past the restraints and move through the coarse fur atop its head. To my surprise, I sense it relax and push its head against my hand.

"Let's see if we can take this awful contraption off you," I breathe, slowly reaching into my dress to retrieve my blade. I'm relieved to find I still have it.

As soon as the beast's eye catches the glint of the dagger, a low, threatening growl rumbles from its throat as it bares its teeth, catching me off guard. I take note of its elongated fangs protruding from its jaws. My eyes flicker back to the blade as I notice the similarity.

"Carved from the fang of a Nymbeast," I repeat quietly to myself.

"You're a Nymbeast," I breathe, our eyes meeting as the snarl dies off in its throat.

"I promise I won't hurt you. But we have got to get this thing off."

As if it understands me, it lies down with a loud thump, lowering its head for me to investigate the metal muzzle. I take in the thick chain locking the two halves of the muzzle in place. I'm taken aback by the sheer heaviness of the chain as I look it over, trying to find a kink in the thick metal. I find the locking mechanism and slip the point of my dagger into it, twisting it around until I manage to prize it open, snapping the lock. The heavy chain slips out of the metal loops and tumbles into a pile on the ground with a loud *clunk*.

Slipping the dagger into my pocket, I slowly reach over the Nymbeast's head and pull the two sections apart, separating it enough for it to pull its head free. As soon as it's free, I throw the contraption to one side, kicking up sand as it lands heavily.

I wince and fall back, regretting the throw as blood wells up once more in my stab wound. The world spins as I fall back into the sand, nausea twisting my stomach into knots from the pain. The beast nudges at me softly with its snout, an odd, almost purr-like sound emanating from its body. I weakly try to push it away, but it persists until I give in and feebly throw my arm over its wide neck, clinging to its fur as it helps me rise to my feet.

It slowly turns us around, and I watch its large paws pad the sand until we're both standing facing miles and miles of trees.

"Where are you taking me?" I ask once I've managed to climb onto its sturdy back.

The Nymbeast turns its head to me slightly and huffs one breath before moving forward, gaining pace, and melting into the trees.

THE DAY DRAGS ON AS WE STUMBLE THROUGH THE WILDERNESS. MY head swims as I brace through the pain with every movement beneath me. The air is thick and sticky, and although I can feel the sweat trickling down my temples, I feel a coldness seep into my body.

So caught up with my delirious thoughts, I slip from its back and fall, catching my bruised ribs on a thickened tree root and reopening the wound. The pain forces me to vomit, rising shakily as I wipe blood and bile from my lips. The beast patiently waits for me to gather myself and regain my grip over its neck before carrying on. I can sense it leading me somewhere, the mountain peaks veering off in the other direction, but I'm too weak to fight it.

I force myself to keep going, a bitter laugh bubbling up my throat as I think back to how simple my life was before. A sudden wistful urge fills me. I was the daughter of a rich aristocratic family, well known and well connected. I went from being a young woman with the world at her feet, to this: a badly injured, naïve girl, alone in the wilderness, and covered in blood, seawater, and vomit.

As I lose myself in these thoughts, my legs wobble. Each step becomes more and more difficult and I mentally beg them not to give out on me. My new friend is patient and keeps a slow but steady pace, though I sense that I'm only slowing her down.

IT'S DARK WHEN WE FINALLY STOP IN A SMALL CLEARING. MY VISION is hazy but I can still make out the den created out of a shallow cave, and the firepit ablaze with crackling flames. In the distance, I hear the forest coming to life as the nocturnal inhabitants wake for the night. Crickets chirp and the sound of the warm breeze rustling through the trees encircles us. Sweat travels down my temples, my body trembling from the cold that has seeped into my bones.

"Well I'll be damned... look what the cat dragged in. Herself," a male voice states dryly.

I try to see past the creature's large head, but to no avail. It growls softly to the man, soft enough for me to realise we're in the company of a friend, not a foe.

"Where the hell have you been? I looked all over for you!" the man's voice is strained as I hear him come closer.

A small whine escapes the beast's throat as it steps around, revealing me to the stranger. The man stops and stares at me with wide eyes, while I look back with wariness and exhaustion. He's a strapping young man, with a similar build to Curly; broad in his shoulders. His jawline is sharp and wide and his lips are set in a thin line. His eyes are dark and stand out against his short, unkempt, blonde hair.

"Who have you brought to me, Maja?" he asks, his eyes still trained on me.

"Maja?" I croak.

"Yes. Maja," he replies, tipping his head toward the Nymbeast.

He steps forward until he's face to face with me, only keeping a distance of a few feet as he takes me in.

"Though I'm more concerned with who you are, and why you're so chummy with my Nymbeast."

"We were cellmates. Helped each other escape," I answer, wincing through my words.

"What?"

His eyes are wide as he looks from me to Maja, concern in his deep gaze and furrowed brow.

"I need help," I whimper.

"You can say that again," he replies as he looks me over.

"Well will you help me, uhm..."

"Nibs is the name," he says, filling in the blank as he holds out his hand for me to shake.

"Nibs," I breathe in surprise, grasping his hand in a feeble handshake.

"That's what I said," he comments.

"I'm Wyn, and I know your old friends."

XX

"So, you're telling me that you're friends with Curly and Slightly?" Nibs asks sceptically as he passes me a hand-carved bowl, filled with a broth meant to help with my fever.

In the short time that I've spent with him so far, Nibs kindly tended to my wounds and replaced my sodden gown with dry, warm clothes. Seeing how extensive the damage was to my torso and the knife wound on top of that, I couldn't help but agree with Nibs when he said that I was lucky to be alive and breathing.

"Yes, and I need to get back to them. We were separated when the pirates set up an ambush."

"Why did they take you?"

"Their Captain believes that I'm Wendy, thinks that I'll help him find something he wants," I explain, unsure of how much to tell him.

"Wendy as in *the* Wendy?" he cuts in, stopping short as he regards me.

"It's a long story that I really don't have time to get into," I snap, frustration seeping into my tone.

He shrugs and gets up from his seat by the fire, babbling incoherently as he brushes away the dust. He reaches over to collect my mangy gown and turns toward the open flames.

"Wait!" I cry as I realise his intention.

"You want to keep this thing?" he asks, crumpling his nose.

"Reach into the pockets, there should be a blade... and a book," I explain, still wary of trusting him fully.

I watch as he does what I ask, my body moving with Maja's breathing. Her frame is curled around me, her warmth and the broth restoring warmth to my body.

Nibs gives each item a once over before handing them over to me. I put the dagger down, anxious to inspect the book. I almost laugh in relief when I see that the book has little to no water damage, only the front handful of pages, the back cover, and binding seem to have saturated with water.

I check the centre pages briefly—checking the ink for any water damage—but the words are still jittered across the page and as legible as when I first laid eyes on the book.

Satisfied, I close it with a sigh and lay the book beside me, intent on reading it properly once I reunite with the others.

"Well, Maja seems to have taken a real shine to you. She's not much of a people person," Nibs observes as he sits back down across from me.

"Who would be if pirates locked you up in a tiny cell and fitted a metal cage over your face?"

"Those bastards," he spits, glaring at the flames.

Silence falls between us as we sit quietly, listening to the sounds coming from deep within the forest. The fire flickers and the stars shine brightly above. It's beautiful.

"Thank you... for helping her," Nibs cuts through the silence, his eyes still trained on the firepit.

"No need to thank me. I owe her my life," I reply, stroking her face with a small smile. "But I can't stay, the others will be looking for me," I add.

"It's a few days travel from here, but in your state, I wouldn't risk it," Nibs tells me.

"You aren't coming?"

He scoffs and meets my gaze, clearly appalled by my question. The fire's reflection flickers in his dark eyes.

"And why would I?"

"You're a Lost Boy, just the same as them. You're a team," I reason.

"I *was* a lost boy, we *were* a team... but that was a long time ago," he points out, his tone grave as he turns away from me.

"Curly mentioned you all went your separate ways, but the way I see it, you're stronger together," I trail off as I read Nibs' grave expression.

I think back to that first encounter with Curly, that first night in the cave with him, and I remember how alone he looked. Thinking back, I realise how much has changed over the last few weeks, how much I've changed too, and as silence envelopes us, I wonder again who I've become and where I truly belong.

'Do I really want to go home?'

How could I go back to London after living out in the wilderness of Neverland? How could I look at the young men my father has lined up for me, without hoping for *his* face? His sharp jawline, his ocean eyes, and his curls, the colour of wet sand. How could I face my mother, with her vacant look of deliria, and tell her that her fantasies are real, but that I could never take her away from that awful place?

"There's more to that story than he's telling you, Wyn," Nibs says with a sigh, cutting through my thoughts like a jagged knife.

"There always is Nibs, but I reunited him with Slightly. This may be your chance to reconnect?" I suggest.

"Don't push it, Wyn," his tone warns me to stop, but I can't.

"They might surprise you. You might even surprise yourself. What's the harm in at least—" I argue.

He cuts me off as he quickly gets to his feet, an anger in his eyes that causes me to shrink away from him.

"I think you've said enough. Just be gone by morning, your *friends* are waiting, remember?" he spits, his chest heaving with pent-up anger.

He storms away toward the mouth of his shallow cave, his boots crunching the dried leaves under his feet. He comes to a sudden stop just before the entrance, a heavy sigh leaving him as his shoulders slump.

"Not that you'd understand, but they're not my brothers anymore. We're not in some fairy tale where happy endings happen like in Wendy's stories. We've grown up."

I can sense the strain and the hurt in his voice but decide it best to keep quiet. Silently I watch him, I notice the defeat in his slumped shoulders and the tiredness in his slouched back.

"Take what you need. There's plenty of medicine, food and water to get you to your friends. But I meant what I said. Be gone by dawn," he says, and with that he disappears into the shadows of the cave.

The sun has cut through the canopy of the trees, making the forest look translucent. It looks almost magical as I trundle through the undergrowth.

After realising there was no point in fighting with him, I respected Nibs' request and did as he had asked. Sneaking away at dawn, I took only a few rations of food, medicine and his largest pouch of water, stuffing it all into a makeshift bag, along with my dagger and Hook's logbook.

From the mouth of the cave, Maja watched me silently, her opal eyes glimmering in the faded light of the early hours. She didn't move an inch as I busied myself with my preparations, but I could sense her angst as she watched on, unsheathing and retracting her claws in a methodical way. It was only when I had packed all that I needed and stood reluctant to leave, that she finally stood up and strode over to me, brushing her rough tongue against the uninjured side of my face. I scratch her head softly; a way of saying goodbye before leaving the clearing. I head toward the trees in the direction of the peaks, sure that they'd lead me back to Stoneshaw.

I pray that my body won't give out before I reach their outpost. I can already feel the drag of exhaustion pulling at me after a sleepless night. Every time I tried to shut my eyes and get some sleep, instead of the usual shadow creature and the clearing of bodies, I see the young pirate clinging to his stomach that gushes with blood, the life draining from his eyes.

The mere thought of it turns my stomach and causes my hands to tremble. I remind myself for probably the twelfth time that I was acting in self-defence—though this does nothing to help diminish my guilt.

As the day grows warm, I'm glad for the shapeless, baggy clothes that Nibs gave me. The thin cotton is damp with sweat and blood as my sodden bandages seep through onto the fabric. I try not to think about how easily it could get infected as I keep a steady pace, my stride a lot steadier after a good rest and being tended to the day before.

Beads of sweat dot my forehead and the nape of my neck as I move through the trees. The day is overly warm, even under the shade of the trees, the air sticky with humidity. Neverwood is quiet and still, any signs of life are hidden away in the safety of the trees and the undergrowth.

I think back to the captain's quarters and the desk packed with scrolls, maps, and leather-bound books. The map on the desk, scrawled with crosses, resurfaces in my mind as I remember Kage's words.

'I want Pan, and you're going to help me find him.'

'For too long I have lived in Pan's shadow.'

"But what does he want with Peter?" I ask myself as I try to connect the dots.

The day is giving way to evening when I finally stop and rest, tipping my head back as I gulp down the warm water from my pouch greedily. As I lean against the sturdy tree, I feel the cloth from my clothes cling to my sweaty body, and for a second, I wish that there were somewhere that I could bathe the sweat and the grime away. Heat rises off my skin in waves and my fever returns slowly as the tonics and medicines Nibs gave me begin to wear off. When I dare to peer beneath my bandages, I see that the wound underneath is seeping and a puffy redness circles the open area.

I mentally kick myself for not packing some fresh bandages, but it's too late now. I know I'll have to wait until I'm reunited with the others to have it seen to properly.

Though I have little to no appetite, I force myself to eat a small portion of the food I have in my makeshift rucksack. Hook's logbook drops out as I rustle through the bag, returning the food.

After a short hesitation, I pull the book into my lap, popping the last morsel into my mouth as I open the cover. The opening inscription is water damaged, the

words swollen on the page. The tendrils of ink remind me of my arm and my eyes subconsciously flit to the burn mark and blackened veins spreading up my arm, though I notice that the mark has faded to more of a grey.

Drawing my attention back to the book, I flip through the pages and past the twelfth entry, searching for another mention of the woman that Hook knew as Mary. As I flick through the pages in the dusk light, I stop short as my eyes fall on her name once more, finding my voice as I begin to read the words aloud.

CAPTAIN'S LOG: ENTRY 15

The mysterious Mary has reappeared!

She was most displeased with her landing in Mermaid Lagoon, she tells me that the mermaids are most unpleasant. I explained to her of their jealousy towards women more beautiful than they, and for my efforts, she gave me the most stunning smile.

We sailed the seas around the coast of Neverland. She told me stories of her amazing world and her life there, until the sun set on the horizon. She bid me farewell with her lips to my cheek.

I must see her again.

As I turn the page and begin the next entry, her name doesn't resurface. The following entry and the next after that are to do only with Captaining The Jolly Roger and the events thereof. I keep flicking until I reach the twentieth entry.

CAPTAIN'S LOG: ENTRY 20

It has been many days and many nights and yet for whatever reason, Mary has not returned to me. She plays on my mind in a constant manner, I can hardly think of anything else!

Pan has noticed a change in me, he senses my distracted mind, but he never asks and I daren't ever confide in him the truth. He would not understand the turmoil within my heart.

My eyes widen in surprise and I reread the entry once more for good measure. But that only makes me more certain of what I just read.

"Surely not," I mutter, shaking my head.

"Peter and Hook were... friends?" I ask myself.

The words sound incredulous to my own ears—it goes against everything that Grandmamma Wendy had told me as a child. Peter and Hook were sworn enemies, that was just the simple fact of it, and yet, in Hook's own word lay a truth that seemed impossible.

As I skim the pages, searching for more, the sky darkens further with oncoming night and I realise that I'll have to wait to read any more.

Taking another swig of water, I place the book back in the folds of my bag and wriggle myself down against the tree trunk. I listen as the quiet forest slowly comes to life as fireflies begin to glow and crickets begin their nightly tune. Though the night is as humid as the day and sticky with heat, the surrounding sounds lull me to sleep.

I'm on a ship, swaying with the rough seas. The sky is dark and angry above, tinges of red can be seen between the thick grey clouds looming above.

The air is cold and the wind sharp as it twists around my body, kicking up my hair as it attempts to lure it into a dance. I don't feel the cold; my body numb is to the elements around it.

My eyes fall to the deck of the ship and I finally notice the bodies, my eyes picking them out one by one. The floor is littered with them, their blood mingling as it spreads across the ground, seeping through the floorboards and painting the decks below red as it rains through the cracks.

My body is tense as I take in each face, each body, waiting for something unknown and dangerous. I can feel the fear beneath my steeled resolve, I can feel it fight for domination, but I refuse to let it swallow me.

When its menacing laugh pierces the stormy sky and echoes through my brain, my gut tells me that this is what I was waiting for. As the angry waves crash into the ship, rocking it violently from one side to another, I tear my eyes away from the faces of the deceased and turn towards the menacing laugh.

The shadow manifests before me only a few metres away. My heart picks up speed as it forms, its violet eyes glowing right through me, yet I grit my teeth and stand firm. Another laugh erupts from the figure as we stand apart from one another.

"Why are you doing this?" I ask, my voice stronger than I expected it to be.

The laugh catches in the figure's throat, its eyes glowing brighter as it regards me. Bit by bit, it grows, its silhouette swallowing the sky until it towers over me.

"What have you to gain by this destruction?" I yell through the thunder.

Lightning flashes through the sky, illuminating the figure and the ship. The being says nothing as it stares down at me, no matter how much I hurl questions at it. Questions that it doesn't want to answer.

As the storm worsens around us, I'm taken aback as the shadow creature rushes at me. The curdling scream that leaves my lips is snuffed out as I'm drowned in shadow. It pours into every pore in my body, creeping up my arms, filling my lungs, and covering me with blackened veins, until I am nothing but shadow, suffocating on the darkness that envelops me.

I gasp as I come to. My lungs ignite as I breathe in and out, drinking in the thick air. My skin burns, every pore tingles painfully, and my body is coated with sweat. I feel dizzy, my head heavy as I reel from the nightmare that is fading from my mind.

As I sit up, a sharp, hot pain shoots through my left side and the wound throbs fiercely through the soaked bandages.

I lean forward gingerly, hissing through the pain. Fumbling through the dark, I rummage through the contents of my satchel. When my fingers come into contact with what I'm searching for, I grab the small bottle hastily and pull the cork free with my teeth with a satisfying pop. I drink the bitter tonic in two gulps, emptying the bottle, and grimacing as the taste lingers on my tongue.

The sky is still dark, the night well under way, but the thought of sleep makes me shudder, and the pain emanating from my festering wound tells me that sleep will no longer come. Grabbing my things and shakily getting to my feet, I decide to keep moving.

My head reels as I stumble through the trees, the fever taking hold of my body. In the dim light of the moons, I manage to make out the outline of the Neverpeak Mountains. A cold sweat runs down my spine as I follow the path, hoping to make it back to the others in time.

XXI

The darkness of the night sky shifts gradually into dawn. Ambers, pinks, and yellows are washed across the navy blue until there isn't a hint of night left. The hours have finally bled into day and I bask in its beauty as it reaches down through the canopy of the tall trees to kiss my swollen face with its light.

I begin to recognise the trees and the trampled path, a second wind coursing through me as I realise that I'm close. The fever still clings to my body, my skin budding droplets of sweat as I surge forward with newfound energy.

I walk without paying attention to the uneven path and trip over a large tree root, collapsing in a heap on the floor. Pain shoots through my body in a white-hot flash, causing me to bring up what little I had left in my stomach. I brush the matted tresses away from my face as I try to catch my breath, the loose strands sticking to my drenched temples.

I notice that the leather-bound book has slipped free from my bag so I reach over and grab it. I let out a shaky sigh, pulling Hook's book close to my chest. If I let go now, it could get lost in the dense foliage. Pushing past the pain, I manage to get back on my feet, my head pounding as I try my best not to vomit again.

After a few shaky breaths, I move on. Weaving through the tree trunks toward the base of the mountains, the earthy ground shifts to a gravellier path that leads me back to Stoneshaw.

I begin to climb the slight gradient, glimpsing my first sight of the outpost. My stomach drops when I notice the stone that hides the entrance to the caves is pushed to one side and a familiar figure paces from one side of the cave to the other.

His head is bent to the ground in concentration. I come to a standstill just on the verge of the clearing and step forward, just out of the treeline, but it takes a few moments for him to notice me.

His head shoots up, his curls bouncing a little as he takes me in. I'm close enough to take in his bright eyes, their colour dark with emotion. His face goes slack as I stumble closer to him, tears spilling from my eyes.

"Please tell me you're not a figment of my imagination," I say, my voice hoarse and edging toward delirium.

He strides towards me with newfound purpose, stopping mere millimetres away. His ocean eyes are filled with concern as he takes my face in his strong hands. He lifts it up so that my eyes meet his.

"It's you, you're here," he breathes as he leans in.

His lips meet mine, gently at first, but soon there's a roughness that causes me to wince in pain. Curly pulls away and for the first time, takes me in fully; the cuts and bruises across my face are on full show and the right side of my face is still swollen from the pirate's strike.

He can feel the trembling in my body as the cold sweat sticks to my skin and the heat rolls off me. I try to hide how much pain I'm in but he sees right through my feeble attempts.

"You're hurt," he chokes.

He touches my forehead, his own creasing in concern as he feels the feverish skin.

"And you're burning up. God, what did they *do* to you?!"

"I'm alive and I made it back, that is all that matters," I reply quietly.

"Khara!" I remember her tied up figure. "Is she ok?"

Curly doesn't have a moment to answer as a low whistle announces

Slightly making his way toward us in his usual suave way—hands in pockets and a grin on his face.

"Well aren't you a sight for sore eyes! Took you long enough, I mean five days, that's really—" He stops short, his teasing tone dying in his throat as he takes me in, ignoring Curly's glare. The grin falls from his face and the playful look turns serious.

"—Jesus, Wyn..."

"It looks worse than it is," I reply, brushing it off.

I attempt to laugh, but end up coughing and spluttering warm fluid, covering my mouth. I take my hand away to see blood dribbling down my palm. I feel a warmth spread across my ribs on my left side as the infected wound reopens again.

"Oh," is all I can muster as I watch the blood stain my shirt.

My knees suddenly give in and I crumple toward the floor; a lifeless ragdoll. My makeshift satchel slips from my shoulder as I fall, the contents spilling across the forest floor, along with the book.

"I've got you," mutters Curly as he catches me in his arms before I hit the ground.

I lean into his chest and close my eyes, the tenseness in my trembling body relaxing as his warmth seeps into me.

"What's this you've got here then?" Slightly asks as he bends down, reaching for the book.

"Don't," I gasp with sudden fierceness, not wanting to share the knowledge within. Not yet.

Slightly frowns, his eyes shifting between me and the book.

"Please. I'll explain everything to you all, I promise," I explain, my breath ragged.

Both of them watch me carefully. Curly with concern and Slightly, with suspicion. Eventually, Slightly gives me a solemn and quick nod.

"Clearly you've been through enough for now. You can tell us everything when you're better."

I just about manage a nod, and he wanders away as Curly carries me into the safe, stone walls of the cave.

"Can you stand?" Curly asks gently, once we're alone in the cave.

I give him a quick nod and he lowers me slowly back onto my feet. I wince as the pain causes my whole body to throb. Curly holds his arm around me to keep me steady, though I have a small suspicion that there is more to his gesture than being helpful.

He turns to look at me when something catches his eye and he hesitates, drawing in a sharp breath as his eyes fall on the pendant hanging from my neck. He slows to a stop, his hand gingerly reaching for it. I watch on, perplexed by this sudden change.

"Beautiful isn't it? It's the pendant I told you about, the one that the pirates stole from me." I ramble, my fingers automatically reaching to fiddle with it as I speak.

Curly drops his hand back down to his side, his eyes still fixed on the pendant for a few more moments before he turns away.

"Yes, I remember," he says eventually.

"You never answered my question about Khara. Is she alright?"

Curly sighs and shakes his head, a small smile fighting to stay on his lips. His curls bounce with the movement and in that moment, it hits me how much I've missed the familiarity of him.

"She's fine, a couple of bruises but otherwise not a scratch. But you..." he trails off, his eyes clouding over as he meets my gaze.

He brings his hand up to my face, his thumb caressing my good side. "You were gone for so long, I wasn't sure if you were even coming back," he says, his voice quiet.

"For a while, I thought you'd left me behind," I mumble.

"What? No! We searched as far as we could, but we lost track of the pirates on the beach," Curly continues.

"They took me aboard their ship and locked me in the brig until we reached Skull Rock," I explain, my feet faltering as another wave of pain washes over me.

"Hey there," he says, steadying me. He looks me over, his face serious as he comes to a conclusion. "Let's get you cleaned up," he says, leading me down the cave path.

The water rushes through the gap high up the stone walls; a familiar and welcoming sight. However, my perspective of the place has changed in the short time that I've been away from it. Now, as I stand between the slick walls, I can't think of anything but Curly's body pressed up against mine and the kiss that started a fire in my belly and an insatiable hunger for more.

I sense the tension between us, the air thick with silence as he helps rid me of the oversized shirt and boots, leaving me in the baggy trousers and my underwear. He cuts away at the filthy bandages to reveal the wound. The gaping hole is swollen, the skin around it raw and seeping. My stomach turns just from looking at it. I quickly look away and turn my attention to Curly instead.

I watch as he disappears for a few moments, reappearing with a handful of different items. He puts them down and pulls his shirt up over his head, dropping it beside them. Even in my current state, I find my eyes travelling the length of his shoulders, arms and torso despite myself. I run my gaze over every inch of skin on his toned body.

Grabbing a cloth, he moves over to where I stand, only centimetres away. His eyes are still on me as he dampens the cloth and rings out the excess water before gently moving it around my face and neck. I relish the coolness of the cloth as he moves it across my skin, wiping away the sweat and grime.

My cloudy mind clears slowly with each brush of the cloth and my burning fever relents slightly as the water cools me down. I sigh with relief. I lean back against the dampened walls and close my eyes, attempting to tune out the throbbing pain that washes over me in waves.

I flinch as I feel the cloth run over my swollen cheek, a hiss escaping my gritted teeth. I sense Curly's hesitation as he mumbles a soft apology and I shake my head quickly, my eyes shut.

"You don't need to apologise," I comment, my voice soft.

When he doesn't respond, I slowly open my eyes to find him watching me carefully. His deep eyes are filled with emotions that I can't read. His face is serious, yet there's a softness to it that I can't quite explain.

"I'm fine, Curly, really," I tell him, giving my best reassuring smile.

He raises an eyebrow at me, unconvinced. After a few moments, his face softens and his hands run over my shoulders to reach my matted braid. Without a word, he untangles the blonde tresses so that they fall loosely over my shoulders.

He grabs my hands in his firm grip before leading me over to the gushing water, immersing us both in the stream.

I gasp in surprise at how cool water is against my hot skin as it runs over my body, soaking through my hair and my clothes. I try to bite back the groan that escapes my lips as the cool water runs over the infected wound, the inflamed skin irritated and angry.

I grab hold of Curly's arms to steady myself as a wooziness comes over me. I grip onto him, my fingers denting his skin as he holds my waist. As the sensation settles, his forehead comes down to rest on mine, the water flowing over us both.

"Thank God you're alive," he murmurs.

I smile at his words, finally feeling at peace as the water creates tiny streams over our skin, running this way and that, connecting the both of us in our silence as we share the same space.

Khara rushes in just as Curly is finishing up tending to my wound.

Her eyes are wild and frantic as she bursts in unannounced, her eyes darting from Curly to me as we stand there for a moment in surprise, our bodies still dripping wet from our shower.

I still feel the fever's hold over me; my skin is still warm to the touch, but after the cool water and a few mouthfuls of a bitter tonic— that Curly insisted I drink—I feel better for it.

"Slightly told me you were back, I just had to see for myself," Khara breathes in disbelief, her eyes scouring me as the words fly out of her mouth.

I take in her bruised face, ugly yellows, purples and blues are splashed around her eye, and the swelling over her eyebrow, eye socket and cheekbone is extensive.

"Khara."

A relieved smile passes over my face and I watch as she relaxes, beaming back at me. The bottom half of her fiery hair tumbles over her shoulders wildly, while the upper half is twisted into a makeshift knot on the top of her head. She doesn't just have the spirit of a warrior; she has the look of one too.

"You look awful," she comments, blowing out a long whistle as she takes me in, while ignoring Curly's glaring eyes, just as Slightly had done before.

Despite myself, I laugh and I regret the decision immediately. Curly gives me a warning look as he wraps the bandages around my torso.

"I've just stitched this up, I'd rather you not reopen it," he grumbles.

"Yes, well... sorry," I reply sheepishly.

"You're one to talk, look at the state of you," I tell Khara, gesturing to her colourful face.

Khara chuckles and shakes her head, the tension in her shoulders evaporating as she relaxes back into herself, back into the young woman that I've come to call my friend.

"Are you done here? I'm sure Wyn wants to change into something a little more appropriate," she says as she peers over at Curly who's already busying himself with packing up the medicinal items.

I watch in silent amusement as his neck turns red, his eyes stealing a quick glance at me before flitting back to the task at hand. I can't help but look down at the oversized and very much see through three-quarter length cotton trousers stuck to my skin, and then to the equally wet brassiere, my cheeks warming with sudden embarrassment.

Curly grumbles a response that Khara takes as a yes and grabs my hand before dragging me out of the room. I'm only able to get out a quick thank you over my shoulder to Curly before he's out of sight.

I let Khara lead me down the passageways and back into her small room, watching as she pulls a drape over the entrance as a makeshift door.

"To shut out any unwanted eyes," she explains as she turns back to me.

We stand apart in loaded silence for a few moments. Khara fiddles with her fingers as she carves lines into the dirt with her boot. I sense that she has something to say so I keep quiet, waiting patiently for her to speak. The tension is enough for me to grow anxious. But instead of speaking, to my surprise, she bridges the gap between us and envelopes me in a long, tight hug.

"I'm so sorry, Wyn," she chokes into my damp hair.

Slowly, I wrap my arms around her as I return the gesture, surprised by her sudden emotion. Her embrace is just tight enough for me to feel the throbbing echoing through my torso, but I don't let go.

"What are you talking about?"

"The ambush. I should've done something, anything," she tells me as she pulls away from me, her eyes shining with guilt and threatening tears.

"There was nothing you could've done, Khara. None of this was your fault," I reply softly, resting my hands on her shoulders.

"I was the lookout, I should've done something," she argues, her gaze dropping to the ground.

"Khara, listen to me," I begin, waiting for her to look at me.

"When they grabbed me, you were already tied up and unconscious. If any of us failed anyone, it was us failing you," I explain to her, my tone sure.

I pull her into another embrace before I release my hold and step back, a grin growing on my lips as we look at one another.

"I never took you for the sappy type," I tease.

Khara laughs and punches my shoulder playfully before walking past me and delving into a pile of clothes.

"I'm not, but you're one of us now and that counts for something," she says, a heaviness to her words that stops me in my tracks.

Her words resonate with me in a way I hadn't anticipated and I smile to myself as a warm feeling spreads through my chest, a sense of belonging. For the hundredth time, I wonder how I'll ever go back to the life that I led before all of this.

"Here," she says suddenly as she walks over to me, handing me a few pieces of clothing.

I hold up the brown leather corset piece with an unimpressed look on my face. Khara chuckles and shakes her head at me, amused.

"It goes over the tunic, plus it'll support your torso, especially while you're healing," she points out.

"Oh. You know I'll probably need help with it or we'll be here all day," I say as I peel the wet trousers away from my legs.

"Duh, what are friends for?" She shrugs, a smirk playing on her lips as she crosses her arms.

"Pretty sure Slightly is itching to hear what happened while I was held prisoner," I add.

"Well he can join the club," Khara laughs. "But maybe we should get a move on anyway," she adds, stepping toward me as I adjust the fabric of the tunic so that it doesn't bunch around my wrists.

Before I have a chance to answer, Khara steps back and leaves the room, giving me a split second alone with my thoughts which lead me back to the Captain's Log Book.

'You can't keep Hook's book a secret forever.'

I dispel the little voice with a quick but violent shake of the head before following Khara, shoving the dark thoughts deep down, for now.

XXII

As Khara and I walk out into the small opening of the cave, I notice both Curly and Slightly are already there, huddled around maps and curled-up scrolls. To my surprise, Hook's leather-bound book is placed beside the unfurled map and as I seat myself by the young men. I reach over and retrieve it, placing it in my lap before anyone notices.

I contemplate its contents and wonder if any of the entries would even be of any use to the others. I think back on Hook's words and the mention of a woman named Mary. I decide to study it further before sharing anything.

The boys barely notice our arrival as they're engrossed in discussion, that is, until Khara clears her throat, watching them expectantly. They both look up, wide-eyed.

"Care to share what it is that you're doing?" Khara asks, tilting her head to one side.

"Trying to work out what our next move should be," Slightly answers, his tone impatient.

"We found nothing useful at Hangman's Tree, and if we don't come up with some kind of strategy soon, we'll be spending the foreseeable here," Curly adds, leaning back.

"We don't have time on our hands to play with," I say as they all turn to look at me.

"Why do you say that? Far as I know you've not been in any rush until now," Slightly points out.

"True, but Kage will be looking for me. Neverwood will be crawling with his men in a number of days."

"But why would he be looking for you, what does he want?" Curly chips in, looking at me over Slightly's shoulder.

Without thinking, I reach up and touch my necklace, twisting the golden acorn in my fingers as I remember Kage's words and his excruciating touch, a shiver running down my spine.

"He thinks I'm Wendy," I answer, my eyes falling on the map.

"But what would he want with Wendy?" Khara joins in the discussion.

"Peter," I reply.

"Pan. Of course. It's the only logical answer," Curly decides with a small shrug.

"If he thinks he has Wendy, Peter would inevitably follow," Slightly adds as the realisation dawns on his face.

But I'm not paying attention to the discussion anymore, my eyes are focused on the map. I travel back in my mind to the captain's quarters and the desk overflowing with notes and scrolls. I remember the map of Neverland with the large crosses dotted on it, and the question that lingered on my lips.

"Of course! Why didn't I think of it before?" I breathe.

The others look at me in surprise as I lean over the map. I feel their curiosity building as they wait for me to say something. Suddenly, I fling my arm out to Slightly, my palm open and flat.

"I need something to draw with," I say, my tone insistent.

Slightly hands me a stick of charcoal and I take it from him, scrawling all over the map as they barrage me with questions.

"Hey! What are you doing?"

"What are the crosses for?"

"Wyn. You're ruining my map!"

"If you all just give me a goddamn minute, I'll tell you!" I snap as I close my eyes.

Trying to conjure Kage's map in my head, I scribble out the last few crosses and sit back on my knees. I drop the stick of charcoal and rub my palms together in a vain attempt to wipe away the black smudges. With a short sigh, I lift my gaze to meet the expectant stares of the others.

"I saw a map of Neverland in Kage's room when I was in his quarters," I began.

"At first, I couldn't understand why his map looked like this; it didn't make any sense. There was nothing except for these crossed out sections and I didn't realise why until now."

The others stare at the map with furrowed brows, their eyes scanning the map as I keep talking.

"He's *looking* for Peter. The crosses must be all the sections of Neverland that he's searched and come up empty-handed," I surmise.

"And if we use it in the same way, we can save time by avoiding all of the crossed out areas—the ones that he's already searched," Slightly says, an excitement to his tone as he leans in to study the map.

"It certainly narrows down where to look," Curly agrees as he joins Slightly.

"All we have to do is search the unmarked spots," Khara says, grinning at me like I'm a genius.

"But that'll take weeks, we'd be travelling all over the place," Slightly points out, slapping the map with the back of his hand as he sits up.

Khara and Curly mumble their agreement as I gaze at the map for myself. I pick out the empty spaces of land and try to come up with some feasible options. My eyes stop drifting when they reach Neverpeak Mountains.

"We need to make sure we don't run into Kage when we're out searching," I tell them. "What do we know about Kage?" I ask the group, meeting each of their gazes.

"We know he killed Hook and took over," Slightly answers.

"Nobody knows what he looks like," Khara adds.

"I do."

That draws them in. I look to each of them, hoping to convey the seriousness of what we're dealing with before I explain.

"I can tell you that he's not human. Black warped skin and bright violet eyes. He looks more like a shadow than a physical person. Yet everything about him says he's made of flesh and blood." I shiver, thinking back to the way his body spewed a black tar-like blood. "Oh. And he has magic," I add.

"They watch me with astounded expressions and a thick silence falls over the group as they process my words.

"If he's able to wield magic, then he's more dangerous than we thought" Slightly speaks up thoughtfully.

"He's a threat to Neverland. Why did you allow him to become such a threat?" I demand, gesturing to Slightly and Curly. "You're the Lost Boys of Neverland, it's in your blood. Hell, it's what you *do*!"

"Things aren't the same as they were back then," Curly argues.

"Maybe Peter was right to flee, maybe he knew what Kage was capable of," Khara adds.

"Maybe someone should've done something before I showed up," I counter.

When none of them say anything, I heave an irritated sigh and shake my head.

"Well, that isn't all I know... he's captained a second ship hidden in Skull Rock, and although his pirate followers aren't the smartest bunch, they follow his orders to the letter."

"Another ship?" Slightly says, his tone shocked.

I hold my hand up to silence him, sending a stern look his way until he grumbles and rolls his eyes, gesturing for me to continue.

"And the magic he possesses is powerful, like nothing I've ever heard of."

I pull up my sleeve to reveal the charred hand mark wrapped around my wrist. The angry mark is slowly turning into a lumpy scar flecked with greying veins twisting up my forearm toward my elbow.

"It's the most excruciating pain that I've ever felt. It was as if he was drawing energy from me while torturing me at the same time. If he'd held on for any longer than he had, I know he would have drained the life from me," I explain as I pull the sleeve back down covering the damaged skin.

"But then, if that's the theory we're working with, how did you—" Khara questions.

"—Escape?" I interject. "I wasn't the only prisoner aboard his ship. We helped each other to escape."

Khara stares at me astounded, but says nothing.

"But that doesn't matter right now. As of now, us and Kage, we share the same goal. We need to be three steps ahead of him at all times," I warn.

"And by the sounds of it, he needs Pan for something, so we need to be prepared. We need to be ready to fight," Curly chips in, his tone grave.

"He gets his crew to do most of his dirty work so it'll probably be his minions scouring Neverland and reporting back," I comment.

"And they'd probably stick to the unmarked areas of Neverwood —" Slightly chimes in.

"—Before they start searching higher ground," I finish. Then I realise exactly where we need to go.

In my mind's eye, I see the snowy passage through the mountains and I'm once again reminded of the nightmarish visions that plague my subconscious. I start to wonder if the setting has any connection as I stare at the drawing of the three peaks on the map.

"I think we should search higher ground," I suggest. The others follow my hand to where I'm pointing, contemplating my suggestion before each looking at me in turn.

"I don't know, Wyn," Slightly starts.

"No, think about it Slightly, Wyn has a point," Curly reasons. "While Kage's pirates are busy searching the forest, it'll give us time to reach the summit and caves, and if they do follow, we have days to outrun them. They don't know the routes like us."

"Plus, it's right on our doorstep," Khara adds with a shrug.

"I guess it's decided then, Neverpeak Mountains," Slightly states, his tone final.

I glance over at Curly and smile, to which he replies with a subtle wink.

THE DAY IS IN FULL SWING AS THE SUN PEERS THROUGH THE CANOPY and warms my skin. There's a tiredness in my bones but my mind is wide awake as I sit in the small grove, enjoying nature's songs. I'm exhausted but I resent the thought of sleep, wary of the terrors lurking when I open my eyes.

Khara and Slightly have gone off to hunt and gather, while Curly offers to hang back with me, despite me insisting I'd be fine alone. I left Curly to collect firewood and made my way into the trees to be alone with my thoughts for a little while.

I take the opportunity to pull out Hook's logbook and skim through the pages until I pick up where I left off.

CAPTAIN'S LOG: ENTRY 29

Ah, Mary. My sweet Maria!

Her adventurous nature knows no bounds, her stubbornness is unmatched and she draws me in like a moth to a flame. I know not from where these feelings have emerged, but they have and with such strength!

How I long for her when she leaves, how the hours fly when she's by my side!

She confides in me her turmoil of home life; her strict father and her tiresome list of responsibilities. I confide in her the plans that Pan and I have built, the Neverland that we envision together. She tells me of how she wishes she could stay here with me forever. I tell her she can.

But alas, in the end she always leaves with the promise of returning to me.

My mind reels as I read through once more, my eyes wide with shock as I process the information. Around me the forest is serene and calm, the sounds of birds chirping and insects buzzing, but my head is in turmoil and my pulse throbs in my ears as I read.

"They *were* friends!" I whisper in dismay. "But what did he mean by plans, and who is Mary?" I ask no-one, turning the pages to find out more.

"I wonder if Slightly and Curly know about any of this?" I question, already doubting their knowledge on the subject of Peter and Hook.

CAPTAIN'S LOG: ENTRY 34

I confessed my love to my Mary; the words rolled off my tongue so quickly I could not catch them quick enough. I thought it a disaster, until she revealed that she felt the same.

Merciful god what have I done to deserve such a treasure such as her?

I am in love. I could scream it from the mountain tops like the foolish man that I am, but then what would Pan think of me? He knows nothing of my darling Mary, only of her lingering effect over me.

What is to become of us? She from her world and I, here in Neverland. How is it that love can conquer such distances?

I snap the book shut as I look up, unable to read anymore as the last sentence rings in my ears, as though the words had come from Hook's own mouth.

"She wasn't from Neverland," I breathe.

Thoughts and questions fly through my mind as I process this new information. If Mary wasn't a Neverlander, then where had she come from and how had she gotten to Neverland? A realisation dawns on me as a new thought flies into my head.

"Wendy, John, and Michael weren't the first people to visit Neverland."

Just as I'm about to open the pages once more, my curiosity overwhelming my better judgement, I hear footsteps wandering my way.

"I'd wondered where you'd got to," Curly calls through the trees.

His voice reaches me before he does, so I manage to hide the small book away and out of sight before he steps into view, with a relaxed smile on his face. He joins me on the forest floor and leans against the trunk of a pine tree alongside me, his shoulder brushing against mine.

We sit in a comfortable silence as we look out through the trees. I admire its beauty as I inhale the fresh, earthy scent of the wild. The musky scent of Curly's skin sneaks its way into my lungs. My heart picks up speed despite myself and I become more aware of the way our bodies lie; so close that we're almost touching.

I feel my skin prickle under the fabric of my tunic, the heat of Curly's body radiating into me. He continues to sit beside me in silence while I try to distract myself from his proximity, and what happens to me when he's this close. I think back to the moment in the cave and I feel my face burn up and not from the diminishing fever.

"What's London like?" he asks finally.

The question takes me by surprise, but despite my surprise I can't help the smile that forms on my lips. I contemplate how to answer for a few moments, before it comes to me.

"It's worlds apart from this place."

"How do you mean, what could be so different?" he asks, childlike curiosity leaking into his voice.

"Well for starters, there are not nearly as many trees as there are here. There are roads and motorcars, and hundreds and hundreds of buildings standing next to each other in long lines. Some of them are so tall, they look as though they might burst through the clouds," I tell him, a passion in my voice that surprises me.

Curly lets out a long whistle that echoes through the trees, silencing the birds momentarily before they burst back into song.

"London sounds so strange," he says finally, fascination clear in his voice.

"Well I suppose it is for someone who isn't familiar with it, but you certainly couldn't compare Neverland to London."

"Really?" he asks as he turns to me with surprise written all over his face.

"Hyde Park is beautiful in the spring, but it doesn't compare to this."

"And the crowds of people are always moving, always in a hurry. Whereas here, I can hear the forest's creatures undisturbed."

"It's nothing like what it was, but I suppose you wouldn't know," Curly says, his voice quiet.

"You're right. I love London, but home feels so far away now that

I'm falling in love with Neverland more and more. Just as she said I would."

"Wendy told you that?" Curly watches me, his deep blue eyes thoughtful.

"She did," I say with a small smile.

XXIII

The sky is the colour of blood as dark clouds roll in from the sea. The freezing wind blows through the mountain pass with unrelenting force, and though I feel rooted to the spot, the mountain peaks are icy and perilous—I can feel how easily I could be carried off over the mountainside.

I see the others nearby, the three of them; Khara, Slightly and Curly in a small cluster to my left. I turn my gaze to the middle and find myself looking at Maja and Nibs, then to the right, I see members of the Piccaninny Tribe with Princess Tiger Lily and Big Chief standing at the front of the mass.

All of them face away from me, staring at something else, and I will myself to move to be nearer to them, as all of a sudden, a strong sense of dread knots my stomach. Snow begins to fall, creating a light blizzard, and a few metres away the darkened figure shifts into focus. Kage.

My blood runs cold as he moves forward, growing larger with each step in our direction. As if on cue, everyone turns to face me, their eyes vacant and glossy. I try to move toward them but I'm frozen, and when I try to scream at them to run, nothing comes out of my mouth. If it does, the strong winds simply carry it off.

I watch helplessly as Kage's silhouette grows and stretches over my friends and companions, my heart lurching as I see the black veins spreading up their bodies and consuming them inch by inch. I watch in horror as they drop, their lifeless bodies falling into the thick snow. My eyes pass over each face until it stops on Curly's, his wide ocean eyes blackening as Kage drains his life and leaves his body to crumple in front of me. I feel my heart break as it freezes over. The scream that rips from my throat is raw and feral as Kage's shadow falls over me and I'm consumed along with the rest.

For the third night in a row, I wake up in a cold sweat as the scream dies in my throat. To my relief, Khara is still sound asleep, her pillow pressed over her head. And for the third time in three nights, I sneak out of the room and down the darkened passage into the main room, expecting to see the earliest hint of dawn streaking through the opening. But instead, I see nothing but darkness. The only hint of light that I get emanates from the embers that are still burning from last night's fire.

Curly lays on his mat sound asleep. I watch the steady rise and fall of his breath, fighting the urge to rush over and check for blackened veins. A pang of jealousy washes over me as I stare at the peacefulness of his slumber.

'*How can he sleep soundly while my body still trembles from nightmarish dreams?*'

With a sigh, I seat myself by the dying embers and poke at them with a stray stick, trying to rid my mind of the images of blood and bodies that cling to me even when I wake. I can feel the exhaustion in my bones, but I daren't give in to it for fear of another vision.

"Wyn...?" his voice rises from the other side of the fire pit, husky from sleep.

"I'm sorry, did I wake you?" I whisper gently.

Curly leans up on his elbows and blinks the sleep from his eyes. He stares at me for a few moments before he speaks.

"Are you alright?"

"I'm not sure," I answer truthfully.

"Can't sleep?"

"Something like that," I reply as I remember the black veins creeping up his skin and devouring him.

I visibly shudder at the thought and turn my face away from him. For a moment I hear nothing but shuffling.

"Come here," he calls over in hushed tones.

Something in the way he speaks makes me listen and I drop the stick and crawl over to him, sliding onto the mat beside him. He pulls a protective arm around me.

"Try to get some sleep, you'll need it," he whispers, his voice husky and alluring.

I feel his arm tighten around me as he draws the blanket over us. I lean my head against his chest as he lets out a sleepy sigh, his heartbeat slowing toward sleep. The warmth of his body seeps into mine and the trembling in my body subsides as I slip back to sleep.

I feel someone restraining me as my body thrashes, the blankets wrapped around my legs. As I'm drawn out of sleep, I blink my eyes open, my vision blurred.

"Wyn, wake up it's just a bad dream," Curly's voice cuts through the panic.

I blink a few more times to focus on his blue eyes staring down at me, laced with concern, before I stop fighting him. He releases his hold on my wrists and watches me closely as I become more alert.

"I'm sorry," I croak as I breathe out a long, shaky sigh.

I glance over at the cave entrance to see the early morning light seeping through the cracks in the ceiling. When I realise how close I was to him, heat rises up my neck. I'm glad that the others aren't awake yet, knowing I have time to gather myself before they drop in on us and ask questions, ones that I'm not sure I have an answer for.

"How often do you have these nightmares?" he asks after a few moments of silence.

He leans forward, lowering his head to meet my gaze. I rub a hand over my face and take a deep breath before I look at him.

"Was I loud?" I grimace.

"You were tossing and turning a lot, cried out a few times," he says with half a shrug.

"Does it happen a lot, the nightmares?" he asks again.

"Every night," I answer, quickly getting to my feet.

"Woah! Hold on," Curly says as he scrambles to his feet and grabs my hand to stop me from leaving.

"How long for? And why didn't you say anything?" he asks softly, his thumb running over my wrist in a circular motion.

"Long enough and I'd rather not talk about them," I respond, avoiding his gaze as an image of his corpse floats into my mind.

"What's going on, talk to me," his voice is soft as he steps closer.

My eyes lift slowly to meet his and once more I see him as he appears in my visions, when the darkness consumes him. I have to look away, my chest aching from the image.

"They're just nightmares, Curly," I say, my voice quiet.

"There's something you aren't telling me," he states.

I glance furtively at the passageway that leads to where Khara and Slightly are sleeping. I bite my lip as I make a decision.

"Not here," I say decidedly as I shake my head.

I grab his hand in mine and he frowns at me, following my fleeting gaze before turning his head back to me. Giving his hand a reassuring squeeze, I tug him towards the door.

"Come with me," I say.

I weave through the trees, pulling Curly behind me until I feel we're far enough from the outpost. I stop and let go of Curly's hand, who's watching me curiously as he fiddles with his hands, something that I've often noticed him do when he's impatient.

"So, can you tell me why we're out here, instead of at Stoneshaw?" he asks.

"I just don't want to spook the others for no reason," I answer as I pace back and forth.

"Spook the others with your dreams?" Curly asks, clearly confused.

I stop pacing and glare at him. He holds his hands up, his brows raised in surprise.

"Jheez, alright I'm sorry," he says as he steps closer.

"They aren't just dreams though, I get the sense that it's a warning," I say, staring through the trees, my unease knotting my stomach.

"When did they start?"

"The day we arrived at the Picaninny camp, when I met Shikoba the Shaman. That's when the visions started, but the dreams came soon after," I explain.

"You went to the Shaman, alone?" he asks incredulously.

I nod.

Curly runs a hand through his hair, his lips parted as he processes my words.

"Wyn that was *weeks* ago, Shikoba is...*was* no-one to fool around with."

"I know."

"In these dreams you're having, what did you see?" he asks, his face serious.

I open my mouth to answer but the words don't come, my voice suddenly failing me. I think of Kage, his shadowy figure, and glowing violet eyes. I think of what he does to those that I care for, what he will do.

"Wyn!" Curly grabs my shoulders and shakes me out of my darkened thoughts, concern in his eyes.

His appearance is blurry and I realise as I bring my fingertips up to my face that my cheeks are wet with tears. I let out an uneven sigh and lift my eyes to meet Curly's once more as he drops his hands from my arms.

"I don't know exactly what it is that I keep seeing but it's dark," I say, my voice trembling slightly.

"And every time I'm there, and I see it, *him*... I see the blood and the bodies."

"Bodies?" Curly's voice is quiet and even but I can sense the tension building in him.

"Of late it's different. I watch as he slaughters each and every one of you," I continue despondently.

"What do you mean?" his expression is guarded.

"You, Khara, Slightly," I say, gesturing to the path back to the others. "The chief and the princess, even Nibs for Christ's sake!" I keep going, my voice getting shrill as I get worked up.

"Wait, hold on, how do you know Nibs?"

"It's not important, but what matters is that you're all in danger and I have no idea how to stop it!" My voice rises in my panic.

"Woah Wyn, calm down. Nobody is in any danger and it's not your job to keep us safe," Curly cuts in, holding me in place so that I look at him.

I shake my head. "Shikoba told me that I had to prepare myself, that it was up to me to restore the balance," I ramble as the words tumble from my lips.

Curly suddenly lets go of me, his gaze steady as he watches me. His silence fills the air, the presence of it so strong that it seems as though the whole world is mute. No birds chirp in their nests as the sun draws up over the horizon, no warm breeze rustles through the trees, and not even one creature can be heard snuffling along the forest floor.

"She told you that?" he says finally, his voice quiet.

I nod, taking note of the way his eyes flicker as he thinks, the way he furrows his brow and presses his lips together in concentration. I study the hint of freckles on his cheekbones, how tan his skin has become under the summer sun, how his hair has grown out, his curls brushing over his forehead, and the ash-blonde stubble covering his jaw.

He has changed in ways so small that I've barely noticed until now. The maturity in his features tugs at me, igniting the desires that prowl in my abdomen as I pick out the little details of him.

"This changes things, we have to tell the others," Curly announces.

"No!" I cry out, surprising myself.

"Wyn, they'll want to know why when I tell them that we're leaving for Neverpeak Mountains *today*," Curly reasons.

I realise that there's no use in arguing and I nod in agreement. Flashes of last night's dreams flicker in my mind as I think of what Shikoba had told me.

"It's Kage, in these dreams."

Before Curly even has a chance to reply, I blurt more.

"The entity in my dreams isn't human, it's like he's made of smoke and mirrors. But when I met him and saw him with my own eyes, it was as if I knew."

"It may very well be."

"And when he grabbed me, the veins that spread up my arm... it was the same in my dreams, he consumed each of you into this cloud of darkness," I add, subconsciously brushing the scar under my sleeve.

"Would explain the rumours," Curly agrees with a shrug, though I can see the tension in his muscles.

I see the worry that he's masking and that decides it.

"We need to find Peter and fast."

XXIV

We waste no time in heading back to the others. Curly informs Khara and Slightly straight away. Every so often they glance over at me expecting words of confirmation, but all I can manage is a nod, their serious expressions making me nervous.

"Well... I wish this had come up sooner, but I get it," Slightly says finally, running a hand through his hair.

"Look, let's just pack our stuff and get out of here. Sooner we start climbing, sooner we find Peter and sorting this whole mess out," Khara interjects.

She heads to the back of the cave, toward the passageway when she stops and looks over her shoulder at me.

"Wyn, are you coming or what?"

I snap to attention and hurry after her. I steal a quick glance at Curly but he's too busy talking with Slightly.

As soon as we're inside, she moves over to the corner, rummaging around until she pulls out a thick poncho-looking thing and holds it out to me.

"Here, you'll need this. The weather in the mountains is never predictable."

"Thank you, Khara," I reply with a smile, taking it from her.

I'm surprised at how heavy it is, the fabric thick and soft to the touch. Lifting my attention from the poncho, I watch as Khara rushes around the room shoving all sorts of bits and pieces into a sack the length and size of her torso. Out of nowhere, she stops and turns to me.

"How's it healing?" she asks while gesturing to my wound.

Putting the poncho down, I lift the tunic up with one hand and pull down the bandage to reveal the large darkened scab that's formed. The skin around it is pink from healing, the infection no longer eating away at the wound.

"Looks better, but I'll pack in some extra bandages and healing herbs just in case," she decides as she carries on. "Bruising on your face has almost gone too," she calls over.

"Same with that nasty black eye of yours," I reply.

"Won't be needing any extra salve then," she chuckles as she pushes down the contents of the sack to make room for more.

"Anything I can do to help?" I call over.

"Yeah actually, you can take this," she answers as she ties the sack up tightly and hands it to me.

I sling it over my shoulder, stumbling back a few paces as the bag tips me back. As I stumble back, I fall into something sturdy. As I hear it make a noise, I turn to find myself looking up into a pair of ocean eyes.

"We need to hurry, god knows how much time we have to outrun Kage's pirates," he says, his gaze shifting between Khara and me.

"Well we're going as fast as we can," I hear Khara snap from over my shoulder.

"Food and water supplies are already packed. When you're done, be ready to move."

The ascent begins slowly as the sun climbs high into the sky. No-one speaks; all attention is focused on footing—and making sure not to slip on loose rocks—which I end up doing, several times.

The sloping path up the mountainside is steep and slippery, and the climb even harder with the supplies on our backs. The others maintain a steady pace, but I begin to lag behind, caught up with my thoughts and weighed down by the heavy sack strapped to my shoulders.

As the day goes on and we climb higher, the weather changes. The once blue skies turn to grey mist as billowing clouds fill the air, all traces of blue lost behind the darkened grey. As the wind picks up, blowing against us with an icy chill, I find myself beginning to falter. My weakened state slows me down as the niggling aches and pains settle into my bones.

I look on to see the others moving forward, the space between them and me drawing wider with every step they take. I can feel the ache settling into my ribs around the wounded area, the pain slowly worsening as I move. The tight corset rubs against it, irritating the scabbed-over skin underneath.

Traces of snow litter the path as we keep moving, my breath unfurling in puffs of smoke as it leaves my lips. I pull the poncho tighter around me as the first snowflakes fall, lifting the hood over my head to protect myself against the icy wind that cuts past my face. The air turns bitterly cold from the altitude and my lungs burn as they inhale. I try to fight the shivers that have begun to wrack my body, but the cold seems to be winning.

It's hard to tell how late in the day it is, the sky grey and heavy with snow clouds, but even without counting what feels like numerous hours, I know that we've made progress. I dare to glance over the edge and recoil instantly, the drop making my heart plummet to my feet.

I try to distract myself by looking out at the view as I surge forward. I take in the sea of treetops that spreads out in all directions, and the dark blues of the ocean in the far distance.

As I'm so caught up with taking in the sights, I don't notice when my foot snags on a dip in the path. A cry of surprise escapes my lips, echoing over the mountainside, and I crash face first to the floor, my hands only just cushioning my fall.

Before I'm given a chance to pull myself upright, I feel strong hands under my arms helping me back to my feet. I look up to meet Curly's worried eyes.

"Are you alright?" he asks, shouting over the whistling winds.

I'm about to answer him when something just past his face catches my eye and the words die in my throat. I squint at the moving object out at sea. I realise after a few moments that it's a sail and my heart speeds up as I recognise the colours.

"The Redbreast," I murmur, my voice lost to the wind.

"What?" Curly frowns before turning to see what I'm looking at.

As he does, another set of sails come into view from behind a cluster of jagged rocks. I clutch Curly's arm as his gaze returns to me and we rush over to the others.

"What is it?" Slightly calls over to us as we close the gap.

"Look," Curly answers, pointing in the direction of the ships.

Slightly and Khara turn back to us, worry written all over their faces. The wind picks up again, howling all the way through the mountain pass as the snow gets heavier.

"We have to find some kind of shelter before the storm gets any worse," Slightly shouts over the howling wind. "Keep close," he hollers over his shoulder as he surges forward.

We each nod in agreement, following him as closely as we can. The wind thrashes down the mountain, the flurries of snow beginning to burn my face. The sheer volume of the blustering wind makes my ears ring.

The sky is dark, and in the few hours that we've been searching for shelter, as predicted, the storm has worsened. I can see only a few feet in front of me and I cling to Curly for fear of losing them in the blizzard. As the weather had worsened, Khara, very smartly, tied a rope around each of our waists and tied us together for safety, with Slightly leading, Khara and Curly in the middle and me bringing up the rear.

Just as I think that I can't take any more of my face burning and my body trembling, we turn a corner and stumble across a gap in the stone. The mountainside opens up to what looks to be a deep cave. Slightly stops and turns to us, pointing toward the opening. Before any of us can answer he moves towards it, pulling us along with him.

Our footsteps echo as we trudge into the shelter of the cave, the forceful gales unable to reach us in here. Slightly stops a few metres in and unties the rope tied around his waist, his eyes shining in the dim light.

"We'll stop here for now, wait out the storm," he decides.

"Hold on Sly, we don't even know if it's empty. It might be dangerous," Curly points out as he does the same.

"C's got a point," Khara agrees.

Slightly lets out an exasperated sigh, throwing his hand in the air as the sound bounces off the walls.

"Alright fine. Khara and I will scope it out and meet you back here," he says as he slides his sack off of his back, letting it drop with a loud *clunk*.

"While we sit here twiddling our thumbs waiting for you? I don't think so," Curly scoffs, his tone defensive.

"You can make yourself useful and build a fire. Wyn can help you set up camp," Khara reasons, turning toward me and winking, snowflakes still stuck to her auburn lashes.

"You have an hour, and if you aren't back by then, we're searching for you," I add, my lips cracking as they move.

Khara nods with a grin as she unties herself, dumps her bags by Slightly's, and picks up her bow and quiver. Slightly lights a stray branch alight and beckons Khara after him.

"In a while crocodile," Slightly winks at me before turning and wandering into the depths of the cave, Khara beside him.

I shake my head in amusement as I watch them grow further and further away, melting into the shadowy darkness until all I'm able to pick out is the tiny flickering flame of the handmade torch.

As soon as they're out of sight, I turn to Curly, surprised to find that his eyes are already trained on me. He gives me a small smile as he drops the sack from his shoulders and removes the thick hood from his head.

I follow suit and my back and shoulders scream their relief as I try to loosen the taut muscles.

My body aches as I busy myself with picking up the loose branches and twigs scattered across the floor, while Curly begins to set up camp. I hear him fiddling with something behind me as I lean down to grab hold of another twig, my fingers bright red and raw.

Once my arms are full, I head back to Curly, dropping the pile of sticks beside me as he sets up a circle of stones. I sit beside him, crossing my arms in an attempt to keep some heat in my body.

"Do you think we'll get lucky and find him up here?" I ask, cutting through the silence.

Curly falters for a moment before resuming his task. I watch as he fills the stone circle with firewood and begins to start the fire.

"I really don't know, but I suppose there's a chance," he shrugs. "I just hope we find him before anyone else does," he adds with a sigh, before leaning in and blowing on the kindling.

The flames grow steadily and the heat radiates, thawing out the icy chill in my bones.

"Right, let's see if we can sort out some food before the others come back," Curly says as he slaps his hands together, rubbing warmth into them.

"It's so strange, but London feels so foreign to me these days," I say softly, my eyes lost in the flames.

I feel the air shift as Curly stiffens beside me, a silence enveloping us. The only disruption is the crackling of the fire. Slowly, he puts down the parcels of meat and sits down beside me, his gaze watchful.

"What do you mean?" His voice appears soft and calm, but I can hear the hidden restraint.

"Since I arrived in Neverland, I've been kidnapped, attacked, travelled miles of terrain, and I've had too many near death experiences to count. It's been an adventure to say the least."

"London should feel like a welcome thought, and yet it isn't. I've changed, adapted. The young lady I'm expected to be there, I hardly recognise her anymore," I admit, turning away from the flames to meet his gaze.

There is a fiery desire in his eyes, his ocean eyes bright and yet clouded with inner turmoil. His lips part as he opens his mouth to speak, before thinking better of it and clamping it shut.

"The whole reason we're here, Wyn, is for you," he says eventually, directing the words at the flames, his tone hard to read.

"I know that Curly, and it's not as though I don't appreciate it, I really do. It's just..." I try to explain, trailing off as my mixed emotions swarm me.

"It's just what, Wyn?"

"I'm torn. I have reason to stay, I have ties here now," I explain, the truth finally out in the open.

The air feels thick with unexplained tension as silence shrouds us. I glance over at Curly but he doesn't turn to meet my eyes, his attention is focused on the dancing flames. The reflection flickers in his glassy eyes. My chest tightens and my stomach knots as the assumption tumbles from my lips.

"I'll take your lack of a response as an aversion to me staying. Clearly I misread the situation."

Curly's head whips around, his eyes wide with unreadable emotions. His hand tries to reach for me as I draw away from him, surprised at how hurt I feel.

"Wyn, I—" Curly starts.

Just as my name slides off his tongue, the sound of boots against stone echoes through the passageway, cutting him short as both Slightly and Khara waltz out of the shadows.

"Just as I thought, it's completely empty so you can relax your pretty little head, C," Slightly calls over as they make their way over to us.

"Did you miss me, Winnie, darling?"

"Get it? Darling?" Slightly chortles, amused at his own poorly made joke.

Slightly slumps down beside me and grins. I give him a half-hearted smile, knowing I'm not fooling anyone, but he's too distracted.

"How soon will supper be ready? I'm starved!"

Khara sits across from me, setting down her bow and quiver, her eyes flitting between me and Curly with suspicion.

"Anything happen while we were gone?" she asks, her voice laced with unspoken questions.

Curly clears his throat awkwardly, suddenly busy with pulling out rations of meat, fruit, and bread from his sack. As I feel Khara's eyes burning a hole in my face, I rub my neck and mumble something about refilling the water pouches.

"What about food?"

"I'm really not that hungry," I reply before walking away.

I hear Slightly's voice as he speaks to the others, beginning another of his long and admittedly humorous jokes as I grab the water pouches and head toward the mouth of the cave, the warmth from the campfire leaking out of my body as I get closer to the blizzard outside.

I kneel down and slowly begin to fill each pouch with snow, making sure to take my time so as to have a few short moments alone with my thoughts before I rejoin the others. My chest constricts as my recent conversation with Curly runs through my head.

One by one, I shake up the snow in the pouches, encouraging it to melt as I lose myself in my thoughts. My body goes into autopilot as I gaze out into the darkening night.

Once again, I wonder whether I should choose to stay or find my way back home to London, feeling even more unsure after voicing my feelings to Curly. My feeble hopes of him understanding are dashed.

Responsibilities clash with my desires over and over, until I'm left more muddled than when the doubts first began creeping into my mind.

XXV

The sound of idle chatter quietens overtime as I stare out at the flurries of snow, watching them dance on the wind in a battle of strength.

The sound of approaching footsteps draws me out of my thoughts. I glance over my shoulder and to my surprise, I find Curly standing there, shuffling awkwardly on the spot.

"You should really come inside, you'll catch your death stood out here," he says softly.

"I'm hardly in the mood for what passes as mild conversation right now, Curly," I sigh as I turn toward him with crossed arms.

"The others have settled in for the night, we still have a way to go tomorrow before we make it to the higher grounds," Curly utters, pointing over his shoulder to our makeshift camp.

As I glance past him, his eyes flicker down to my trembling hands and he steps forward, pulling my reddened hands into his and rubbing his thumbs over my knuckles.

"You're freezing," he observes aloud.

"You would be too if you were filling the water pouches," I reason with a shrug.

He gives me a pointed look before turning and pulling me gently back to the shrinking flames of the fire. Dropping my hand briefly, he adds some more firewood to the flames, the heat cracking and splintering with a satisfying sound as I sit beside it.

I glance around the space, my gaze flitting between our sacks, the firepit, and all the spaces in between, but neither Khara nor Slightly come into view, and I turn to give Curly a quizzical look.

"They've gone behind that wall, figured we'd be safer in case of any unwanted guests," he explains as he hands me my rations.

I shake my head and avert my gaze as I push his hand away. With a sigh, he draws back his hand as I mumble through an excuse for not eating.

"You have to eat something, Wyn, you'll waste away," Curly comments in exasperation.

"I've lost my appetite. I'll eat it tomorrow," I reply, my tone warning him not to pursue it further.

I watch as he gives in, swallowing the argument that had been balancing on his tongue. He places the rations back, folding them beneath a number of cloths to preserve it as well as possible.

"Wyn, look... I—" Curly starts, moving to sit beside me.

I hold my hand up to silence him, shutting my eyes and shaking my head as I realise that he wants to continue the previous conversation. With my pride already wounded, I'm not sure I want to hear what his explanation is.

"I think you've already expressed your thoughts on the subject, Curly. No need to rub it in," I scoff.

"Dammit, Wyn, will you just let me talk?" he snaps.

"Why? So you can tell me that I don't belong here, that I have people waiting for me at home?" I demand, my voice breaking as I turn to him, my eyes turning glassy. "A crazy, incarcerated mother and a stubborn, stuck-up father," I spit.

Curly watches me silently, his mouth set in a thin line as he processes my words.

"Those *people* that you think are so desperately waiting for me to return home, are most likely busy living their lives. I owe them *nothing*."

My blurred sight clears slightly as a single tear slips down my cheek, only for Curly to gently wipe it away with his thumb.

"But you…" I trail off, my voice uneven as I cup his face in my hands, a hesitance in his expression that I choose to ignore.

"I owe you everything… my life, my loyalty," I say softly, my heart speeding up in my chest.

Curly remains silent, his skin hot against my cool palms. As my heart hammers in my chest, echoing in my ears, I'm suddenly aware of the change in atmosphere. The air around us buzzes with tension as we sit across from each other, our eyes trained on one other in an unrelenting, fixed stare.

"So now, by all means, tell me you think I shouldn't stay," I say, hammering in my final point before I fall into silence.

I watch him closely, bracing myself for his reaction, but for a few moments nothing happens.

Curly blinks once before he leans forward, his arm wrapping around my waist under the thick hide of the poncho as he pulls me into him. His lips crash into mine as my heart explodes in my chest as a sense of deliria overwhelms me. He teases my lips open with his tongue, relishing the taste of me as he pulls my body closer to him.

My mind is fuzzy as I return the kiss, the blood pumping loudly through my body as I inhale his musky scent, filling my lungs with him. My stab wound aches as I move closer, but right now I don't care.

I feel rather than see him remove the thick poncho, lifting it over my head and chucking it to one side. I hear the sound of it as it crumples to the floor as I run one hand through his hair, my fingers getting lost in the curls, and the other runs over the muscles under his clothing, from his shoulders, all the way down his spine.

He groans into my lips as my hands explore the map of his body greedily, tugging at his shirt. He pulls away for a few seconds to drag the material over his head, before bringing me back to him. The heat radiates from his skin through the tiny holes in my tunic.

Before he can deepen the kiss, I follow in his lead and gently lift the clothing over my head before dropping it to one side. Curly makes quick work of the brassiere, slipping it off my shoulders as he drops soft kisses along my neck.

His lips soon return to mine as he presses his bare chest against mine, our hearts mimicking each other's unrelenting pace before he lowers me down. My lungs scream for air, but my mind is in a fog, unable to think clearly as lust takes over. There's nothing to do except succumb to the unrelenting need.

He says nothing as he lowers himself onto me, fitting between my thighs and filling me like a puzzle piece that I never realised was missing. He looks at me with unyielding desire and admiration in his eyes as he breaks his lips from mine. It's only for a moment, but it's enough for me to fill my lungs again before I pull him back in. An insatiable need claws at my stomach as his body covers mine, as his scar brushes mine.

We move together in rhythm, slow at first, then speeding up as we succumb to our mutual desire. I wrap my legs around him as he moves, my fingertips tracing the muscles in his shoulders, my delirious mind craving and savouring every passing moment of us as one entity.

That night, as I slip into a deep slumber with my body wrapped around Curly's, the nightmares leave me alone. Instead, I'm finally graced with a peaceful rest as I relive the memory of Curly's touch.

I wake alone beside the dying embers of last night's fire. A blanket carefully placed over me, an empty space beside me, the only sign that the events of last night didn't just occur in my mind. I notice my brassiere and tunic crumpled over in one corner and grab them, quickly manoeuvring under the blankets as I hurriedly redress before anyone notices. Though I realise that Curly isn't the only one that's absent. The light of dawn hasn't even begun to light the sky.

Footsteps reverberate through the room as I turn to see Curly walking over from the deeper sections of the cave, a warm smile painted onto his face as he sits himself beside me, planting a quick kiss on my swollen lips.

"Morning," he whispers, his voice husky.

"Good morning," I smile as I lift myself up.

"You seem to be in a rather good mood," I add, stealing another glance at him.

"Why wouldn't I be, when the others get up, I'll tell them about the change of plans," he says with a smile.

"Change of plans?" I frown, not understanding what he means.

"Well we don't need to go searching the whole mountain for Pan now, do we?" he replies, his tone shifting as he eyes me.

"Kage's threat to Neverland is still a threat, whether I stay or not, Curly," I reason.

The smile drops from his lips, his eyes darkening as they search mine. But my resolve is final and no matter what he says next, I know that I won't change my mind, we both do.

Without another word, he gets to his feet and walks over to the mouth of the cave, disappearing around the corner before I can call after him. Though my heart squeezes in my chest at the sudden conflict, I decide it best to leave him and give him his space while I busy myself around the camp.

As daylight begins to pour through the mouth of the cave, I stand back dusting off my hands as I admire my work.

A fire blazes brightly in the firepit, the provisions and blankets are neatly stored away, and evenly spread out rations are lined up, ready for when Khara and Slightly finally rise from their slumber—though from the sound of the snoring coming from behind the wall, it might be a little while longer.

I can't help but steal yet another glance at the opening, my thoughts travelling back to Curly once more. With a resigned sigh, I pull my poncho over my head and tug my hair loose, letting it flow freely over my shoulders as I make my way toward the opening.

I'm stunned to a stop as I walk outside, taking in the surrounding view. Snow blankets the mountains with copious amounts at a surprising height against my boots. I take it in as the icy wind kisses my neck.

I stare out at the view, amused by the green trees and icy mountains living side by side. I'm wrenched from my thoughts as I pick out the sails of the two ships just beyond the trees, The Redbreast anchored to the right, and The Jolly Roger anchored to the left.

My heart picks up in my chest and I turn around, focusing on the task at hand. I notice footprints in the snow leading around the mountainside and further up the slope. I follow them silently until they stop. Sat amongst the snow, with his back against rock, is Curly.

His eyes are vacant as they stare out at the horizon, though it is all too soon that they fall on me.

"You know you'll catch your death that way," I say, cutting through the silence as I step closer.

"I've suffered worse conditions," he mumbles as he slowly gets to his feet.

I bridge the gap between us, staring up at him through my thick curtain of lashes, and give him a small smile.

"Don't you think it's a little stupid to be sitting out here alone when there's a warm fire and breakfast waiting for you back inside?"

I lift a hand to his face and give him a soft smile before stretching to kiss him. He pulls away, his fingers wrapping around my wrist and gently lowering it back to my side. The rejection is like a punch in the stomach and for a few moments I'm left breathless and embarrassed.

"All these mind games..." I start, trailing off as I look at him. "I don't understand why you're doing this, Curly," I continue, my voice cracking as the emotion fights to get through.

"I'm not doing anything, Wyn. At least I'm not trying to."

"You open up to me and then you shut me out."

The anger spikes within me when he says nothing, avoiding eye contact.

"You have nothing to say to me?" my voice cracks as it rises, echoing down the mountainside.

"Well?"

When he stays silent, I let out a shaky breath and turn to leave. Tears blur my vision as I walk away, my chest tight with anguish.

"Wyn, wait," he calls, his voice pained.

"I can't. I mean I just—"

"Can't or won't," I reply, refusing to turn and face him.

"You don't belong here Wyn," his voice mutters, his mind seemingly made up.

I spin on my heels and stare at him, the hurt in my chest blossoming into anger. Marching back over to him, I point a finger roughly at his chest, while he watches me with wide eyes.

"And who gives you the right to decide where I go and what I do?" I shout.

"I deserve to stay just as much as you, but there are more pressing matters to contend with than what I want. All of Neverland is at risk, why couldn't you just focus on that, instead of deciding my fate for me?"

"I can't let myself love you, knowing that you don't belong with me, Wyn," he says softly, his tone defeated.

I hiccup as the words leave his mouth, the tears I'd been fighting to stay put, now cascade down my cheeks as my eyes rise to meet his.

"But instead you let me grow these feelings, knowing that you are incapable of loving me back," I say quietly, my voice shaking.

He stares at me with widened eyes and his lips parted, before his eyes spark with new emotion.

"Wyn I—" he starts.

I hold my hand up and turn my head away from him, my chest tightening as I fight to keep more tears from falling.

"You've said all that I need to know," I choke as I walk away, back down the mountain.

XXVI

For the rest of the morning I stay quiet. When the others finally awake and join me by the fire, I find myself unable to join in on Slightly's high spirits or even explain to Khara what's bothering me when she leans over to ask.

My stomach knots up when Curly returns. He sits across from me with his eyes wide, imploring me to meet his gaze. I don't, not after our words outside. They ring in my mind, each word stinging as I replay them over and over.

"Weather's cleared by the looks of it, should be an easy shot to the top now," Slightly mentions between mouthfuls.

"Should be able to make it to Boulderswift Passage in around four hours or so at this rate," Khara adds with a nod.

"Great, then we'll leave as soon as we've finished up here," Slightly decides, bumping shoulders with me, and sending a playful grin my way.

I manage a weak smile in return, but even that takes copious amounts of effort.

The rest of the day revolves around climbing the long, twisting route up the mountain, one after another in a single file line. No-one speaks, each one of us focusing on maintaining our strength.

My heavy breaths unfurl from my parted lips as I move forward, keeping a reasonable distance from Khara, and watching as her auburn hair shines brightly in the late morning sun.

I feel my neck burning with Curly's stare as he walks behind me, but I refuse to let myself acknowledge him, still unable to look him in the eye. To distract myself from him, I draw my mind to another topic, pushing all thoughts of Curly deep into a dark corner of my mind.

I think of the near future and try to consider what lies ahead of us. My gut tells me that Peter is up in these mountains hiding out somewhere, but I wonder if we'll even find him. I wonder what condition he'll be in, and if he'll refuse our sudden presence in the world of isolation, he may have created for himself.

There are so many possibilities, so many alternative outcomes.

'What if he refuses to help? What if the conflict I feel about belonging is pointless because ultimately it will not be my choice but his? What if he refuses to help us fight against Kage?'

Or worst of all, what if he's no longer alive?

I glance around our surroundings, taking in nothing but rock, snow and the sheer drop down to the forest floor below. While it's plausible for someone to live up in the mountains, there are numerous risks to consider. What could start off as a secluded home could then end up becoming a perilous death trap.

The hours pass by slowly as we keep moving along. The snow is much thicker here and slows us down considerably. My legs are numb from the constant cold and my head is light from the altitude, but I stumble forward regardless, intent on moving until suddenly my legs buckle and I drop into the snow, my head reeling as I try to calm the dizziness.

I feel someone come up beside me as Curly's voice fills my ears, but I shrug him off as I get back to my feet, my legs a little wobbly as I straighten myself.

"I'm fine," I mutter.

I hear him sigh before moving back a few steps and though I hate to admit it, I'm grateful for the space. I look ahead to see both Slightly and Khara turned in my direction, a look of concern etched on Khara's face.

"Keep going, I'm fine," I call over.

They hesitate for a few short moments before each of them turn and keep moving, trundling through the snow. The wind howls above us as it curves around the high peaks, though the sky is clear and bright, the air is cold. It cuts through my layers of clothing easily and kisses the back of my neck with its taunting, icy lips.

My skin prickles as the wind picks up, whipping my hair across my face as it whistles through the tight gaps of the rock face and roars down the mountainside. I stop short as a noise reaches my ears, cutting through the commotion from the wind.

My head turns as I follow the ghost of its echo, my eyes lifting up towards a steep ledge to my left. Snow drowns out most of the grey rock and I squint, staring at it for a few moments, my gut telling me that something's out of place.

"What is it?" Curly asks as he stops beside me.

I'm about to answer him when I hear a cry of surprise ahead. Instantly, both Curly and I whip our heads around to see Khara fall forward into the snow, her foot snagging on something hidden beneath the folds of white. I feel Curly move as, out of the corner of my eye, he steps toward Khara, just as Slightly turns back toward her.

I'm about to follow when the scuffling sound reaches my ears again and I spin around, my eyes cautiously scanning the snowy ledge as my hand slowly goes to reach for the dagger. For some reason that I can't seem to explain, an uneasy feeling settles in the pit of my stomach as my eyes scour the untarnished purity of the snow.

"See anything interesting up there, Wyn?" Slightly calls over, his tone mocking as he helps lift Khara from the snow.

I hear her hiss as, with the help of the boys, she gets back on her feet and begins to hobble on one leg.

"Think I've twisted my ankle," she comments, grimacing as she tries to put pressure on it.

"Well we aren't going to get much further if you have," I hear Curly comment gravely.

"Great observation there, Curly," Khara retorts, I can almost hear the eyeroll that accompanies her words.

"As fascinating as whatever's up there may be, Wyn, we have more pressing matters to worry about," Slightly calls over, his tone turning impatient.

"Just a minute," I breathe as I keep my eyes trained on the ledge.

"Wyn, Slightly's right," Khara says.

Her voice reaches my ears, just as my eyes fall on a silver pair. My heart palpitates suddenly, causing me to choke on my breath as I realise what the pair of eyes belong to.

It moves slowly, drawing away from the camouflage of the snow and I can finally see its size. I start to distinguish its white frame from the freshly fallen snow. I hear the others calling me, but my eyes are locked with the wolf, its silver eyes unblinking as it bares its teeth.

I just manage to grab my dagger as it howls before lunging for me with an aggressive snarl. There's no time to warn the others before it's upon us, bodies colliding as we crash to the ground. Clumps of snow go flying into the air as we each scramble for the upper hand, the wolf pinning me to the ground snapping at me, as I hold it back as best as I can, swiping at it with my blade.

The dagger cuts through the air with a swishing sound as I try to embed it in the beast, desperate for any type of advantage. I hear myself grunt as, with all my might, I kickback against the torso of the beast, sending it sprawling backwards a few metres. I take the opportunity to get back on my feet, flipping the dagger in my palm so that it juts out, giving me more room to twist my wrist.

The wolf and I circle one another, our eyes locked. Out of the corner of my eye though I notice the others aren't coming to my aid, I hear Curly's and Slightly's voices cut through the wind.

"Looks like we have more company."

I hear them, but I try to ignore the distraction as I focus on my opponent. My heart beats in such a way that I'm surprised it hasn't beaten straight out of my chest, my hands giving away the fear that I'm feeling.

The howls of the other wolves reveal themselves, howling to the wind as they glare and snarl at us all, drawing my attention from my wolf for only a moment as I glance at the others, their backs up against each other's as they take in the wolves that close in on them, as a team.

I only look away for the shortest moment, but it's enough for the wolf and it lunges at me once more, all claws and teeth. The bloodcurdling scream rips from my throat as a green blur barrages into the wolf, stopping the wolf in its tracks.

I fall back into the snow, panting breaths rattling from my lungs as I stare at the blur of green and white with widened eyes. I hear the snarls and the snapping of jaws as I scramble to my feet. The other wolves abandon their attacks, joining their leader in circling the green beast and bringing it down.

Frowning at the unfolding scene, something bothers me, tugging at my mind as I watch on. The creature swipes its large elongated claws at them, is snarl deep and menacing as the wolves taunt it, nipping at it at every opportunity that presents itself.

Suddenly as if a switch has been flicked, they all dive towards the creature. It howls in pain, snarling and swiping at its attackers as Curly runs over to me, grabbing my hand and dragging me towards the others and away from the violent scene.

"Hurry up Wyn, we need to get out of here, now!"

"But it just saved us, we can't just leave it here to die," I argue, turning back to look.

"Better it than us," I hear Curly say over my shoulder as I drag my heels.

But my attention is on the creature as it battles the pack of wolves. I see the blood that stains their white fur, and the blood that stains the creature's. From where I am, I can see it's doing all it can to keep the smaller beasts at bay, but it's still heavily outnumbered.

I watch as one of the wolves in the pack steps too close and the creature's jaws snap around it, a sickening crunch as its teeth cut through flesh and muscle before it throws the wolf against the rocky ledge, its blood painting the snow red.

It's then that I finally get a good look at the creature's face and my heart lurches as our eyes connect. The familiarity registers in my brain as I stare into the opal eyes before her attention is drawn back to the wolves still circling her.

Curly's grip pulls me a few steps backwards, but I rip my arm away as a sudden protectiveness washes over me. I'm filled with a fiery anger as I watch the wolves beat her down slowly.

"Maja!" her name rips through the air as it tumbles from my mouth.

I swivel around, grabbing hold of Curly's sword and unsheathing it as he cries out in dismay. Before he can grab me, I surge toward the wolves with the sword raised above my head. I drop it heavily down on the first, cutting into its back before I slice it along and yanking it out, its body crumpling with a loud whine as I turn, ready for the next.

Another wolf runs toward me, leaping at me with wide jaws. I duck at the last second, the warrior in me coming to life as this wolf too, falls on my blade, its blood staining the steel as I draw it out of the ribcage with a popping and crunching sound.

I quickly turn, expecting another to run at me, but I find that the rest are running away from us kicking up the snow as they go. I then glance over at Maja, expecting her to need help, but it seems that she's beaten me to it, having killed the pack leader while my back was turned, its lifeless silver eyes staring up at nothing.

My eyes meet Maja's just as the sword drops from my bloody hands. Before I can move, a blur passes me as Curly grabs the sword and stands between me and Maja, the tip of his blade pointed at her. Maja's eyes narrow at him as a defensive growl grows in her throat.

"Wyn, get back! I'll deal with it," he snaps at me over his shoulder.

"Curly, stop you don't under—" I begin, rushing through my words.

"—I said I'll deal with it!" he cuts me off, anger rolling off him in waves.

With no choice, I roughly butt him with my shoulder causing him to stumble, as I quickly take the opportunity to move around him and stand in front of Maja.

"What are you doing?!" Khara calls out in shock.

"Do you know how dangerous those things are?" Slightly joins in, striding forward as he twists his dagger in hand, eyeing Maja cautiously.

"You will not lay a goddamn finger on her, do you hear me?" I snap coldly, my glare moving from Slightly to Curly, their expressions beyond surprise.

"It's a Nymbeast, Wyn. You know that right?" Curly says slowly, eyeing me closely.

In a spurt of anger, I grab his sword from him and bash him over the head with the hilt. He scowls at me, reaching up to rub the spot I'd hit him.

"*She* is a Nymbeast yes, but Maja is a friend," I retort, turning to her and resting my forehead on the bridge of her snout.

"What are you doing here, girl? Are you alright?" I ask when I finally draw away from her, my eyes searching hers for an answer. I take in her wounds and realise thankfully that they're only superficial.

"Where's Nibs?" I ask realising that she's come alone, my chest tightening.

"Nibs? You know Nibs?" Slightly asks, looking at me, confused.

"Not important," I reply dismissively.

"I'd say that was a pretty important piece of information you decidedly *forgot* to share," Slightly says pointedly.

"She belongs to Nibs. She was my cellmate aboard The Redbreast."

"Well this is news," Slightly scoffs at me.

"Maja, where's Nibs?" I ask her softly, choosing to ignore him as Maja whines quietly.

"Wyn's right, now's probably not the best time to pick stupid fights," Khara chimes in, her voice distant.

"What, so now you're siding with her?" Slightly starts bickering childishly.

"Sly shut up and look," Khara snaps.

"Slightly," Curly suddenly speaks up.

We all fall quiet as we follow Khara's outstretched arm, her finger pointing at a lone figure across from us, high up on a ledge. The figure doesn't move from where they're standing, the wind blowing their scarf out behind them. The fabric covers their face, shrouding it—and their identity—in shadow.

"You don't think it's...?" I breathe, not daring to move.

"I mean, who's to say it isn't?" Khara replies quietly, the wind picking up her voice as it sails past.

As soon as the words leave her mouth, the figure darts along the ledge with incredible athleticism before somersaulting down and landing in a crouch. They stand up straight, watching us momentarily before they dart down the long passage ahead, growing smaller with each passing moment.

"They're heading down Boulderswift Passage," Curly observes.

"Let's get moving before we lose them completely!" Slightly shouts, surging forward.

"Hey, wait! What about me?" Khara yells after the boys, raising her arms in exasperation.

I glance over at Maja who understands and quickly lowers herself for me to clamber on. Khara turns to look at me, her irritation turning into appreciation as I hold out my hand to her.

"Climb on."

XXVII

As soon as Khara is on, Maja surges forward with incredible speed, her body built for this. Her large paws pad the surface of the snow with no trouble as she weaves forward. It isn't long before she's caught up with the boys.

The figure ahead rushes away, moving eerily fast through the thick snow without any problems, while Slightly and Curly are much slower, weighed down by the sacks over their shoulders.

"Go, get after them, we'll catch up," Curly calls out as we come up beside them.

I tighten my grip on Maja's fur and lean into her body as Khara reinforces her hold around my waist. As though she's read my mind, Maja flies forward, kicking up the snow as she speeds through the mountains. I squint as the wind rushes past my face, making my eyes water.

I follow the figure with my eyes as he darts diagonally along the passage before suddenly veering left and kicking against the mountain wall. I watch in amazement as they swivel in the air while lunging for the other side, grabbing the ledge and scrambling up to the higher level, and out of sight.

"Maja!" I say, desperation leaking into my tone.

In the next moment, Maja leaps toward the ledge, her claws unsheathed as we collide with the rock. The air rushes out of me on impact. Unfazed, Maja claws her way up, pulling herself onto the ledge before scanning along the path until she locates the stranger.

I glance down at Boulderswift Passage and see the boys as they run in our direction. In the second before Maja breaks into a run, I call out to them, their heads swivelling up just as we're whisked away.

The path winds around the curve of the mountain, blurring past as we follow the stranger. As soon as we're close enough to pick out the details of his clothing, Maja leaps over him and stops, causing us to slide backwards through the snow a few feet, her back paws just reaching the edge of the ledge as the stranger is forced to stop running.

I watch as they consider running back the way we came, but to my relief, I see Curly and Slightly rushing towards us. The stranger glances over at the ledge in what looks like contemplation, but before they can even make a move, I jump down from Maja's back with my hands up.

"We aren't here to hurt you," I say cautiously.

"Wyn, what are you *doing*," Khara hisses at me from atop Maja, whose eyes are still locked on the stranger figure.

"We're looking for someone, maybe you know where he is," I continue, taking another step forward.

The stranger stops and stiffens, watching me from under the shadows of their hood. Slowly they lift their hand and lower their hood, and out of shock, I stop. The person standing in front of me stares with parted lips. His face is slightly tan and a tad grimy, with a jagged scar running across the right side of his face from his eyebrow to his cheek. His good eye is a warm shade of brown under a fringe of dark lashes, where the other eye should be, is an empty socket, the scarred skin bumpy. His auburn hair, wild and unkempt stands out against his dark attire, the thick stubble on his chin forms into a beard as red as the hair on his head.

He steps toward me with a look of amazement and awe while I lower my hands, watching him warily.

"It's you, you came back," he says softly.

Before I can brace myself, or even react, he grabs hold of me and pulls me into him, his lips pressing roughly against mine. I squirm in his hold as I fight him off, pulling away from him as I shove him hard in the chest.

I watch as he stumbles back a few paces, hurt evident in his expression as I wipe my mouth with the back of my hand as Curly marches toward us.

"Get your hands off her!" he spits.

"Wendy, it's me, Peter."

I stare at him wide eyed as his words hit me square in the chest. Curly stops in his tracks, his jaw slack as he processes the same words that I am.

"Peter?" I repeat.

"Yes Wendy, honest, it's really me," Peter replies, stepping closer.

"I'm not Wendy," I tell him, glancing past him at the boys.

"Of course you're Wendy! Peter would know the real Wendy when he saw her," he argues.

"But you just said that you're Peter," I stop, confused.

"I did and I am, just like you're Wendy. Wendy Moira Angela Darling," he tells me, memorising my great grandmother's name.

"Pan?" Slightly walks over, eyeing Peter cautiously as he turns to face him.

As Curly moves to join them, Khara slides off Maja and hobbles over to me. We stand silently, waiting in anticipation as both Curly and Slightly stare at Peter, their gazes wide and full of conflicting emotions.

The surrealness of the moment hits me as I watch the Lost Boys reunite with their leader. In my mind I drift back to the townhouse, my home, number fourteen along a rather dreary street in Bloomsbury. I think back to the quiet evenings laid out beside Grandmamma Wendy as she would retell the many adventures of Peter and his gang of Lost Boys, while my Grandmother Jane would brush my hair.

It amazed me how, as the years went by, and she grew frailer and more forgetful, her stories about Peter would never be forgotten. She spoke of him less and less as we grandchildren grew, and I'd find her often sitting alone by the fire, mumbling about Peter as she held her pendant tightly in her small, wrinkled hand.

"You're really alive," Slightly breathes in disbelief, finally cutting through the silence.

"I am," Peter replies.

"What happened to sticking together?" Slightly's tone turns to one of anger as he suddenly shoves Peter.

Peter says nothing, wide eyed as he stumbles back in surprise. But Slightly doesn't stop, he runs to shove him again, portraying a side of him that I'd never seen before.

"You disappear up into the mountains. No word, no nothing?!"

"Hey Sly, this isn't getting us anywhere," Curly tries to cut between them, his voice even and eerily calm, though his body is rigid.

"Dammit Curly, are you kidding me? He abandoned us!" Slightly spits, seething with anger and pent-up emotion.

He turns back to look at Peter who's watching silently from a few feet away, his stare almost vacant.

"You don't even give a crap, do you? About me, or Curly, or anyone!"

"Nibs, Tootles, the Twins. We were your comrades, and this is how you repay our loyalty? Things got too tough and you abandoned us!" he yells as he swings for Peter once more, his voice breaking.

Curly grabs him as he hurls his fists at Peter who quickly jumps back. Peter opens his mouth to speak, but soon thinks better of it and shuts his mouth, his lips tight as he stares at Slightly.

Slightly pushes away from Curly and staggers back a few paces, glaring angrily at Peter as we watch in utter silence. The wind whistles around us as the evening begins to roll in with thick, heavy-looking clouds. The sky has shifted from blue, to peaches and warm pinks as the sun sinks below the horizon.

"We were there every time you needed us. Where were you when we needed you?" Slightly says evenly, though I can hear the anger that bubbles away beneath his words.

He turns to look at us, roughly wiping away the few tears that streak down his cheek before he shrugs it off and wanders away, his shoulders tense.

"Slightly," I call.

I make a move to stop him, but Khara's gentle yet firm hand on my shoulder stops me. I turn to her and she shakes her head, her face sombre.

"I know you want to help, but probably best to leave him for a while," she explains, giving me a small smile.

With a sigh, I nod, and return her smile with my own.

"He'll come back when he's ready," Curly says with a sigh. "But he's got a point, Pan."

Khara and I watch silently as Curly walks up to Peter until he's inches from his face and I feel my stomach twist in angst as I watch the two young men square up to each other.

"The Pan I knew would never have deserted us."

To everyone's surprise, Peter throws his head back and laughs. The action is odd and despite myself I feel the seed of doubt being planted in my mind as I watch him.

"My Lost Boys are much younger than you. Besides I didn't abandon them, they died," Peter explains casually.

The shock that registers on Curly's face is delayed as he stands frozen to the spot. Khara and I stare at Peter in disbelief as he turns to face us, giddy excitement registering on his face as he strides over and grabs my wrist.

"Come Wendy, we mustn't waste any more time, I have something to show you," he says eagerly, with childlike excitement.

He pulls me along behind him with surprising strength, following the path along the ledge of the mountains. I can only glance worriedly back at the others before I disappear around the corner and out of their sight.

Peter leads me along the mountainside until we arrive at a hollowed out space in the rock wall. The place is damp and cold and I find myself perplexed, confused at how a person could survive the harsh wilderness of the mountains with nothing but the clothes on his back and an empty space.

The others are close behind after recovering from their momentary paralysis. Maja skulks in after them as we step into the small space.

"Hardly what I'd call homey," Khara comments quietly.

Peter chuckles to himself and grins over his shoulder at her for a moment before he lets go of my wrist. We watch in silence as he lifts a corner of what looks to be a grey tarp, to reveal a lit-up space behind it.

"Come on, hurry up," his voice trickles through, an insistence in his tone.

I glance warily at the others before I step forward and lift the fabric just as Peter had, letting the others through before looking expectantly at Maja. She blinks once at me before lying herself down in the space outside the tarp.

"Suit yourself," I tell her before joining the others.

I'm stunned into silence as the tarp falls back into place behind me, my eyes taking everything in as Curly and Khara do the same.

The space is much bigger than I imagined, the hole more of a tunnel running along the inside of Neverpeak Mountains, stretching much further on into the inky darkness.

The hollowed out space is musty with an oddly earthy scent to it, despite being thousands of feet above ground level. It's quaint and seemingly a replica of what once was Hangman's Tree.

The space overall is warm and inviting with handfuls of furs lining the stone floor and small candles hanging from the ceiling in little nets, lighting the space quite cleverly. I walk past a little nook fashioned into what I assume is a bed, when my eyes fall on the inscriptions carved into the walls, my lips parting.

Some of it are simply scribbles and gibberish fashioned into looking like words and sentences, but when I step back, I notice the bigger picture, embedded into the rock wall. I take in the swirls of the carving forming land and sea, I recognise some of the areas on the biggest section, Neverwood, and the Indian camp high on the cliff edge, and Skull Rock on the other side of the island.

Then my eyes flicker to what is carved past the sea just as Khara's voice picks up, cutting through the silence.

"Nice place you have here, Peter."

"Yes, yes," Peter snaps impatiently as he walks over to me.

"Peter," Curly calls firmly.

Peter turns to him and gives him an impish grin.

"The Lost Boys didn't die," Curly continues firmly.

"And you would know, would you?" Peter counters with an odd giggle.

Khara and I share a look before we both return our attention to Peter. His strange behaviour is making me feel uneasy. I can't quite put my finger on what it is, but there is something not quite right about Peter, though all these years of solitude clearly haven't helped.

"I would because I am, *was*, one of them," Curly argues.

"Of *course* you were, you strange fellow. I think I would know who my Lost Boys are, don't you think?" he replies with another laugh.

Khara hobbles over to me and leans over as the Curly and Peter continue to bicker amongst themselves.

"I think Pan's well and truly lost it," she mutters into my ear.

"I'd be inclined to agree with you," I mumble back.

"Here, have a look at this," I tell her, nudging her as I turn back to the wall mural.

"What is it?"

"A map of Neverland, I think. But what do you suppose they are?" I point to the carvings further out, outside of the larger scaled map of Neverland.

"They look like other islands," Khara surmises, glancing over at me with widened eyes.

"But I thought that Neverland was one island."

"Well it is, though there are rumours amongst people that Neverland isn't the only land floating around in these seas."

"What people?"

"Villagers in the port, some of the Picaninny folk," Khara shrugs indifferently.

"In the stories, I was only ever told about a single island," I say quietly as I turn back to the mural.

"Wendy wouldn't have known anything about it. They're just a myth. This is just proof that Pan's well and truly lost it."

"I'm not sure, Khara, as far as I knew, this place was a myth until I was dropped smack-bang in the middle of it. Maybe he's not crazy, just onto something."

We look over to where Curly and Peter are having heated words, though by the looks of it, it's Curly's words that are heated. I can see just by Curly's posture that this isn't the reunion he had hoped for. There is a tightness in his shoulders and his brows are furrowed into a frown, his lips twitching with irritation as he speaks.

Peter's expression on the other hand, reminds me of my mother. There is a vacancy in his stare, his lopsided, cheeky smile sitting odd on his face as though he were on some sort of sedating medication—like the pills my mother is forced to take every day.

Once more, I'm riddled with guilt at the thought of my mother alone in that small, white room, staring out of that barred window. All those years I disbelieved and doubted her, believing her to be losing her mind when she'd been right all along.

"Peter," I choke.

The boys stop mid-sentence and turn to me, their eyes expectant.

"What are these?" I ask pointing to the wall.

Peter rushes over and lets out a ragged breath as he looks at the wall before turning back to me. Curly reaches us soon after, his eyes taking in the mural with a serious expression.

"Peter drew it. There are more islands, many more."

I glance over at Khara in the middle of Peter's rambling, a concerned look on my face before she subtly points at her temple while circling it with her finger. I frown at her and quickly shake my head, turning back to Peter's excited rambling.

"Said he'd be going there, away from it all, that way Peter would be safe, safe from *him*," he says as he points to the closest of the other islands.

"But you're Peter," I say slowly, forming it into a question.

He stops short and turns to me, a wild look in his eyes and suddenly laughs.

"Peter? Of course I'm Peter. Peter Pan, that's me."

"Who's him?" Khara cuts in.

A shadow falls over Peter as he stares at the wall, his bubbly nature suddenly dulled by the question.

"Peter's enemy," is all he says before he switches back to his former self.

"Right. Girls, a word?" Curly says finally.

Khara and I turn to him in surprise, but his mind is made up.

"Uhm, ok," Khara drawls as we both turn to face him.

I watch as his eyes narrow as they flit over to Peter, who is still rambling on about the scrawled out map, before returning to us and tilting his head towards the way we came in.

"Not here, outside."

I open my mouth to protest, but suddenly think better of it. We move toward the door as Curly explains to Peter we'll only be a moment, but I feel his desperate gaze fall on me as we turn to leave.

"Only a moment, I promise." I reassure him and thankfully it works.

As soon as we're back outside, leaving Maja in the comfort of the cave opening, Curly leads us back to where we cornered Peter and stops, rubbing a hand over his face as he searches around. As we stand there waiting for him to speak, out of the darkness we hear someone coming.

We brace ourselves, expecting some form of enemy, but relax as soon as we realise it's Slightly.

"Took you long enough," Curly scoffs as he walks over to us.

Slightly mutters something under his breath as he stops in our small circle but it's inaudible over the wind curling around the mountain.

"So, what's this all about then?" Khara asks, turning to Curly.

"It's about Peter," he replies sombrely.

"I can't be the only one who thinks he's nuts?" Khara replies.

I nudge her hard and she gives me a look before shrugging. Curly pulls our attention back to him, looking each of us in the eye before he speaks.

"That isn't Peter Pan."

XXVIII

"Whoa, wait, hold on. You think we're dealing with an imposter?" Khara replies. "I mean... it would explain why he's acting so weird. It's like he's got a screw loose in that head of his," she reasons with a shrug.

"I don't like it," Slightly grumbles, his eyes cast downwards.

"His wall mural and mumblings were a little odd, but that's no reason to make claims like that, Curly," I reason, trying to be the level-headed one.

"Whoever that is in there, he's not who he's claiming to be, I just know it," He argues, his gaze steady.

"What makes you so sure that you're right," I reason. "He's clearly been up here for far too long. You heard him yourself, he thinks the Lost Boys are all dead and yet here you both are."

Slightly suddenly lifts his eyes to Curly, with an even stare.

"What?"

"I'm telling you, the person in there is not Pan. Call it a gut feeling, but *he isn't Pan*," Curly says.

I look at the others as Curly's words sink in, weighing up our options. In the pit of my stomach, I know that Curly may be right. Whilst I know that Neverland and its inhabitants aren't the same ones told to me in tales as a little girl, there is something off about Peter and his mannerisms.

I think of my mother and what the doctors referred to as a '*fractured mind*' and wonder to myself whether her misdiagnosis was the very thing we could be dealing with now. As Khara and Curly update Slightly on what he's missed, I step away quietly, my mind drifting to the mural on Peter's wall.

I consider his rambled words of further lands and islands across the sea from here, of the potential truth to the myth surrounding it. A plan begins to formulate in my mind as I look out into the darkness, the tug of home becoming less alluring as my priorities shift.

"I should speak with him alone," I say eventually as I turn back to face the others.

Their hushed tones cease completely as they each turn to look at me, baffled

"That's out of the question," Curly says, a sudden drop in his tone.

"He thinks I'm Wendy, he trusts me, and we can use that to our advantage," I reason.

"She has a point there," Khara comments, addressing the boys.

"I'm with Curly, Wyn, by the sounds of it, Pan's clearly unhinged," Slightly says, joining the conversation.

"I think you'll find it's not up for discussion," I reply bluntly.

"We're a team, we make decisions together," Curly argues.

As if someone has flipped a switch within me, I feel the burning anger fill me, snaking its way through my veins with incredible speed. I glare at him, striding over until I'm a few centimetres away, my head tilted back as I maintain his gaze.

"Does it make you feel like a man, telling me what to do? Making all these decisions for me? Does it make you feel powerful trying to maintain control?" I snap at him, my voice getting louder with each word.

"Hey, now," Slightly says, trying to come between us as Curly and I glare at each other.

"You toy with people's feelings and expect all to be well. I'm not your puppet Curly," I spit, fuelled by rage.

"Maybe if you knew what the hell you were doing then I wouldn't have to protect you constantly, like some irresponsible child!" he retorts, his voice raised.

Before I know what I'm doing, my hand is flying through the air, connecting with Curly's cheek with an echoing *thwack*. I release a shuddering breath as I drop my hand, my palm stinging as I look at Curly in shock.

"Whoa!" Slightly calls out as he steps between us.

Curly and I stare at each other. Neither of us say a word, Curly cradling his reddened cheek as my trembling hand tingles from the blow, both of us in shock over my actions.

"Curly I—" I start, my voice faltering.

"Look, it's been a long day. Let's just go back to Pan's den and get some rest, we can figure out our options in the morning," Khara says evenly.

"When we're all thinking calmly and we've cooled off," Slightly adds, giving both Curly and I a pointed stare.

Curly turns and walks back towards Peter's hidden home, without uttering a single word, though I can tell by the way he holds his shoulders that he's angry. I decide to stay put, despite the urge to run after him as guilt twists in the pit of my stomach.

"Want to explain what the hell that was all about?" Slightly asks suddenly.

Not wanting to betray myself, I look away. He lets out a long sigh whilst running a hand over his face.

"He is right though, your actions don't just affect you, they affect us all," he says quietly, before following after Curly.

"I never asked you to come," I choke when he's out of earshot.

"You didn't have to, that's what friends are for," Khara pipes up as she moves over to me, still hobbling as she tries to keep the weight off her bad ankle.

We stand together in mutual silence for a few minutes and I appreciate her not pushing me to explain, knowing deep down that I couldn't do it without explaining my complicated feelings toward Curly, and the conversations we had shared earlier.

"He cares for you Wyn... deeply," she says softly as she leans in to gently knock shoulders with me.

"I know," I reply, my throat tight.

When I follow the others back inside after some time alone to clear my head, I find them all curled up in each of their makeshift beds, every one of them heavily covered in furs. I climb over them as silently as I can. Maja still lies outside the tarp, happily guarding the entrance, the only thing stopping me from spending the night alongside her is the bitter cold from the open space.

Peter sits up atop his pile of furs, leant up against the corner with his eyes shut and his arms crossed over his chest, a blade jutting out from his left hand.

As I step through the masses of bodies, his eyes fly open in alarm until they fall on me. An impish grin flashes beneath his beard and I can tell from his body language that he intends to move over to me. Acting quickly before he has a chance to move, I lift my finger up to my lips and quickly shake my head. His gaze drops to the others seemingly asleep and nods in understanding before he slowly closes his eyes again and releases a long sigh as he settles back into sleep.

I move over to a cleared-out space a little further from the others, and seat myself opposite the mural as I pull a fur over me, withdrawing the leather-bound book from the folds of the contents of my sack.

Warily, I glance around the dimly lit room before I open up the pages, my eyes squinting in the poor light to read the fancy, swirly handwriting and the splattered dots on the worn pages. I skim through the talk of tides and storms to reach the rare entries involving the mysterious woman named Mary.

. . .

CAPTAIN'S LOG: ENTRY 35

Pan has discovered me and my wonderful secret which I thought I held tight to my chest. But alas he discovered us together in the cove. I had no excuses to give, my distracted mind now makes perfect sense to him.

My best friend has given me the cold shoulder and Mary blames herself. I could not think of a worse outcome. This is not the meeting that I envisioned.

"But what were their plans, what did Hook and Peter have in common for them to be working towards the same goal and together?" I whisper under my breath as I try to make sense of it.

CAPTAIN'S LOG: ENTRY 38

Pan continues to elude my attempts at reconciliation. I am unsure what steps to take next, it would seem our friendship is irreversibly damaged. In our usual meeting place, instead of Mary, I discovered a letter from her. In it she expresses her guilt at causing the rift between Pan and I.

I am angered by this turn of events, but until she returns or Pan's aloofness ends, I shall sail the seas and Captain to the best of my ability.

CAPTAIN'S LOG: ENTRY 43

After numerous weeks of exchanging letters, Mary has finally returned to me. I watch her, deep in slumber in my quarters, as I write this entry.

My heart is full once more, the emptiness that consumed me is gone with the brightness of her presence. I realise now I no longer desire to join Pan in his efforts to make Neverland great, though the fact of the matter is while our friendship has survived, it is highly improbable the dreams we once shared could ever become a reality.

I wish to leave with Mary back to her world of London. To make a name for myself, to marry her, and have a family.

My life here in Neverland is one I no longer wish to lead.

I have to bite back the gasp in my throat, my eyes wide as I read and reread the entry, mouthing the words as disbelief shocks my system.

"I don't believe it... Mary was from *London*, but how can that be? Who *was* she?" I ask myself, now desperate for the answer.

I flick through the pages, my eyes greedily scouring for any sign of her identity, any words from Hook himself, but there is nothing that shines out in his version of events.

As someone exhales a heavy breath, my eyes dart up and I slam the book shut. I pull it close as if I've been caught in the act of something awful and I question why I feel this way as I know I will have to share this new information with the others eventually.

When no-one stirs, I exhale and continue where I left off searching for answers. To my disappointment, the letters he mentions are not among the pages and not folded away within the front or back covers, so I'm inclined to read on.

CAPTAIN'S LOG: ENTRY 44

I have never seen Pan in such a jealous rage as I have today.

I told him of my love for my sweet Mary and my desire to leave. It was foolish of me to think he could ever understand. He has stripped me of my ability to fly, he has turned our friends against me.

I watched with helpless desperation as she left, thinking I was right behind her and yet I was not. Unable to follow was the cruellest torture, but how I am to go to her without the ability to fly? How will I ever escape this god forsaken place to be with her once again?

CAPTAIN'S LOG: ENTRY 50

I waited for days, weeks, months, but my sweet Mary never returned to me. I wonder if she thought I had abandoned her, or if Pan somehow banished her.

Without her I am nothing.

My broken heart has twisted me into this cruel image. My new crew fears me and for that I am glad. No-one will be allowed that close ever again.

People I once called friends, are now enemies. He took everything from me, he stole my dreams, my future, and crumpled it to dust in his filthy hands. James is gone, Hook is all I have left. As my hope dies, so does my once everlasting youth.

I will have my revenge.
Pan, I will kill you for this. If it's the last thing I do.

I turn the page but to my surprise, the page is empty, just like the rest of the small booklet.

"It just cuts off..." I say softly to no-one.

Shutting the book quietly and returning it to my sack, I lean back against the cool stone walls as I stare at nothing in particular, my head buzzing with information and questions. My eyes drift over to where Peter lies asleep, a sudden eagerness to wake him and unleash the barrage of questions hurling themselves around my mind with an insistence that I struggle to quell. As my eyes fall, I see three coloured glass marbles resting in his relaxed palm. The sight of it niggles at me, something about it not quite right, but my mind is too distracted to pinpoint why.

I glance over to where the others lay and I'm reminded of Slightly's words. With a reluctance, I realise that he's right and I resign myself to wait until morning to question Peter, knowing that this interrogation will put a rest to the doubts of Peter's identity.

With one last glance in Peter's direction, I direct my gaze toward the wall, stopping when it falls on the map. I silently regard the piece one last time before I finally close my eyes and after a short while, hesitantly fall into the realm of dream.

Once again, I find myself soaring above the clouds, the luscious greens of the forest giving way to the cold greys and whites of the snow-capped Neverpeak Mountains, the chill running through me as the temperature visibly drops.

As I swoop down through the billowing clouds, the distant sound of thunder rolling through the sky, I'm greeted with the familiar feeling of dread as the hairs on the nape of my neck stand on end. I land gently as the first snowfall breaks free from the heavy skies above.

Familiarity tugs at me as I glance over the edge of the mountain peak, the icy chill of the strong winds whistle down the mountain. I turn in anticipation for what's to come.

His menacing laugh can be heard before he twists and forms into the usual figure that haunts my dreams. I notice how we've swapped positions, with me standing by the mountain ledge, the sheer drop mere footsteps from my current position, while he's situated further inland and seemingly out of harm's way.

In the split second it takes for me to focus on his shifting figure and glowing violet eyes, they turn violet, and bodies have appeared just like before, scattered all around me in twisted and uncomfortable positions.

I don't have to look at them to know that they are no longer amongst the living, but I do anyway, taking in all their faces and stopping when my eyes fall on Curly's body. My heart contorts in my chest as the suppressed feelings come bubbling up to the surface. My face betrays me as I stare into his lifeless ocean eyes, curtained by thick, curled lashes.

It takes everything within me not to run to him, and for my eyes to move away from his pale face and onto the others, the faces of the innocent, faces that I recognise as I scour them, not giving the darkened figure the pleasure of my undivided attention.

Before I know what I'm doing, I feel myself move forward until I reach Curly, kneeling down in the snow as I reach out to caress his face.

As soon as my fingertips touch his frozen skin, his body shifts to black and the wind carries the ashes away, leaving only the space where he lay indented in the snow. The sight turns my stomach and I feel the silent tear run down my cheek, as one by one, the others shift to ash before being carried away. Thunderous clouds hover above cutting through the darkened figure's evil laughter.

"Enough with these mind games, reveal yourself!" I demand angrily as I get to my feet, my voice bouncing along Boulderswift Passage as I surge towards him, glowering at his violet stare.

The figure grows bigger as I move forward, but to my surprise, despite the fear I feel bubbling in my chest I'm not deterred.

"Dammit, what do you want?" I scream at it as I stop mid stride.

The figure chuckles, the sound ringing in my ears as it looks down at me; a god gazing down at its puny worshippers. Its eyes blind me with their brightness as they zone in on me.

"Bloodshed will come," it speaks, its voice eerily familiar.

My heart stops dead in my chest as I recognise the voice, goosebumps travelling up my body as I slowly turn to stare at the evil being in disbelief, my eyes as wide as saucers.

"No," I breathe, the wind carrying my voice far off.

Before I can even release the scream fighting for release in my throat, the figure lurches down at unmatched speed, surging through the ice and snow toward me. I shield my face with my arms and inhale sharply as it consumes me, pouring into every part of me.

XXIX

I bolt upright, my cry cutting through the still air, leaving a bad taste in my mouth. My body trembles, covered in a slick layer of cold sweat, beads of it dribbling down my temples as I breathe in and out heavily.

The others jump up, ripped from their slumbers, weapons at the ready. Both Slightly and Curly's eyes dart over to me, but I stare through them as I try to catch my breath. The remnants of the dream linger on the edge of my memory, threatening to slip away at any moment. But I remember the pain, my every pore tingling like pins and needles.

"What happened, are you ok?" Slightly calls over.

I visibly jump as his voice draws me out of my own mind and back into the present. Not trusting myself to speak as my eyes turn glassy with the threat of tears, I quickly nod. Before either of them can speak or move toward me, I grab my thick poncho and hurriedly head toward the exit, before they can ask any questions.

Once outside, the cool morning air hits my face and I sigh in appreciation, my breath unfurling from my lips like smoke from a dragon's mouth.

As I wander around the ledge back to the wider space around the curled path, I notice Peter rushing towards me, his brow creased in concern before his maple eyes fall on me.

"I heard screaming," he says by way of explanation.

"Nightmares, sorry," I explain sheepishly.

"Oh, right."

I watch him visibly relax as his eyes remain locked with mine, a warmness in his gaze. As I keep eye contact, I think back to last night and the revelations from the pages of Hook's logbook.

I consider Curly's claims as I watch Peter thoughtfully for a few moments, considering how I should approach the subject without having him clam up or snap under the pressure of my desperate need for answers.

As I turn to watch the horizon, the light from the rising sun reflects on the small section of my necklace that's on show. The reflection catches Peter's eye and he bridges the gap between us, gingerly pulling out the pendant from under the many layers and folds of clothing that I have on.

"You kept it, the kiss... you really kept it after all this time," he breathes giddily.

His eyes shine with glee as another episode of giddiness makes me feel uneasy. Peter twists the acorn pendant between his rough fingers as a smile forms on his lips, a wicked and not entirely lucid one that solidifies Curly's opinions of Peter in my mind. I remind myself that I have to be sure before jumping to conclusions.

"I know your secret, Peter," I say eventually.

Stepping back as he releases my pendant from his finger's grip, he turns his head and narrows his eyes, a small smirk forming on his lips as he takes in my serious expression. I'm surprisingly grateful for the distance between us, realising that with all that I know now, and all I've been through, I don't fully trust him.

"And what is my secret, Wendy?"

"I'm not—" I start, stopping short as I let out a short, frustrated sigh, knowing my protests will fall on deaf ears.

"Something that you've kept close to your heart for a long time, something you couldn't even share with the Lost Boys," I continue slowly as I gage his reaction.

"Go on," he says slowly, clearly intrigued by where the conversation is headed.

I glance furtively over my shoulder, in the direction of his hideout, making sure there are no unwanted ears before I turn back to him. Peter watches me silently, but there is a light in his maple-coloured eyes that unnerves me, a gaze intended for another woman.

"You know what I mean, don't you?" I ask, suddenly unsure.

"Well if you tell Peter, then maybe Peter can help answer that," he responds, an ambiguity to his somewhat odd sentence.

"Hook. Your relationship with him, the friendship you shared," I utter to him under my breath in one quick rush.

Peter's face contorts into anger, his eyes igniting with a fury that makes me want to shrink away, but I stand my ground, knowing that this may be my only chance to hear Peter's version of events.

"*Friends* with that... that Pirate fiend?!" he spits incredulously.

"I know it's the truth, you were friends, with plans for Neverland. I read the whole of Hook's account. Of the events that lead to your betrayal, Peter, you can't lie to me," I argue, my voice even and to the point.

"Peter was never friends with that, that codfish. He's an enemy, always was and always will be!" he counters childishly, his immaturity shining through.

"But what about the woman Hook fell in love with? Mary? If you refuse to acknowledge Hook, at least tell me you remember her," I press, desperate to know the truth.

"How would I know what he did in his spare time, I told you, Peter Pan would never be friends with that scoundrel," he argues, his voice raised as his fury emanates from his pores.

"You've either chosen to forget or you aren't who you say you are," I blurt out, surprised at my own forwardness.

We both stop, stunned into mutual silence at my words. I watch as the anger dissipates from his eyes leaving them hollow and the bright maple colour of his irises visibly dim. His face turns pale as the words echo around us, silently taunting him.

"The real Peter would know the truth, these are some of his

deepest, darkest secrets," I breathe finally cutting through the thick silence brewing between us.

"Curly was right, you aren't Peter." I continue, my gaze levelled with him.

"I am Peter, and Peter is me," his voice cracks as he speaks, a hollowness in it that causes me to wonder how fractured he really is.

"But what does that mean?" I press, confused and suddenly tired by his odd ramblings.

I watch as he suddenly begins to pace up and down in the snow, his face twists and contorts as he scrambles for details and answers. The way he moves, and the way he expresses himself I realise as my gut clenches, that he's a broken young man. Khara and Curly were right to doubt him and his reliability. I see that his mind is fractured and not capable of differentiating between reality and fiction.

"Tootles followed Peter into the mountains and Peter... Peter tried to send him away," he says finally, his voice soft as he stops abruptly.

"Peter was going to leave Tootles all alone, so Tootles made it that he'd stay with him forever. In here," he continues softly, pressing his fist against his chest where his heart lies.

"What did you do to Peter?" I ask in a whisper, my eyes wide in horror.

"Peter couldn't leave again, he just couldn't... leave... Peter was going to..." he trails off as he stares off into the distance, slowly lowering himself down into a crouched position amongst the snow. He reaches into a pocket and retrieves the same three marbles from the night before.

I stare at him in silence, shaken and visibly disturbed by the words that he spoke and the gesture that followed. Though despite the growing unease I feel, I still feel a sense of confusion at the complicated truth he just shared.

I glance down at his fiddling hands, watching the marbles as they move around his fingers as a thought surfaces in my mind. Before I realise what I'm doing, I've backed away from the imposter's rocking frame and I'm rushing back to the others, my heart beating faster than ever.

I come crashing through the tarp breathless, despite the run back only being a short one. The others look up at me surprised, waiting for me to speak. I stumble through the words incoherently until Slightly stops me.

"Alright, first you need to calm down and then you can speak," he says slowly as he holds me at arm's length.

"Curly's right, that isn't Peter," I spout quickly, my eyes flitting between each of them.

"You spoke to him, *alone?*" Curly cuts in as he strides over to us, anger in his eyes.

"We agreed we'd wait and decide on what was the next step together, Wyn," Khara says, a warning tone in her voice as she watches from across the room.

"I know and I'm sorry, but I went outside for some air to clear my head and he was there, and it just happened. I didn't plan it," I rush as I ramble through my explanation.

"What makes you think he's not Peter?" Slightly asks dubiously.

"I don't think, Slightly, I know."

I pull myself free of Slightly's grasp and walk over to my sack, pulling the leather-bound booklet from within and hold it up for the others to see.

"I asked him about something only the real Peter would know, and he couldn't answer," I begin.

"But that doesn't prove anything," Slightly argues with a shrug.

"Oh really? When I confronted him about it, he just cracked, started rambling about Tootles following Peter into the mountains, saying something about how Tootles made it that he'd stay with him forever," I explain.

"And then he pulls out marbles of all things!"

Slightly and Curly share a look before turning back to me, their expressions serious. With a deep breath I move back over to Slightly and hand him the book.

"This book belonged to Hook; he wrote more than just his Captain's log in those pages. There are parts about Peter. It mentions how they had a friendship a long time ago," I explain.

"And you waited until now to tell us about it?" Curly cuts in, his brow furrowed.

"I took it at first thinking Kage may have added to it, but when I realised it was only Hook's entries, I wasn't sure it would be of any use," I confess.

"But after reading the last few entries, I wasn't so sure," I add, opening the book to reveal the entries I read through last night.

I step back as the three of them lean in, silence ensues as they each read the pages I pointed out, taking in the information at their fingertips. I stand silently, my fingers anxiously tapping my palm as I wait for them to finish.

"I don't believe it," Slightly breathes.

"You're right, this is something the real Pan would know about," Curly comments with a sigh. "Dammit, I didn't want to be right, but I know it. I *knew* he wasn't Pan, from the start something just didn't feel right," he adds as he turns away.

"He really must be crazy to take on a whole other identity," Slightly says, his voice hollow as he stares at the open pages in his hands.

"But then, who is he if he isn't Peter?" Khara asks the group.

The boys glance at one another somewhat expectantly, as though they hope the other has the answer to Khara's question, but I can see that neither one of them has any idea.

"Do you think it could be Tootles? I mean he was rambling about him following Peter into the mountains, and well didn't Tootles own marbles?" I suggest, an uncertainty to my voice.

"I mean it's a pretty strong possibility," Slightly agrees as he tilts his head in thought.

"Only way to know for sure is if we talk to him, make him speak some sense," Curly states.

"And even if he isn't Peter, he may know where the real one is," I add thoughtfully.

"Well then, what are we waiting for, let's get some answers," Khara chirps, slinging her bow and quiver over her shoulder.

The imposter claiming to be Peter is still crouching in the snow, exactly as I'd left him when I return. Only this time, I'm returning with Khara, Curly, and Slightly in tow. Maja hangs back, slumping lazily into the snow a few feet behind us, resting her head on her crossed front paws as she watches.

I don't dare to speak, stepping forward with the others as we close in on him. The sky is dark with heavy storm clouds, not a shred of blue to be seen across the sky. I find myself feeling uneasy at the thought of being high in the mountains when another heavy storm hits.

Curly steps forward while the rest of us hang back. For a few moments no-one speaks, the moaning sound of the wind curling around the peaks the only sound. I watch the back of his head in anticipation, the curls that twist down towards the nape of his neck swinging sideways with the strong wind and realise that what I had thought would be my last few days in Neverland may actually turn out not to be.

I wonder how I'll manage to make it through the countless days that follow with this visible strain between Curly and I. I wonder how long our search will continue if the fraud before us isn't able to give us any valuable information on where the real Peter may be.

"We have questions and we aren't leaving until they're answered," Curly calls, his voice steely as he cuts through my train of thought.

The young man stands silently from his crouched position but doesn't turn to face us. His shoulders are slumped and his head hangs low. He looks utterly defeated and I feel a pang of guilt as I realise that I'm responsible for all of his undoing.

As if he can read my mind he turns and his eyes fall on me. They look pained and confused all at once and though the main emotion is pain, I can tell by the way he clenches his jaw that there's also anger brimming under the surface.

"Careful, he's still somewhat a stranger, we don't know what he's capable of," I warn Curly, suddenly nervous.

"Don't worry, C, we have your back," Slightly calls over.

Curly turns his head over his shoulder a fraction to give us an acknowledging nod before turning back to the task at hand. My thumb runs over the hilt of my dagger subconsciously as I wait anxiously to see what happens, I'm grateful that I have it close.

"We know you aren't Peter, Wyn told us everything," Curly states, his voice echoing slightly as it fills the space. "So, who are you really, or is your mind too screwed to answer that?" he continues bluntly.

The imposter's gaze sticks with me for a few more moments, as if Curly hadn't even uttered a word, and I find that I can't look away from his emotional eyes. They cut through me before something causes his gaze to shift to something past me.

"I'm talking to you!" Curly strides forward a few paces, his tone impatient.

I follow the young man's gaze past me to the snowy ledge and the Boulderswift Passage further on, a sense of dread washing over me as I stand rooted to the spot. My mind drifts back to my nightmares and the location that continues to appear in most of them and I bite my lip in angst.

"Wyn, you ok?" Khara quietly calls over to me, concern laced into her expression.

"I think so," I reply, the words drawn out by my distracted state.

As I turn back around, I see the imposter suddenly glance back over at the same spot and my stomach knots up once more. He strides forward, bumping shoulders with Curly as he goes, a sudden steely determination set in his maple eyes.

"Something is coming," is all he says before he heads down toward Boulderswift Passage.

The others look at each other and then at me, frustration clear in Curly's eyes, their colour dark and his brow furrowed. "Who the hell does he think he is?!"

"He's right, something's coming," I cut in, my voice monotone as I stare after the imposter, now running through the snow.

I feel all of their eyes on me as I speak, but I don't turn to them. Subconsciously I touch my charred forearm, the knotting in my stomach unable to subside, slowly realising what is about to happen.

"You all need to stay here," I say finally, stepping away resigning myself for what's to come.

XXX

"Oh no you don't," Curly cuts in, jumping forward and grabbing my arm before I can go any further.

"Wyn, he's right. We do this together as a team," Khara adds, stepping forward.

I pull my arm from Curly's grip and shake my head as I back away a few paces. I look each of them in the eye.

"You don't understand, it's not safe."

"If you haven't noticed sweetheart, none of this has been safe and yet here we are," Slightly points out with a shrug.

"This time it's different," I choke.

"This is about your dreams isn't it?" Curly questions, his voice surprisingly gentle.

"You aren't coming with me, it's not safe," I counter, stepping back a few more paces.

Before any of them can stop me or even argue, I call Maja over.

"Make sure they don't follow me... please," I tell her, searching her eyes for a few moments before I dart away.

I hear Curly call after me while the others shout in protest, but I clench my eyes shut and shake my head, trying to block them out before I carry on my way, unsure exactly what I'm running into. Unprepared and alone.

I make my way towards Boulderswift Passage as quickly as I can, thunder echoing through the darkened clouds as I catch sight of the imposter standing a couple of yards ahead of me, where the passage opens up to the air. When I reach him, he doesn't even acknowledge me, his eyes trained are on something else that's making its way up the mountain pass.

When I follow his gaze, my stomach drops. Out of the whole group, I pick out several of the pirates that I recognise from my earlier encounters, none of which have been pleasant.

"You need to get out of here, they're looking for Peter," I mutter hastily to my companion.

"I'm staying," he replies adamantly.

I sigh, knowing that it's too late now to argue. As we stand, silently united, they stop a few yards away from where we're standing, leering at me. The group suddenly splits in half, and out of the crowd of pirates, comes a well-dressed figure in a long, red and gold dress coat and overly large captain's hat, decorated with large, white plumes. He lifts his head to reveal two violet eyes that pierce through me as he saunters forward, dragging something alongside him before he thrusts it forward.

"Ah... Miss Wendy, so good to see you again, it's a shame our last meeting was such a disappointment." Kage remarks as he stops in front of his crew.

I sense the underlying anger in his words, but I don't respond, my attention, instead, drawn to the writhing heap laid out in front of him. A sinking feeling spreads in my stomach. Kage's glowing eyes follow my gaze and his pulsating figure shifts as a twisted smile forms on his darkened face.

"I see you've noticed our little tag along. Sadly, he wasn't any more helpful to my cause than you, dear," he comments as he steps forward and yanks the heap upright.

Kage grabs him by his hair, pulling the man's head up as he winces in pain. I gasp as I take in his swollen face, the bruising an awful tinge of black and blue. His lip is busted and split, and blood runs down his chin. His crooked nose is visibly broken and soaked in blood. One of his eyelids is swollen shut while the other squints and streams tears from the pain. And as I look into his one good eye, I see a flicker of recognition and a strangled cry escapes my lips.

"Nibs! What did you do to him?" I demand, my voice pitching as I step forward, but I'm stopped by the young man beside me.

"Oh, I only roughed him a little, he'll survive," Kage responds, bored, as he shoves Nibs' head down.

"You brute," I spit, venom seething in my words.

"Wendy dear, you're so ill-mannered to not introduce your friend here," Kage chides with a grin, ignoring my insult.

I open and shut my mouth, scrambling for a believable lie, my brain frazzled as I find myself suddenly on the spot.

"No matter, I'll find out soon enough, introductions are such a trivial thing when your life is about to come to an end," Kage says nonchalantly, sending a chill down my spine.

"You won't find what you're looking for up here, Kage," I say, my voice a lot steadier than I feel.

"Oh, but you see my dear girl, I have," he replies, his violet eyes challenging me.

"I don't understand," I utter, my voice faltering.

He steps around Nibs and saunters forward a few more steps, too close for comfort despite the several feet between us. He paces back and forth while his eyes remain on me, their eerie violet glow causing my skin to prickle.

"You say you don't know where Pan is, and yet you've befriended the very people who would know," he explains, his tone unnaturally cheery.

Thunder rolls over the sky above us as another frosty storm commences from above, his plans abruptly clear. I stare wide-eyed at the snowy ground as he walks back to his crew, kicking Nibs in the gut on his way past.

This small, unnecessary act causes my blood to boil, but before I can move toward him, I hear a familiar snarl and out from the ledge above, Maja leaps down, the snow flying in all directions as she lands, claws unsheathed and fangs bared. Even though I know deep down she'd never harm me, a part of me shrinks away from her in this protective and primal state.

After the shock of her arrival passes, the realisation dawns on me. If Maja is here, then without a doubt, so are the others. I mentally curse them as Maja charges at the gang of pirates, and out of the corner of my eye, I notice a movement on the ledge that Maja had dropped down from.

I'm not the only one who notices the slight movement, and before I can stop it or shout a warning, a silver dagger slices through the air, spinning rapidly until it connects with flesh, and a familiar cry cuts through the air.

I watch frantically as Khara steps out into the open and staggers forward, plummeting over the ledge and landing in a crumpled heap in front of me, snow flying in all directions upon impact. I feel like I'm underwater, unable to hear the blood curdling scream that rips from me. Ignoring the hands that are trying to hold me back, I scramble forward and drop down onto my knees beside her.

Behind me, I hear all hell break loose as Kage screams with unmatched fury.

"I told you I need them alive, you worthless *idiot*!"

I barely hear the screams of the unlucky pirate whose screams echo along the mountain canyon, my eyes are focused on Khara's face.

"What... why didn't you listen? You should have listened to me, Khara I—" I ramble softly as my hands hover over the hilt of the dagger embedded in her chest.

"Couldn't let you stare into the face of danger alone, now could we?" she jokes, her voice raspy.

I take in her pale face as she chuckles, her laughter turning into a fit of coughing, blood spraying from her lips as her body begins to tremble from shock. I hastily remove the thick poncho, lifting it over my head and laying it over her as lightning flashes above us.

Behind me, I hear the boys run toward the pirates alongside our new ally with no name, their battle cries just loud enough to be heard over the roar of the pirates. Their swords clash as the thunder sounds above.

"You're dying because of me," my voice catches as I speak, tears welling in my eyes as I cradle her head, The Sight shifting my eyesight.

The blood that stains her lips can instantly be seen that much clearer, the crimson colour brighter and deeper. Small blotches of blood ruin the pattern of freckles splashed across her paling face. Her usually bright amber eyes are now a faded brown, and my heart breaks as I watch the life leak out of her.

"You're wrong there," she rasps, the effort it takes for her to form words is unmistakable.

"You can't, Khara, not like this," I say quietly, my voice breaking as the first tear falls down my cheek.

"It is what it is, Wyn, we can't change it. You still have to get out of here," she replies, her words slurring.

I try to argue as I notice the blood spreading across her chest, staining her clothes as she grows weaker. She stops me, placing her shaking, icy hand over mine as she stares up at me.

"It'll be ok, Wyn. It's time to go."

"No! No, you aren't going to die, you can't!"

I shake my head violently with my eyes clenched shut, denial set deep in my bones as a wrenching pain claws at my chest. She gives me a small smile as she squeezes my hand.

"Wyn," she breathes affectionately with a soft sigh.

When she doesn't continue, I open my eyes and look down at her, finding her lifeless in my arms, her amber eyes staring out at nothing. The golden flecks were now dull and empty.

Pain and grief consume me as I lay her down gently, my fingertips brushing her eyelids shut. Through teary eyes, I glance down at the dagger sticking out of her chest and anger swells within me. I pull it free, dropping it in the snow, staining the pure white snow red as I draw the poncho up over the wound and up to her shoulders.

Slowly, I get to my feet and turn to the chaos behind me. Curly, Slightly and the nameless young man are in the middle of the scene, wielding swords and daggers, all bloody and bruised, but they don't back down. I watch on, as if in slow motion as I step forward, a sureness in each step as I get close to the action.

I pass bodies of dead pirates as I walk forward, pulling a sword free from one of their corpses as I go, the anger growing within me turning to unquenchable rage. I ignore the pirates, dipping out of their reach as I make a beeline for Kage, my heart calling for blood.

My eyes glance down for only a moment, but it's enough for me to stop short as my gaze falls on Nibs, curled-up in the bloodied snow, amongst the fighting and lifeless corpses. In a matter of seconds, I push down the rage and focus on Nibs, knowing what I have to do.

I weave in and out of the bodies littering the floor, adding to the numbers as a few pirates break away from the masses surrounding the Lost Boys and Maja—the sword in my hand is steady as the blade cuts them down. A numbness creeps over me as I show no remorse. When I finally reach Nibs, I'm splattered with blood.

Without a word, I grab him by the shoulder and drag him up. For a moment, he looks up at me startled, until he sees that it's me and he visibly relaxes. I can tell that he's in a lot of pain, just by the way he leans into me and winces as I lift his arm up over my shoulders.

I drag him clear of all of the debris and lower him down in a little nook hidden away from the action. He leans back and scrunches up his swollen face as he lets out a strangled sigh.

"You should be safe here for a little while, but when you have the opportunity, you should leave," I tell him, my voice sounding cold and blunt to my own ears.

I turn to walk away, but his hand on my wrist stops me and I turn back to him briefly. He watches me through his good eye and I take in the severity of his wounds, his face swollen and bruised—almost beyond recognition. I'm surprised I even managed to identify him.

"I had no choice but to lead them here, I'm sorry," he says, finally mustering the words.

He lets go of my arm and I draw it back to me, unsure of how to respond, the pain and anger flowing through me is too much for me to be genuine or even remotely forgiving.

"It is what it is," I reply bitterly, unintentionally echoing Khara.

Without another word, I stand up, searching through the fighting bodies for the being that I'm after. I find his shifting, darkened figure hunched over a newly dead pirate, drawing energy from his victim. I narrow my eyes, my fury flaring as I stride forward.

The Sight takes over as my emotions overwhelm me and I let them, relishing the idea of cutting Kage down until he is nothing but a worthless, powerless inkblot on my blade. Despite my morals, I want him to suffer, to feel the cool kiss of death as he meets his maker.

Khara's lifeless eyes are at the forefront of my mind as I rush toward Kage again. As if he senses me, he glances up, his violet eyes glowing bright. His darkened frame begins to show signs of natural skin colour across his face and hands; drawing energy from those around us must be working for him. I steel myself as I get closer and this time, there is nothing to stop me, nothing that could possibly get in my way. Until suddenly, there is, in the form of Curly.

He stands before me, sweaty and bloody and his ocean eyes dark with inner turmoil. For a single short moment his eyes flicker to where Khara's body lies, before they return to me.

"Get out of my way," I order through gritted teeth.

"You need to get out of here now, while you still have the chance," Curly argues, blocking my path.

"No, he's mine Curly!" I cry as I try to push past him.

Without another word, Curly whistles and Maja tosses the pirate she'd had locked in her jaws before bounding over to us. He grabs me roughly and plants a kiss on my temple before he lets go and rushes back over to help the others.

"Get her out of here Maja, *NOW*!" he yells over his shoulder.

I'm stunned by his action for only a few moments, but it's enough for Maja to comply.

"No!" I yell as she grabs me and slings me onto her back before breaking into a sprint.

I have no other choice but to hold on for dear life as the lightning flashes around us. We reach the mountain edge in little time, but suddenly, over the rolling thunder and battle cries of the remaining men, I hear the humming sound of an arrow cutting through the air.

"Look out," I cry.

But it's too late, the arrow buries itself into Maja's shoulder and she stumbles sideward, her left paw slipping over the mountain edge. I watch in horror as Maja loses her balance and we plummet over the mountainside. The last thing I see is Curly's shocked face before I lose my grip on Maja, free-falling down the mountain.

My screams cut through the air as I fall. I squeeze my eyes shut, unsure how to feel, now, in my last moments.

A rush of something foreign hits me square in the chest with a loud thump and with my ears ringing and my head spinning, I quickly lose consciousness.

My head feels like I've been hit by a ton of bricks when I come to, my eyes still shut tight. I feel nauseous as I realise that I'm swaying on my feet, sure that my weakened knees could buckle at any moment.

'Is this what death feels like?'

As the ringing in my ears subsides, I hear the rush of what sounds like motorcars and the sound of people as they hustle and bustle down busy streets. The air smells polluted—this isn't the fresh air of Neverland. The familiarity of all it tugs at me and I can't resist opening my eyes.

As my blurred vision clears, I find myself speechless, unable to believe it. I slap myself once, then twice in disbelief, until I realise that the people around me have begun to stare.

"But how did I..." I begin, trailing off in astonishment.

"I was falling, and then I..." I try again, trying my best to make sense of my muddled thoughts.

All around me, dandelion-looking flowers float around me before rising through the air, and up into the dusky sky, disappearing from sight. The way they float gently through the air reminds me of the whisps, and my breath catches in my throat as I take a good look at my surroundings.

The cobbled streets below my feet are slick with rain and I realise, with a start, that I'm in the middle of a busy street; a motorcar beeps its horn at me, signalling for me to get out of the way.

I jump and stumble across over to the pavement to let it pass, staring at it dumbfounded. The sight of a motorcar seems odd and not *normal*.

I notice that more people have stopped to stare at me, looking me up and down with horrified glances and hushed whispers as they put as much distance between them and me as possible.

Glancing down at myself, at my ripped and blood-spattered attire, I see that their horrified expressions are justified. I also realise—as one woman looks at me blushing—that I'm still wearing tight-fitting trousers, albeit a bit ripped in some places.

I stumble down the street, pushing past people as I pick up speed. Without thinking, I break into a sprint, my body leading me right to the bridge that runs over the river Thames. One of the most well known pieces of architecture in London stands in front of me, the building towering high into the sky in all its glory, standing watch over the city.

"Either this is true or I'm dreaming," I breathe.

I feel the stares of passersby burn holes in me as I stand there gormless. I don't know how this happened, or why, but I know with a sinking certainty that this is real.

"I'm back," I breathe in bewilderment.

My hand subconsciously reaches for my dagger, my fingers wrapping tightly around its hilt as I furrow my brow and look up to the sky, a fierceness burning in my heart.

"Mark my words, Kage, I'm coming for you," I vow, as my voice is drowned out by the chimes of Big Ben.

COMING SOON!

Wyn's adventure continues...

NEVER NEVER

ELORA BURRELL

eloraburrell.com

inkandfablepublishing.com

ACKNOWLEDGMENTS

Writing Neverlander has been an interesting journey and such a learning curve as a writer with big aspirations. There have certainly been many moments of trial and error, some that I never even thought about before I decided to publish my book.

That being said, none of this would have even been made possible without my amazing team at Ink & Fable Publishing, to whom I am eternally grateful for making my dream of becoming a published author a reality.

There have been moments where I thought my stories would never become anything more than a stack of manuscripts, so to be able to say that I have actually published one of hopefully many books, and made my lifelong dream a reality, is beyond incredible.

I would like to give a special thanks to my best friends and writing confidants, Sophie and Des. You have both helped shape Neverlander into what it is now. From our lengthy chats about plot development, to helping me decide how the story carries on through the series, you have both been imperative to my progress and development as a writer —with all of your inspiration, lengthy chats, and motivational speeches.

Secondly I would like to thank my good friend and fabulous editor

Britt, who has been a fantastic support throughout the editing stages as well as willingly been available at all times for if I was ever unsure.

I would also like to thank Kristin and Art By K Huggs who created the beautiful cover art and face of the book, as well as some amazing merchandise for the book and its series. You have been a wonderful artist to work with and you have outdone yourself with Neverlander's artwork.

This leads me to thank another talented artist, James, for the beautiful illustrations within Neverlander. It has been a pleasure working with you.

Thank you to Morgan Wright for bringing Kristin's artwork to life with Neverlander's moving cover art, which is both captivating and mesmerising.

A huge thank you to my wonderful husband, Jac, for being my constant cheerleader, as well as my friends and family for their support and belief in me and my abilities as a writer.

And finally, I want to thank you, my readers.

Thank you to you all for your eagerness and excitement for Neverlander's publication, and thank you for believing in my dream.